The
Cursed Half Moon

The Cursed Half Moon – Book 1
The Cursed Half Moon – Book 2

Other books by
Danielle N. McDonough

THE LEGACY SERIES

BOOK 1: THE PREPARATIONS
BOOK 2: THE TRIALS
BOOK 3: THE RETURN
BOOK 4: THE BROKEN

www.thecursedhalfmoonbookseries.com

The
Cursed Half Moon
Book 1

Danielle N. McDonough

Story by
Danielle N. McDonough & Charles Gilbreath

Ideas contributed by
Collin Glaess, Makenna Glaess, Anna Castro,
& Joe Martinez

Illustrated by
Aleasha Ford, Rebecca Coker, & Danielle N.
McDonough

Edited by
Terry McDonough & Rebecca Martinez

The Cursed Half Moon – Book 1
by Danielle N. McDonough

Printed in the United States of America
ISBN (Paperback): 978-1-950296-12-5
ISBN (Hardcover): 978-1-950296-13-2
ISBN (eBook): 978-1-950296-14-9

Written by Danielle N. McDonough
Story by Danielle N. McDonough & Charles Gilbreath
Ideas contributed by Collin Glaess, Makenna Glaess, Anna Castro, & Joe Martinez
Illustrated by Aleasha Ford, Rebecca Coker, & Danielle N. McDonough
Edited by Terry McDonough & Rebecca Martinez

This series and other books by Danielle N. McDonough are available online at www.daniellenmcdonough.com.

This book is dedicated to my party,

Collin, Makenna, Anna, and Joe, who experienced this adventure with me and fought bravely by my side.

And for our amazing Dungeon Master, Charles, who guided us the whole way through and only tried to kill us occasionally.

Planosia

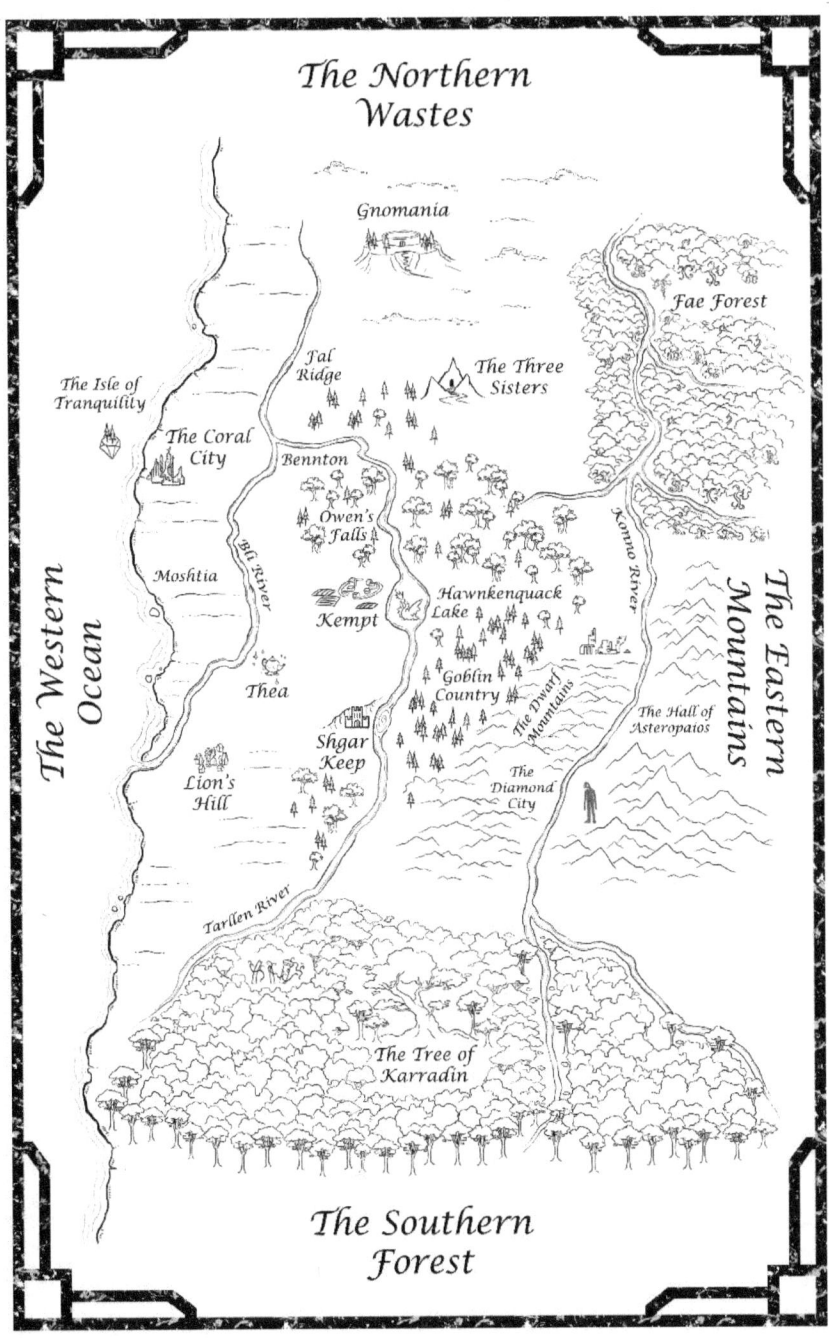

The Northern
Wastes

Gnomania

Fae Forest

The Isle of
Tranquility

Tal
Ridge

The Three
Sisters

The Coral
City

Bennton

Owen's
Falls

Konno River

Moshtia

Bli River

Hawnkenquack
Lake

The Eastern
Mountains

Kempt

The Western
Ocean

Thea

Goblin
Country

The Dwarf
Mountains

The Hall of
Asteropaios

Shgar
Keep

Lion's
Hill

The
Diamond
City

Tarllen River

The Tree of
Karradin

The Southern
Forest

Prologue
The Cursed

Unseen, a half-elf child glided through the dappled sunlight and shadow within the forest. She wore no shoes, and a few leaves were tangled in her dark brown hair. There was a trail nearby, going in the same direction she was. It led to a waterfall, which cascaded into a pool of cool, mountain water. However, the girl chose to find her own way, passing among the woods in silence.

As she walked along the trunk of a fallen tree, the child held out her slender arms for balance. With a triumphant smile, she reached the end and leapt, doing a full flip in the air, before landing in a crouch on the leaf-carpeted ground.

The smile died on the girl's lips when she caught sight of a small stream in front of her. It was one of many that ran out of the pool fed by the waterfall.

Slowly, the child straightened to her full height, eyes locked on the water. She began moving forward as though in a trance and only stopped once she stood on the edge of the bank.

Delicately, she stretched out a foot, slowly brushing the surface for a single moment before jerking her leg back. The girl froze, watching carefully for signs of danger, but the brook trickled on as if she did not exist.

Again, the child reached out to touch the water, this time leaving the tips of her toes submerged. Her body was taut, prepared to spring away at any moment. She remained in the same position for nearly a full minute, then, cautiously, she took a step forward. Her foot disappeared up to the ankle in the placid water.

The girl's hesitation was shorter this time. Carefully, she placed her second foot beside the first. Almost as soon as both were fully submerged, she began to slip uncontrollably toward the center of the stream. The child's eyes widened in horror, and she made a mad scramble for the bank. Despite the minuscule depth of

1

the water, her efforts were in vain. Surging forward, she almost managed to escape, but a large wave shoved the child to her knees and carried her into the middle of the stream.

The cry of terror that came from the girl's throat was cut off as a wall of water struck her from behind, spinning her around in the now raging torrent. The child struggled, trying to keep her head above the surface. Another, even stronger wave, forced her down, pinning her small frame to the rocky riverbed.

Wriggling like a fish, the girl attempted to fight her way free but was unable to escape the grasp of the current. She opened her mouth in panic, releasing a cloud of bubbles in a scream that no one heard. Her lungs burned, and her heart thundered in her chest as darkness pressed on the corners of her vision.

With her hands, the half-elf scrabbled among the pebbles on the bottom of the stream, desperately trying to claw herself from the water's sinister clutches.

Suddenly, her head broke the surface, and she took a long, choking breath.

"Candra, are you okay?" the human boy who was holding the back of her shirt asked in concern. He was the one who had lifted her from the bottom of the waist-deep water.

"I'm fine, Kraster!" she spat at him, attempting to pull herself free of his hand.

The boy didn't release Candra; instead, he started towing her toward the nearby bank. The stream behind them was as calm as it had been when the girl first laid eyes on it.

"Are you sure you're all right?" Kraster asked, guiding her to the safety of land.

As soon as she was no longer touching the water, Candra savagely ripped herself out of Kraster's grasp and turned to face him.

"Leave me alone!" she snarled, backing away.

The girl's wet hair was plastered to her pale face. Her brown eyes were hot with anger, igniting the specks of gold in them. They were strange eyes, even for a half-elf. Sometimes, the golden flecks seemed to glow inexplicably with an inner fire.

Confusion clouded Kraster's countenance.

"I was just trying to help," he told her.

"I don't need your help," she snapped bitterly. "Yours or your *family's*."

"Don't you mean our fam–"

"No!" Candra shrieked. "Never!"

Without another word, she bolted away from him, back into the forest.

Kraster pursed his lips as he watched his half-sister vanish from sight among the trees.

Chapter 1
The Teapot

I'd learned a long time ago that there was absolutely nothing remarkable about me.

I didn't stand out as being particularly beautiful, intelligent, or witty. Others weren't interested in befriending me or even engaging me in conversation. Being overlooked was such a common occurrence that I often felt invisible. In a crowd, people tended to unconsciously shy away from me. When I spoke, my words were rarely well received, as though the listener heard a negative undertone in everything I said.

As a child, these realities caused me a lot of pain. However, as an adult, I used them to my advantage by making stealth operations my specialty.

Over the last decade, I'd mastered the art of going unnoticed, completing my objective, and slipping away without leaving a trace. Although to be honest, I probably wouldn't have been nearly so successful without Kraster, my half-brother, as my partner. Magical abilities were rare, especially among humans, but he'd been blessed with them and was incredibly gifted. He was also the only person I'd ever met who was immune to the negative effect I had on those around me. I'd always assumed it had something to do with his magic, but he'd been friendly to me even before his powers manifested.

From what I knew, our current mission was unlikely to require Kraster's special skill set. Yesterday, my brother and I had been briefed on the assignment by General Greyward, the commander of Kempt's army.

He hadn't given us very much to go on. Our only instructions were to locate and gather information about some kind of ancient artifact. The relic was believed to be in a small, quaint town called Thea, which was a few days' ride southwest of Kempt.

I'd never been there before, but I knew Thea was considered a sacred place, with a shrine and an enclave of acolytes.

As soon as Greyward had told us our objective, I suspected it was some kind of test since everything seemed so simple and straightforward. However, there was a tense expression on the general's face that I'd never seen before. Not that I got a very good look, since Greyward's attention was primarily focused on Kraster, as usual. Whenever we met with the general, it was always the same; he'd gush over my brother's talents and achievements while barely bothering to register my existence.

For the last several years, our assignments had been growing more numerous and more dangerous, with little explanation given to us either before we were dispatched or after our return. Even still, this time I'd been left with the strong impression that something wasn't quite right.

Humans were short-lived compared to most other races, and Greyward was nearing the age of sixty. Was that when they started becoming soft in the head? The general certainly had plenty of wrinkles and gray hair. If he was going senile, it would explain his curious behavior of late.

Speaking of odd behavior, three weeks ago, General Greyward had gathered most of the army at a temporary camp two days' march from Kempt, leaving only the city guard behind for protection. The rumors I'd heard seemed to indicate that none of the captains or other officers had any clue as to why he'd done this. Neither did Kraster, Greyward's protégé. My brother's best guess was that this was all some sort of training exercise. I didn't think he was right as it didn't seem like a good enough reason for the general to have left the city so vulnerable.

Kempt was one of the three major human cities in Planosia. Once, many centuries ago, all of mankind had been part of a unified kingdom called Aurum, but not anymore. While Kempt wasn't currently in conflict with any of its neighbors, trust wasn't something I believed in, due in no small part to my line of work.

Case in point, Kraster and I were currently disguised as pilgrims, riding down the dusty road to Thea. The red sun was high in the sky without a cloud in sight. It was early summer, so the plants were still small, just beginning to grow toward the heavens. The last few weeks had been very pleasant, with only a hint of frost in the air on the coldest of nights.

We'd departed camp at dawn and had made good progress. I knew we were getting close to our destination when we started to pass fields of wheat, groves of tea trees, and rows of grapevines. There were plenty of other travelers on the road, most wrapped in rough, handspun, pilgrim robes similar to our own.

Mine was itchy and uncomfortable. Even worse, donning it meant I couldn't wear my swords and had to hide them in a bundle of clothing among my luggage. I felt naked without the two blades on my belt. However, I was far from defenseless, as there were several knives concealed on my person in case of an emergency.

Less than twenty minutes later, the town came into view. The small cluster of stone buildings was nearly white. The one in the center was taller than the others, its roof rising to a sharp steeple many feet in the air.

"I'll bet you a month's pay that's the shrine," I said, pointing to it.

"Thanks, but I'll pass," Kraster replied. "That sounds like a terrible bet."

I scowled at him.

"Don't turn into a storm cloud," he chuckled. "Candra, if you won, you'd just drink the coins away and regret it in the morning."

"I regret nothing," I told him.

Even in the beginning, when I'd tried to be clever, I'd never been able to hide my chosen vice from Kraster. I knew he worried for me, but sometimes I wanted to be less lonely, and sometimes I wanted to be happy, and sometimes I wanted to forget, and sometimes I wanted to feel something, and sometimes I wanted to feel absolutely nothing. It didn't seem to matter what mood I was trying to capture, the answer could almost always be found at the bottom of a flagon or two... or three now. A few days ago, it had even taken me four, but I'd eventually gotten there just the same. No one else seemed to care, as long as it didn't interfere with my assignments, but I knew the habit didn't sit well with Kraster.

Pushing away the guilt, I focused on the town in the distance. I'd never heard of anyone being sent on a mission to Thea before, and, the closer I got, the easier it was to understand why. The first building we came to was more of a hovel than a decent dwelling.

A hunched, old woman, dressed in the garb of an acolyte, sat out front tending a fire over which hung half a dozen metal tea kettles. Her hair was frizzy and gray, and she had a pair of large warts on her very prominent nose. It seemed that the woman was offering tea to travelers as they passed. Some stopped; others did not.

Kraster halted his warhorse, Raspberry, and dismounted. My brother had chosen the name because of the reddish tones in the beast's chestnut coat. Currently, the stallion was disguised as a carthorse by a layer of mud, so little of the vibrant color was visible.

After handing me Raspberry's reins, Kraster stepped off the road and politely accepted a small cup of tea from the woman. He took a sip and dropped a few coins into the donation bowl on her table, then headed back in my direction.

Quickly, I swung down from my black gelding. His name was Tempest. I'd picked it for him because I thought it sounded powerful. However, Kraster had started calling him Pest, which didn't sound powerful at all, and, of course, that's what everyone else started calling him too.

"How's the tea?" I asked my brother quietly.

"Hot," he replied with a grin.

I rolled my eyes at him.

"Greyward was right about you," I retorted. "You don't miss a thing."

Kraster beamed. "Greyward said that about me? He's too kind."

"You've got that right," I muttered under my breath, as I pushed past my brother and handed him both sets of reins.

With a pleasant smile plastered on my face, I reached the table and also deposited several coins into the woman's bowl before waiting to receive a cup of tea. The woman turned away from me and offered the next three cups to a group who had approached from the opposite direction while Kraster and I were talking.

"All out," she said gruffly and without a hint of remorse when she finally acknowledged my presence.

"Of course," I murmured with a polite dip of my head as I turned back to Kraster.

He was scowling, but there was no way he was going to make a scene while we were working.

"Are my ears still covered?" I mouthed to him as we began leading our horses further into the town.

Kraster nodded, but I still raised one hand to my hair to check. We had both inherited our father's dark locks. I almost never cut mine, using them to conceal my ears, which came to traitorously sharp points at their ends. Kraster's hair was just long enough that he could tie it back with a leather thong when needed. However, unless we were training or preparing for combat, he usually left it loose.

I patted my hair back into place and struggled to hold in a sigh. It was so much easier to make the slights of others feel less personal when it was only the result of my mixed blood. That way, I could pretend it had nothing to do with me and me alone.

"I think that's an inn," I announced, motioning to the only two-story structure.

Kraster nodded and led the way to the door. In less than half an hour, we had secured a room for ourselves and stalls for our horses. Now it was time for the real work to begin.

The view from our room couldn't have been better. We were on the second floor, and the window looked out on the center of the tiny village with the pointy-roofed shrine smack dab in the middle.

I spent about twenty minutes mapping the layout. It did seem like overkill, since the town was so incredibly small, but this mission was clearly very important to Greyward, and, if anything went wrong, I was sure to be blamed.

Kraster and I had been a team for many years. We were usually dispatched to gather tactical information, track down a fugitive, or liberate an object from its illegitimate owner. We'd even been sent on a few assassinations. This time, Greyward had told us to learn all we could about the item, but not to touch it. He'd been very clear on this point.

Once I finished sketching, I poked Kraster, who'd fallen asleep on one of the two beds.

"Nap time's over," I told him. "Let's get busy."

We leisurely stepped out of the inn onto the unpaved street. It didn't take us long to determine the purpose of each building. There was a dormitory where the shrine maidens lived and a row of small villas for the acolytes. Both groups were made up solely of women and girls. The only males in the town were the pilgrims and other travelers.

Several large sheds scattered throughout the village housed the items used in the shrine and the tools for working the surrounding fields. Closer to the inn, there was a bakery, a trinket shop, and a winery, which I resolved to visit later.

Lastly, there was the shrine itself. I took careful note of where the doors and windows were located on each structure so I could add the details to my map later.

Even though it was the central building of the town and clearly the main attraction, the shrine was pitifully small compared to others I'd seen. We waited in a line of pilgrims as only a few visitors were admitted at a time.

"Here's where we find the relic," I murmured to Kraster, who nodded.

Just as it was about to be our turn, the shrine maidens on duty switched. Four new women, one of them young enough to still be a teenager, walked past us in a diamond formation. Their feet were perfectly synced with each other, almost as though they were marching in a military maneuver.

Suddenly, the young one tripped and bumped into the woman in front of her, who was closer to my age. Scowling, the older shrine maiden turned around to chide her clumsy companion. "Wren, how many times must I tell you to watch where you place your feet?"

The young shrine maiden, Wren, dropped her eyes and looked at the ground, mortified. "I am very sorry," was all she said.

The three other women shook their heads as they all started forward again.

I stared after them in shock. The shrine maidens wore white and teal uniforms that covered nearly every inch of their skin and included a hooded robe. However, when the young maiden tripped, her hood had fallen back to reveal ears that were slightly pointed. She was a half-elf, like me. Although from her fine features, I imagined she was descended from a high elf bloodline, instead of merely a wood elf one, as I was.

The presence of another half-breed surprised me. We were rare. Not only did the races of the world tend not to mix, but their offspring often found it hard to fit into either parents' world. Besides that, I hadn't seen any elves serving among the shrine maidens or acolytes, only humans, as was common in this part of the world. It was likely that this girl had been given to the sisters not from a sense of religious vigor, but for convenience. If there had been a shrine near Owen's Falls, where I'd grown up, I'm sure I would have shared the same fate.

Kraster touched my shoulder. "Come on," he murmured. "It's our turn."

We stepped forward and both put three coins into the donation box. One of the maidens pulled back a threadbare curtain to let us inside the shrine.

The interior was dim, and it took a moment for my eyes to adjust. When they did, the first thing I saw was the teapot.

I'd never drunk much tea and knew very little about the beverage, much less about the vessels in which it was brewed;

however, even I could see that there was something extremely special about this one. The teapot was a crystal orb, gilt in an intricate weaving of gold, which formed the handle, legs, and spout. Within, was a mint green, slightly luminescent liquid. It was too opaque to see through but moved as though the tea was being stirred, even though it sat untouched on its pedestal.

I glanced to my right, where Kraster stood staring with his mouth hanging open. Suppressing a smile, I gave him a nudge. He snapped his jaw shut sheepishly.

Aside from the teapot, the interior of the shrine was very plain. It had clean, white walls and a few open windows close to the ceiling. The space was cut in half by a pair of teal green curtains, shielding half of the room from our view. A shrine maiden stood close to where the curtains met. I recognized her as the half-elf who had tripped earlier. Now that she was indoors, her hood was down, leaving her pointed ears exposed as they poked through her brown hair. I tried to recall her name. Robin, maybe?

After one more long look at the teapot, I moved to her, trying to see if I could make out anything through the slit between the curtains. The opening was only an inch or two wide. No light filtered through the cloth, so the windows on that side of the building must have been shuttered.

"Good afternoon," I said to Robin–or whatever her name was–giving her a smile. I tried not to overdo it; I'd been told I often overdid it when attempting to be friendly.

"Greetings to you." The shrine maiden dipped her head to me respectfully.

"Where did it come from?" I asked, nodding toward the teapot.

"Only The Great Shal'eth knows," she replied in that insanely annoying way people did when they'd said the same thing over and over again because they were told to, but really had no idea what it actually meant.

"The Great Shal'eth?" I asked, wondering why that name sounded so familiar. All the while, I was cocking my head slightly, trying to get a better angle to peer into the shadows on the other side of the curtain. Even with my half-elf eyes, which were better at seeing in the dark than a human's, I still couldn't make out anything in the gloom. Although I had the strangest sense that someone was watching me.

"Yes," the young woman replied, drawing my attention. Her voice was the same as before, except it had now taken on a dreamy tone. "It is he who protects this place and gives us sanctuary here."

"Well, he has done a wonderful job," I told her, doing my best to come off as sincere. "This place is so… preserved?" My words came out more as a question than a statement.

"Indeed," the shrine maiden answered, not seeming to notice my uncertainty. Her doe-like eyes were unfocused as she continued. "The order has lived this way for centuries and will continue as we are forever, under his watchful eye."

I nodded. Now that I'd confirmed there was no way to sneak a peek behind the curtain, it was time to escape this conversation. Thankfully, another of the shrine maidens approached us.

"Forgive me," she said, eyes looking me up and down disapprovingly, "but the next group of pilgrims is eager to enter."

"Of course. My apologies." I smiled at both of them.

"Wren, please fetch some water for those accepting donations," the second woman continued to the younger shrine maiden.

Wren. Her name was Wren. Both wrens and robins were birds starting with "r" sounds, so at least I'd been close.

Kraster was waiting for me by the exit where we, once again, made a donation on our way out.

"If you care to join us," the maiden holding the box said to Kraster, "Mother Imin will be hosting a tea ceremony for all to see in the square at sunset."

"We'll be there," I told her, even though she never turned her eyes in my direction.

"Learn anything?" Kraster asked as we walked back to the inn.

"Not really," I shrugged. "They follow someone called Shal'eth. I feel like I should know who that is, but I can't recall."

Kraster considered for a moment. "I think he's a dragon."

I rolled my eyes. "Whatever, you're making that up to try and look smart."

We got to our room, and I plopped down on the nearest bed.

"No, I'm serious," he insisted. "I remember reading about him in one of Noral's books."

I nearly flinched at the name of one of my half-sisters.

"Then what else did the book say?" I challenged.

"Not much. He was on a list of the great dragons of old."

"Right," I said, my tone disbelieving. "I'm sure the sacred relic of one of the great dragons is a teapot."

"It has to be more than just a teapot," Kraster protested. "I mean, did you get a good look at that thing?"

"Of course," I nodded. "I'm just not sure why a dragon, or Greyward for that matter, would find it important."

Kraster shrugged. "It's clearly a magical artifact of some type."

"Yes, but it's a teapot," I couldn't help pointing out again. "If it were a sword or a shield or something like that, I wouldn't have nearly as many questions as I do now."

"Regardless, I'd better give the general an update on our progress." Kraster took out a small, gray charm with a purple rune carved on the top.

General Greyward had a matching charm with the same rune. Once a day, each charm could be used to send a brief message to the other. The general would want a full report at the conclusion of our investigation, so I took out the map once more and started adding the details I'd collected.

Chapter 2
The Ceremony

An hour later, Kraster and I headed down to the inn's main room for dinner.

"We should stop by the winery after the ceremony," I told him.

Kraster glanced at me, then gave the mug of ale in my hand a pointed look.

"Come on," I sighed. "This is just to wash down dinner. The winery will be an experience. Didn't you notice the vineyard on the road here? They grow their own grapes and make their own wine. We may never have the chance to try it again, and I, for one, don't want to waste this incredible opportunity."

Kraster pursed his lips but relented. "Fine. After the ceremony, we can go for *one* drink at the winery."

I grinned at him. One never meant one to me.

Just as we finished our meal, a gong sounded, summoning everyone in the village. Kraster and I divided, each taking an opposite side of the town square, so we could observe everything from two angles. It didn't seem like there would be much to see, but it was good to maintain our training.

A low, wooden table was carried to the center of the square by six shrine maidens. Three others stood slightly off to the side, making music with a set of chimes, some handbells, and the gong we'd heard earlier. It was very pleasant and fit the time of day perfectly. The sun, large and maroon, was just touching the horizon, streaking the clouds deep purple and pale pink.

The tempo of the melody changed as a procession of women emerged from the shrine. They took each step together, slowly making their way to the table.

The two in front carried candles. They were followed by four others who each held a teacup. The design of these matched the teapot in the shrine. The only difference was that they were empty, which made them far more ordinary than I would have thought possible. Next came Wren and a girl who couldn't have been more than twelve. Each of them held one end of a rolled-up piece of fabric. The cloth was white with thin swirls of teal.

Last came a tall shrine maiden who looked to be in her late thirties. In both hands she clutched the teapot, which was glowing brightly. The liquid within churned wildly despite the slow and careful steps of the woman.

As the candle and cup bearers reached the square table, they split, half going to the left and half to the right. When Wren and the little girl approached a moment later, they unfurled their cloth over the wooden surface. The younger girl was flawless as she released her end and allowed the fabric to gently roll down the length of the table, never touching the dirt.

Wren was less perfect. She wasn't quick enough to keep the hem from hitting the ground, and the cloth on her side didn't lay quite flat. Hastily, Wren straightened it with her hand before stepping back.

Ironically, one of the things high elves were known for was their gracefulness, but, as I well understood, being a half-breed was a mixed bag. You got some traits from one side and some from the other, with no regard as to what would make sense.

The candles were set in the center of the table, and a cup was placed on each of the four sides. The other shrine maidens withdrew as the woman carrying the teapot reached the table. All of their movements were so practiced that the entire ceremony was like a dance. Even Wren moved with an innate agility. She wasn't as skilled as the others but still performed far better than I could have.

Circling the table slowly, the maiden with the teapot began to pour the tea. Once she'd finished filling all the cups, she stepped back, still holding the completely full teapot. I made a mental note of the fact that it was never put down.

Everyone's attention shifted to the right, where an ancient woman, who could only be Mother Imin, approached from the direction of the acolytes' villas. She used a cane, which appeared to be more reliable than either of her legs. Finally, she reached the table. A girl of six or seven had been following with a cushion, which she slipped under the old woman as she sank to the ground directly across from the shrine.

Mother Imin picked up the teacup in front of her with a shaky hand. "We give thanks this night to The Creator for the ever-rising sun," she said in a surprisingly strong voice.

Almost before I realized what was happening, one of the shrine maidens had stepped forward and picked up the steaming cup of tea on the eastern side of the table. After quickly pouring its contents on the ground, she stepped back to her place.

"And we ask for grace for the fallen who seek redemption," Mother Imin went on as another shrine maiden poured out a second cup on the opposite side of the table.

"We offer a hymn of mourning for Alora, The Blessing that was lost so long ago." The cup of tea across from Mother Imin was poured out by Wren.

"And voice our gratitude to The Great Shal'eth for his provision."

I glanced at Kraster, wondering if he knew anything about the different beings Mother Imin had referred to. I'd always understood that there were many powerful forces in the world, both seen and unseen, but I couldn't name more than a handful.

Mother Imin lifted the final cup to her lips and drank deeply. The surrounding maidens and acolytes bowed their heads. After finishing the tea, the old woman set the cup back down and rose.

The dance of the shrine maidens started again. In no time, the cloth, candles, cups, and table were removed, and the music came to an end.

I made my way to Kraster.

"That was interesting," he said.

"Yeah, I guess." I nodded. "Not sure what they were going on about, but at least it was short and sweet. Now, with regard to that winery…"

Kraster sighed but followed as I turned around and set off with purpose.

The winery was delightful. It had an open courtyard full of tables where we could drink and watch the stars come out one by one. To my surprise, there was a full-blooded high elf woman sitting alone at the table to our right. She wore an elegantly woven tunic of thick thread that was a masterpiece of many rich shades of orange. Her legs were sheathed in brown pants of a similar design. They weren't elvish garments exactly, but certainly looked expensive and ornate.

There was a glass of wine in front of the elf, which she was gazing at more than drinking. In the time it took for me to down two glasses, she hadn't taken more than a few sips.

I was about to order a third, but Kraster seized my wrist to stop me.

"We have work to do tonight," he reminded me quietly. There was concern in his brown eyes. They were several shades darker than mine and lacked the golden flecks that I'm sure came from my unusual parentage.

"I do my best work when I've been properly watered," I informed him, waving for another glass. The workers here weren't shrine maidens, but the older acolytes.

"Besides," I said, turning back to Kraster, "what is there to find out? It's a teapot. It holds tea. Do we really need to know more?"

"More is always better," Kraster insisted.

"You're just trying to impress Greyward," I muttered.

"You should try it sometime," my brother retorted.

"Won't help," I announced, accepting another glass from the serving acolyte.

"It might–" Kraster started, but I gave him a sharp look, and he fell silent. We both knew that in our first two years serving under Greyward, I had run myself ragged attempting to earn the general's favor. My efforts had all been in vain. The only reason I received any promotions or special assignments was because of Kraster, whom Greyward couldn't praise enough.

"We should investigate anyway," Kraster started again.

"Fine," I sighed. "I am curious about what they are hiding behind that curtain."

He nodded eagerly. "Then it's settled. When the town grows quiet, we will make our move."

After I finished my final cup, Kraster helped me to my feet. Even still, I clumsily bumped into the table next to me.

"Sorry," I said to the high elf.

"Pray, don't mention it," she replied in a tone far friendlier than that of any high elf I'd spoken to before, not that there had been very many.

"It is I who should apologize to you," she went on.

I glanced at her and realized that she didn't look much like other high elves either. Her rich brown hair was cut short, barely reaching past her chin, and her eyes were a vivid shade of orange I'd never seen before.

"Are you really a high elf?" I blurted out. "You don't seem like one."

"Do I not?" the elf asked. In her words was the sound of tinkling bells, and her small mouth twisted with mirth at my observation.

"Sorry, she's had more than she should," Kraster apologized.

"It's fine," the elf told him, then turned to me. "My name is Lucille. Long has it been since I lived among high elves, so it is not surprising that my mannerisms should be different."

"Why has it been so long?" I wondered.

The elf pressed her ruby lips together, and a sad look crossed her perfect face. "I've been waiting for something. Waiting for a very long time now." Lucille's orange gaze settled on me. It was intense, as though she was looking through me.

"What are you waiting for?" I asked, feeling suddenly quite sober.

"The right time," she replied.

"The right time for what?" I pressed. Now she was sounding more like a high elf.

18

"Candra, you're being rude," Kraster said softly, but Lucille waved him off with a few of her fingers.

"The right time to find someone," she told me. There was finality in her words, and I knew we had reached the end of our conversation.

"I wish you luck," I called over my shoulder as Kraster led me away.

I felt Lucille's eyes on me as we crossed the courtyard and headed back to our accommodations for the evening.

"You didn't have to make such a fuss," I told my brother.

"And you shouldn't be bothering people in your state," he snapped back. "We are trying *not* to draw attention to ourselves, remember?"

"I'm not that drunk," I said. "I'm just trying to enjoy the region's delicacies!"

Kraster rolled his eyes as he marched me up to the inn.

Once we were back in our room, I perched by the window, keeping watch on the square. A moment after I'd gotten settled, I saw Lucille leave the winery and head for the shrine. A few of the maidens were by the door, and others were coming in and out, probably on cleaning duty. None of them tried to stop her when she entered.

A quarter of an hour later, a saddled horse was led to the front of the shrine by an acolyte just as Lucille walked out. She took the horse with a nod of thanks, mounted it, and left the town, vanishing from sight into the darkness.

Chapter 3
The Great

The town grew quiet early, with most of the pilgrims retiring shortly after nightfall. From our window, Kraster and I could see that, while the square was empty, oil lamps were refreshed every hour or so. There were also processions of shrine maidens and acolytes that didn't seem to follow any sort of set schedule. Sometimes, they ventured into the shrine momentarily; sometimes, they merely passed it by.

Around the third hour of the morning, I nudged Kraster, who was dozing at my side. The lamps had just been filled, and the processions seemed to be fewer and farther apart.

Kraster watched as I took out a length of rope. The inn's stairs were creaky, and going out the window would be faster anyway. The large wardrobe in the corner was the only piece of furniture in the room heavy enough that it might hold Kraster's weight. He'd received our father's sturdy frame, and military life had added ample muscle.

As with all things, I'd inherited a little from both sides. I was taller than most wood elves but had their willowy build. My arms were long and a bit disproportionate, but ideal for climbing down ropes from second-story windows in the middle of the night.

"You coming?" I whispered over my shoulder as I clambered onto the windowsill.

Kraster hesitated and glanced at the wardrobe, then shook his head. "I'll watch from here," he decided.

I nodded before slipping out the window. A moment later, I was down the rope and crouched in the bushes below. After several moments of stillness, I carefully started across the square, trying to be a mere shadow. It was not an easy feat considering how brightly the lamps shone.

20

Just before I reached the shrine, I heard the tramp of feet. Diving to the side, I flattened myself against the wall as three figures appeared. I held my breath, hoping they would stop or turn, but they didn't.

As they continued, their pace slackened. For a terrible moment, I feared I might have been spotted, and then all three slowly crumpled to the ground.

I looked up at the inn's window where I could just make out Kraster's hand pointed toward the downed trio. Sleep was one of his most useful spells, as it left no witnesses and also no carnage. We were lucky there had only been three, since that was about all Kraster could manage to drop at one time.

Heaving a sigh of relief, I slipped into the shrine. I paused on the threshold and held my breath. All was quiet and still. I'd been expecting it to be dark inside, but there were lamps burning behind the cloth curtain. Slowly, I moved forward, using all my skill to create as little noise as possible. The first thing I noticed was that the teapot was gone, its place on the pedestal barren.

Probably removed for security, I decided.

It was most likely stashed somewhere close by, in a locked chest or something. None of my senses detected movement on the other side of the curtain, so I carefully pushed my way through.

Immediately, I froze, because sitting in front of me was a dragon!

Okay, not a dragon exactly. He was human–a very large, very muscular human, with a dragon head on top of his broad shoulders. The proportions were incredibly strange since there was no neck, and the long snout of the dragon head protruded nearly as far as the human arms would be able to reach.

The dragon-man-thing wore no shirt, which wasn't strange because how would he have put it on? His lower half was wrapped in a white sarong, which ended mid-calf. However, I hardly noticed the clothes. All I could do was stand there and stare at the head, trapped in the gaze of its brilliant teal green eyes.

"Hello," the creature said in a calm, regal voice that rumbled deep in the back of his scaly throat. He was seated on a comfortable-looking, velvet chair. Beside him was a wooden table which held the teapot and a matching cup half full of tea.

I wonder how he drinks it, I thought, then mentally slapped myself. That was the last thing I should be worried about. I needed to make a choice: run, fight, try to explain I'd gotten lost on my way to the bathroom, or beg not to be eaten.

"You're The Great Shal'eth, aren't you?" I asked, amazed at how calm my words sounded.

"You are correct," he replied with a slight nod of his head, then his gaze intensified to a level I hadn't thought possible. "Who are you?"

"I'm– I'm nobody," I told him, the words coming to my lips almost unbidden. In my defense, it is really hard to keep your wits about you when facing down a dragon, even if it's just the dragon's head. If Shal'eth had stood up, he would have only been a foot taller than Kraster, but that mouth looked like it could swallow me in one bite.

"Everyone is someone," Shal'eth said, his eyes running over me. I prayed he wasn't thinking of having a midnight snack. "We all have a story, a mission, a journey." His eyes flicked back to my face. "A future."

I wasn't so sure about that last one anymore, unless I managed to escape quickly.

"And your arrival heralds the start of the end," he went on matter-of-factly.

"The end?" I asked.

"Indeed," Shal'eth said, voice softer. "But we have some time yet, I think, before tragedy befalls us. Please, sit, so we may speak."

I glanced at the chair across from him. It was identical to the one in which he sat.

"I'm good," I said, preferring to remain as close to the exit as possible.

Shal'eth made no response; he only watched me with those depthless eyes of his. If you have never been within ten feet of a dragon, then you will never understand the power of their gaze.

I swallowed and made my way to the empty chair, choosing to perch on the very edge of it, like a bird about to take flight.

"Where are you from?" Shal'eth wondered.

My mind went blank. This was not the direction I'd expected our conversation to take. I'd been caught sneaking into the forbidden section of a sacred shrine in the dead of night, and this Shal'eth fellow wanted to have a friendly chat about my early life? I was starting to wonder if the wine I'd had earlier was a lot stronger than I'd thought. Maybe I'd passed out back in my room, and this was all some kind of dream.

"A town outside of Kempt," I hedged. In case this wasn't a dream, the less the dragon-man knew about me, the better.

"Which one?" he asked smoothly, as though he understood exactly what I was doing.

"Owen's Falls," I admitted, feeling certain that Shal'eth would be able to tell if I lied to him. Even though I was a spy, lying was never really my thing. It was easy for me to simply blend in and go unnoticed in a sea of other names and faces. However, Shal'eth had definitely noticed me and was now giving me his full attention–not something I was used to.

That's what happens when you're a bumbling idiot and interrupt a dragon at tea time! I scolded myself.

"Owen's Falls," Shal'eth mused, eyes growing distant. "A humble, quiet place. So out of the way and nearly forgotten." His gaze returned to mine. "But not by all."

I didn't know what to say, so I nodded, figuring that agreeing with a dragon was always a good idea.

"You're here with your half-brother, are you not?"

My jaw dropped open at the question, because Kraster and I never mentioned our family tie when we were working.

"The man you serve, Greyward, can no longer be trusted," Shal'eth went on, ignoring my silence. "He has given himself to something ancient and evil."

"What?" I gasped.

"Have you not noticed changes in him recently?"

23

"I'm– I'm not sure," I muttered.

"Would you believe me if I told you he is on his way here right now to massacre my people?" Shal'eth asked calmly.

"He would never do that," I spluttered. "Yeah, he's kind of a jerk sometimes. At least, he is to me, but he'd never attack a village without provocation."

"We shall soon see," Shal'eth replied, eyes sliding closed in a very reptilian fashion. "I can feel him. He's currently working to break through the barrier of protection I've placed around these lands to keep evil away. Once he succeeds, my people will begin evacuating to a safe place I have prepared for them."

Shal'eth leaned forward, making my breath hitch as his teeth got within a few feet of my face.

"The question is, what will you do?" he asked.

"Umm…"

"Will you engage in slaughter and blindly follow orders? Or will you protect those who have turned their backs on you?"

His questions were very confusing to me.

"I would never hurt the innocent," I said.

Shal'eth studied me carefully. We were so close, I could have reached out and touched him. Despite this, my feelings of fear were melting away. He clearly knew quite a bit about me or was a mind reader. Something about him felt familiar, though I was sure we hadn't met before. Even if he was in his fully mortal form, I doubted I would have forgotten him.

"I would never hurt the innocent," I repeated more firmly.

He nodded slowly. "I believe you. That is why I must ask you to do something for me."

I hesitated and waited for him to continue.

"I want you to go with my people," he began. "There is one among them, a shrine maiden, who will need your protection. Her mother has already died in my service, and only she can help save the future. Protect her from Greyward and from all who mean her harm, for there will be many."

I stared at him as though he had– well, as though he had a dragon's head.

"I can't," I all but whispered. "I've taken oaths. I'm sworn to the Kempt army. I cannot betray and abandon th–"

"Even if they have fallen under the shadow of evil?" Shal'eth interrupted me.

I tried to speak, but no words came out.

Shal'eth closed his eyes for a moment, then they snapped open.

"The time has come; you must leave," he said, rising to his feet. Even as he towered over me, I didn't feel any fear.

"What do I do?" I asked him, standing as well.

"What you know to be right," he replied.

Slowly, I nodded, as resolve hardened in my heart.

"I am very sorry," he whispered so softly I almost couldn't make out the words.

Just then, Mother Imin and several acolytes hurried through the curtain. A few of them gave me looks of surprise, but none stopped to speak to me. Instead, they bustled around the shrine, gathering items and stowing them in wooden chests. I narrowed my eyes as I noticed the old woman working beside them. She was walking without the use of her cane and seemed much more spry than before.

More acolytes and shrine maidens surged through the curtain. It was getting quite crowded as I pushed my way to the exit.

Outside, the first light of dawn was touching the sky, painting the horizon blood red. The square was as busy as an ant colony. Robed figures were rushing here and there, loading carts, packing boxes, and ushering pilgrims toward a line of waiting horses.

A hand fell on my shoulder. I whipped around to find Kraster behind me.

"What happened?" he demanded. "You were inside for nearly an hour without a peep, then, suddenly, everyone started rushing around."

"They– they are about to be attacked," I said.

"Attacked? By who?" Kraster wondered.

"By Greyward, I think." Kraster's face fell. "Did he contact you?" I asked.

Kraster nodded. "He said that the teapot isn't the relic he wants, but it is proof that what he is searching for is here. He told me he was on his way, but I don't think he'll attack a shrine..."

Kraster trailed off uncertainly.

"Are you sure?" I asked.

He licked his lips, then continued. "He's been– strange lately. Keeps talking about needing more strength, more power."

My heart skipped a beat.

"What are we supposed to do?" I wondered, taking in the chaos surrounding us. "Should we help them?"

"They'll never escape in time," Kraster said, looking at the two dozen wagons being quickly loaded. "Even if they make it out of the village, Greyward will catch them before they get far."

"Then what?" I asked softly.

"Then, for their own sakes, I hope they give him what he's looking for."

We both stood watching in silence for a moment. All the pilgrims were long gone, but the inhabitants of the village were still packing with incredible speed and coordination. I glanced to the east, squinting against the rising sun. In the distance, I could just make out a long line of dark figures on the horizon, black silhouettes against the red light.

"Honored guests," a voice said behind us. We turned to find Wren standing there. Her hands were clasped together, and her head was slightly bowed. "For your own safety, we must insist that you depart immediately."

Wren moved away to continue helping her people pack, revealing my black gelding, Tempest, and Kraster's enormous bay, Raspberry, tied to the post in front of the inn. They were saddled, and it looked like all of our belongings had been strapped in place as well.

I stepped forward and reached for Tempest's reins. It took me a moment to realize Kraster hadn't followed me. He'd gone after Wren and was speaking to her. I untied both horses and moved closer to hear what they were saying.

"But where will you go?" Kraster was asking.

"To the new home The Great Shal'eth will provide," Wren assured him unconcernedly.

"I don't think that's going to happen," Kraster told her. "It would be better to surrender and plead for mercy. I will speak to the general myself on your behalf."

Wren gave him a smile as she continued with her work of taking down the oil lamps from around the square and wrapping them in cloth curtains.

"Thank you for your concern and your offer, but it won't be necessary. The Great Shal'eth will save us," Wren assured him.

Kraster opened his mouth, but just then, The Great Shal'eth himself appeared. He left the shrine closely followed by Mother Imin, with whom he was speaking. As they moved from the shrine to the middle of the square, Shal'eth glanced directly at me. Our eyes locked for a long moment. Emotion churned in my stomach, and I knew what I was going to do.

Kraster was staring so hard at Shal'eth that it looked like his eyes might pop out of his head. "What," he gasped, "is that?"

The dragon-man was walking toward the center of the space in front of the shrine, fitting several golden rings onto his fingers as he went.

"It's The Great Shal'eth," I hissed to my brother, forcing Raspberry's reins into his hand.

Kraster turned his amazed expression toward me.

"I met him earlier and– well, he's the one who told me about the coming attack," I explained.

"But what *is* he?" Kraster demanded more loudly than was probably polite.

"You should be telling me," I replied. "Didn't you say you'd read about him in some book?"

Kraster never responded, because at that moment, Shal'eth raised his arms in a great, sweeping motion then pulled them down before thrusting them straight forward, palms out. The rings on his hands started to glow, and a portal of glimmering teal light opened in the middle of the town square. Carts, guided by the women of Thea, started pouring through it in an orderly fashion.

There was a shout from the distant army, and the attack trumpet was sounded. A moment later, a wave of arrows crashed into the streets. I flinched back, pulling Tempest closer to the wall of the inn for cover. Fortunately, no one was hit, but I could hear the thunder of a thousand hoofbeats.

Since Kraster and I were posing as pilgrims, I wasn't wearing my leather armor. I hadn't imagined I'd need it, but then I hadn't imagined Greyward was planning an attack either.

I glanced to the right. The cavalry was charging, their weapons glinting in the morning light. Greyward was at the front, his sword held aloft. A knot pulled tight in my gut. I rushed to the portal, Tempest trotting behind me to keep up.

"What are you doing?" Kraster called.

"Come on," I yelled back at him. "We're going too."

Tempest and I reached the portal and stepped through into a woodland grove. Kraster, leading Raspberry, followed a moment later. I glanced back through the portal. A couple of stragglers hurried after us, then Shal'eth lowered his arms. The portal started to shrink, but not before I saw the dragon-man turn to face Greyward and the onslaught of charging soldiers.

Chapter 4
The Stone

The portal closed behind us, leaving Kraster and me in the middle of a forest. We were surrounded by shrine maidens and acolytes who were hurrying to unload the carts they had so quickly packed less than an hour before.

"What are we doing here?" Kraster asked urgently. His words were spoken close to my ear, but not quietly enough to avoid attracting attention.

"I'd like to know the same thing," an acolyte said, stepping forward and crossing her arms. The woman had dark, curly hair, and the expression she wore was far from friendly.

"These two are members of the Kempt army," the acolyte accused. "I saw their uniforms when I was saddling their horses. They are spies and must have been the ones to signal the attack!"

My mouth went dry as many of the other acolytes stopped their work to glare at us.

"Peace, Tayer," Mother Imin said, placing a hand on the shoulder of the scowling woman. "The Great Shal'eth has sent them to us in our time of need."

"Ummm–" Kraster started, but was cut off almost immediately.

"For even though The Great Shal'eth has delivered us from the present danger, evil times are fast approaching." The old woman's words stilled everyone in the clearing, even those who hadn't noticed us yet.

"Tayer," Mother Imin continued, "fetch the chest containing my personal effects."

Still wearing a disgruntled expression, Tayer headed to one of the wagons across the clearing.

"I have never doubted the wisdom of The Great Shal'eth," Mother Imin announced, as she approached Kraster and me. "That is why I am now entrusting you with–"

Kraster held up a hand to stop her words.

"What is going on?" he demanded, looking questioningly between Mother Imin and myself.

"A darkness is coming," Mother Imin replied softly. "The Great Shal'eth has foreseen it, as he has foreseen that you will help us."

I glanced at Kraster. He wasn't convinced. I was confused myself, but when I thought of my conversation with Shal'eth, the uncertainty cleared.

"Shal'eth told me some kind of ancient evil has taken hold of Greyward," I told Kraster.

"That's ridiculous," he scoffed.

"Are you sure? You heard him sound the attack," I reminded my brother. "He was planning to massacre the entire town."

"Maybe," he mumbled, looking away.

Before I could say more, Tayer returned with a large chest. The box was made of a light brown wood, and it took three women to move. They set it down and then stepped back respectfully.

Mother Imin glanced around. "Now, where is Wren?" she called.

Everyone was completely still for about five seconds until a stunned-looking Wren stepped forward. "Here I am," she squeaked.

"Good." Mother Imin motioned for her to come forward.

Wren approached us hesitantly as Mother Imin opened the chest and folded back a few layers of cloth to reveal the teapot along with its matching set of cups. Even though it had been packed on its side and was still filled with glowing liquid, the pot didn't appear to have leaked so much as a drop of tea.

"Wren," Mother Imin began, "I have something of your mother's that she wanted passed on to you at the proper time."

Wren's eyes widened. Mother Imin reached deeper into the chest, beneath where the teapot lay, and pulled out a polished, teal stone. It was just large enough to fit in the palm of her hand. As Wren took it, I caught sight of a rune engraved on the top.

Future. I read the word to myself, and a warm feeling filled me. The stone was like looking at something out of a dream.

Kraster and I exchanged a glance, and I knew we were thinking the same thing. This was what Greyward had really sent us to look for. It actually made me want to laugh that we'd ever considered the teapot as a viable possibility.

"What– what is it?" Wren wondered.

"It is The Scrying Stone," Mother Imin replied. "Very few are blessed with the ability to use it, but your mother, Elise, was. Since you are of her blood, you will be able to use it as well." Wren nodded eagerly, looking down at the stone cupped in her hands.

"You must take it and go," Mother Imin went on, drawing a gasp from the crowd of women.

Wren looked up sharply, all the color draining from her face.

"Go?" she asked in a small voice.

Mother Imin nodded. "The forces of darkness are seeking that stone. They will use its powers for evil. You must not let that happen."

Wren didn't reply; she just stared at the older woman in horror.

"Take the stone to The Oracle of the Three Sisters. She will be able to guide you on your path," Mother Imin continued, before pointing to Kraster and me. "These two will escort you there."

"We most certainly will," Kraster declared, eagerly stepping forward. His eyes were locked greedily on the stone.

Slowly, Wren's attention shifted to us. Kraster gave her his most winning smile, and she couldn't help but smile back in a shy manner very befitting of a shrine maiden.

"The Great Shal'eth has left this for you too," Mother Imin said, holding out the teapot. "I believe you have already been trained in its use."

Wren nodded and accepted the teapot, then stood there awkwardly with both hands full.

"Fetch Wren traveling clothes and supplies, along with a horse," Mother Imin ordered Tayer and those beside her.

The old woman turned to Kraster. "If there is anything you will require for your journey, you have only to ask."

"We will need a map," Kraster told her. "And if you could point out our location, that would be helpful since I have no idea where we are now."

Mother Imin nodded. Kraster turned to see if I had anything to add. After a moment, Mother Imin looked at me as well.

"I don't suppose you brought any of that lovely wine with you?" I couldn't help but wonder.

Twenty minutes later, Wren was mounted on a sturdy horse that she called Valor, Kraster was studying the map Mother Imin had given him, and I had three bottles of wine stashed in my saddlebags. I'd carefully wrapped them in a spare cloak so they wouldn't shatter.

Gently, I nudged Tempest into a trot and led our small procession away from the clearing. Wren was just behind me. She twisted around in her saddle and called farewells to many of the other shrine maidens, who wished her luck as we rode past. While the younger women in the group seemed confused by how events were unfolding, I saw fear and concern on the faces of the oldest acolytes. They definitely knew more than they were telling us.

Kraster brought up the rear of our party, trying to look at the map and steer Raspberry at the same time.

When we'd left the forest glen behind, Wren fell silent. The path was wide enough for all of us to ride abreast. I stole a glance at the other half-elf. She'd changed out of her mostly white uniform and now wore something more akin to a robe, which ended just below her knees. It was a murky teal color and was tied at the waist with a dark sash. Wren was looking down, so I

32

couldn't see much of her expression, but there was a tear trickling down the bridge of her nose.

When I'd left Owen's Falls, I walked away determined to never return. That decision had literally made me giddy with delight. Wren, however, was not having a similar experience.

"So, who are these three-sister-oracles?" I asked, hoping to distract her.

Wren glanced up. Her eyes were mostly dry, for which I was thankful. I wasn't so good with the emotional stuff.

"There's just one oracle," Wren said quietly. "She resides where three mountains converge. One has a peak that points to the east, another points to the west, and the one in the middle points directly up at the sky. The mountains are the sisters."

Wren gestured forward, and I peered through the trees ahead. Far in the distance, I could just make out several rocky shapes rising into the sky.

"Have you been there before?" Kraster asked.

Wren shook her head. "No, I've never been this far north."

"That makes three of us," I said.

"Really?" Wren wondered. "Since you were chosen by The Great Shal'eth as my guides, I assumed that you'd traveled all over Planosia."

"Hardly," Kraster chuckled. "We're soldiers of Kempt, and our patrols rarely take us farther than three days' ride from the city."

"But what about Moshtia, Fal Ridge, Lion's Hill, Bennton, and The Coral City?" Wren wondered. "Aren't those part of the human kingdom too?"

"What kingdom?" I asked her. "Humans haven't been united under a single banner for hundreds of years. The three major cities have ruling councils and guard the regions close to them, but that's about it. The smaller cities fall under their protection or are on their own."

Wren considered for a moment, then she spoke up sadly. "Wouldn't it be better if they all stood together? Like in the histories about the time of the kings?"

33

Kraster and I exchanged a confused look.

"Maybe," I replied. "But that was a long time ago, before The Great City was razed and King Ardit was slain. He died without a known heir. Although there were rumors of an infant daughter, she was never found. If someone appeared now and tried to claim the kingship, it would doubtless lead to war. So, I think we are better off as we are rather than being forced to unite unwillingly."

"You don't– you don't think that's what Greyward is planning, do you?" Kraster asked uncertainly.

"I don't know," I told him. "You would probably have a better idea of that than I would."

Kraster considered and then shook his head. "No, that doesn't make any sense," he muttered under his breath. "It must all be a misunderstanding."

No one replied, and we rode in silence for the next few hours.

"The mountains don't seem any closer," Wren observed when we stopped for lunch beside a stream.

"I'd say it'll be at least another day or two before we reach them," I guessed.

"That long?" Wren asked in surprise.

I nodded.

"What happens after that?" Kraster inquired.

"We do whatever The Oracle tells us," Wren answered him confidently.

Kraster gave me a skeptical look. *What have you gotten us into?* his expression demanded. I merely shrugged.

"Can I see that stone you were given?" Kraster asked, turning to Wren.

She stiffened slightly, but pulled it from her pocket. Kraster held his hand out, but she shook her head. "Mother Imin said I need to keep the stone on me at all times so I can attune to it."

"What will happen then?" I asked, stepping forward for a better look.

"I'm not sure," Wren admitted.

34

"Your mother never mentioned anything about the stone?" I pressed.

Wren shook her head.

"What happened to her?" Kraster asked softly.

"She died seven years ago, after suffering from a mysterious illness," Wren murmured. "She was in a lot of pain, and even The Great Shal'eth couldn't help her."

"I'm so sorry," Kraster whispered.

I held my tongue; loving parents were not a subject I could relate to.

"What about your dad? Maybe he knows something," my brother suggested.

"I've never met my father," Wren told us. "He was someone who passed through our town one night, leaving my mother with only a kiss and me."

"Men," I snorted.

Wren merely replied, "That is the way of it with my people."

She went on to tell us more about her childhood and what it was like growing up in Thea. The stories of her shrine maiden training were very interesting. She and the others were educated in etiquette, dance, poetry, music, gardening, and martial arts. It honestly sounded worse than a finishing school for ladies, not that I would ever have been admitted to such an establishment.

Wren also revealed that she had been chosen for additional instruction by The Great Shal'eth himself in meditation and mental fortitude. I really couldn't have told you what either of those things were, but they sure sounded impressive.

Once the horses were rested, we set out again and rode until nearly dusk when we happened upon a small town with an inn.

"What luck!" I announced in delight, wondering what kind of drink they had on tap.

"Is it safe?" Wren fretted.

"I don't see why not," Kraster told her.

"But what if we're being hunted?" she argued.

"Even if someone is after the stone," I began, "they'll have no idea where we are or even who they're looking for."

Wren nodded reluctantly and let us lead her to the inn. It was well-lit and cozy. Once the horses' stalls and our rooms were sorted out, I ordered a drink. It was a delightful dark ale sweetened with molasses.

Kraster had a pint too. We tried to talk Wren into trying a sip, but she resisted. Her embarrassed blush made me suspect it was her first time in this kind of establishment. The inn in her town had been much smaller and lacked the raucous ambiance.

A young bard sat in one corner of the room strumming on a lute. He kept starting songs, but then seemed to forget how they went halfway through, drawing the laughter of all the patrons. The way he chuckled each time and made a self-deprecating remark led me to believe he was blundering on purpose. The comments were certainly bringing in more coins than the music ever would have.

My second ale went down just as smoothly as the first. It felt like fire in my veins, racing through me with impossible heat and speed. The third only added to the sensation. If I'd had wings, I knew I'd be able to fly. Before I finished the flagon, I was singing along with the bard, continuing the songs even when he trailed off.

I would have been game to drink the whole night away, but Kraster reminded me we wanted to make an early start in the morning, so I allowed him to guide me up the stairs. I was sharing the larger room with Wren while Kraster took the tiny one next to it.

Wren hesitated when she saw Kraster heading for the smaller room and I for the larger.

"I– Are you two not a couple?" she asked, following me through the door.

I bellowed with laughter, dropping my pack on the closest bed.

"He's my brother," I told her.

Wren cocked her head slightly, and I could see the questions that flooded her mind clear as day on her face. "That means…" she started.

"It means I'm his father's 'wild oats', and he's his mother's revenge against my mother," I clarified. "Not that it was necessary. It was pretty clear early on that my parents were never going to be together. My father already had a family, a big one, and he wasn't going to accept me and jeopardize the life he'd built."

Memories of the years I'd spent watching Kraster and his siblings filled my mind. They had been so happy, and I was nothing but a shadow, casting darkness on their joy.

"Everyone knew," I went on, my voice filling with sorrow. I tried to stop my words, but I'd had too much to drink and they just kept coming. "Everyone knew who I was. *What* I was."

"What you are?" Wren asked in confusion.

"I'm half," I told her.

"Half what?"

"Half everything. Half elf, half human, half of the forest, half of the village, and right now, half drunk." I laughed a little at my joke. "I even go by half of my name. My name, my full name, Bankimcandra, means half moon. So, apparently, my mother had a sense of humor at some point in her life."

I stopped myself. I should have drunk more. I should have drunk until I couldn't remember anything. Oblivion was amazing. I glanced around for my saddlebags. There was wine in them. Wine would help me forget. The bags were nowhere to be seen. Kraster had probably taken them.

Much as I wanted to stop the pain, the effort of trying to wrestle the saddlebags from Kraster or of braving the stairs back down to the inn's common room seemed too exhausting. Instead, I clumsily removed my boots and fell into bed fully dressed. Sleep came easily and lasted through the night.

In the morning, I had only a slight headache. I'd gotten so used to those that I hardly even noticed. I was awake before Wren and had just secured a plate of eggs and sausages in the common room when I saw Kraster coming to join me. He looked perturbed. I took a bite of sausage as he sat down.

"Sleep okay?" I asked innocently.

He nodded.

"Then what's with the sour expression?" I pressed.

Kraster sighed and pulled out his communication charm.

"I forgot you had that," I stated tensely. "Did you get a message?"

"I did," Kraster nodded. "It came through this morning. Greyward wants to know where I am and if I've found any kind of special stone."

"Getting straight to the point now, isn't he?" I observed before swallowing a spoonful of eggs.

"What should I do?" Kraster asked.

"You haven't told him anything?"

Kraster shook his head.

"I think you should throw that thing away," I replied.

Kraster furrowed his brow. "I can't. Not after everything Greyward has done for me. I don't believe he's the villain in this. There has to be a logical explanation for what he's done."

My brother heaved a great sigh, then his eyes narrowed as he looked at me. "And what's your explanation?" he snapped. "You abandoned the mission and somehow managed to drag me into this! Now we're both traitors!"

"Greyward doesn't know that, and he doesn't need to," I said, attempting to placate my brother. "Tell him we didn't know what he was looking for yesterday, which is true, and we saw the townspeople of Thea escaping, so we went along to continue our search. Again, most of that is true.

"Then see if you can casually ask Greyward what's going on and what's so special about the stone. Maybe that will give you the explanation you're looking for."

Kraster sighed, but nodded.

"In the meantime, we can see what The Oracle says. Maybe it is all a misunderstanding, and we can find a way to make everything right."

"That's a good idea," Kraster agreed. "It wouldn't hurt to work both sides for a bit until we discover what's going on, then we can decide what to do."

"I'm really smart like that," I told my brother, making him roll his eyes at me.

Still, Kraster looked much happier as he went to get some breakfast for himself. Wren joined us a little later, and we set out, heading once again toward the distant mountains, where I hoped we would find the answers to all of our questions.

Chapter 5
The Genie

In the morning, we passed through several towns and villages, but all signs of civilization vanished by late afternoon. When the shadows started to grow long, we stopped to make camp.

"We'll probably reach The Three Sisters in the morning," I observed as I dismounted.

"I hope so," Kraster muttered. Despite sending Greyward the message we had agreed upon, Kraster had been growing more and more agitated all day. He kept checking his communication charm, despite the fact that he knew the enchantment only worked once a day, and he'd get nothing in return until sunrise when the magic was restored.

After tending to Tempest, I started gathering firewood.

"I should have asked Mother Imin for a tent," Wren chided herself.

"We have tents," Kraster told her.

Wren turned and watched as he laid out his bedroll. "Then why aren't you setting them up?" she asked curiously.

"No need." Kraster shook his head. "It's a nice night."

Wren glanced around the clearing warily.

"I'm guessing you haven't traveled much," I remarked.

"I've been on a few pilgrimages to other local shrines," Wren replied. "But we always slept in wagons. What's going to stop wild animals and bandits from attacking us if we are in the open like this?"

"We'll leave someone on watch," I explained. "I'll go first."

"No, you won't," Kraster called from where he was using my pile of wood to build a fire. He turned to Wren and explained, "Candra likes to watch first, so she can have a few drinks when she's done."

"That's the responsible way to do it!" I protested, rolling my eyes.

"Unless something goes wrong on any of the other watches," my brother countered.

Wren's eyes were the size of saucers.

"I will leave off the drinking… for tonight," I sighed before taking my bow and walking into the woods.

I returned twenty minutes later with a fat rabbit to roast over the fire. We finished setting up camp while it cooked and then gathered around to eat. Wren brought out the teapot and poured us each a cup. I looked at the minty green contents and raised an eyebrow. Steam rose from the liquid even though the pot had not been close to the fire.

"What is it?" I asked.

"Tea, of course," Wren replied, taking a sip of hers.

I narrowed my eyes suspiciously. "Where does it come from? What exactly is in that pot?"

"I'll show you," Wren said, rising to her feet. She lifted the teapot in both hands, then began to move it in different directions. Suddenly, she thrust it upward, holding it aloft over her head while spinning in a quick circle. She mumbled some words under her breath that I didn't hear as she sat back down.

The teapot was glowing brighter than usual, and thin, pale green wisps of smoke trailed out of it. Some of the mist wrapped around Wren, hardening into three bangle bracelets on her right arm.

"What–" Kraster began, but was interrupted as the remaining smoke twisted unnaturally, forming into the shape of a female humanoid.

I was on my feet in a moment, both of my swords drawn and pointed at the being. Her face wasn't quite human, with skin that had an aquamarine, iridescent sheen. The mint green hair floating around her head was completely ignoring gravity, as was the hem of the white, dress-like robe she wore. Her hands were webbed, and each finger ended in a sharp claw.

The creature turned to look at me with eyes of solid black. A sense of danger, unlike anything I'd ever felt before, lanced through me. I wanted nothing more than to run her through. It took every drop of willpower I possessed to keep my hands still.

"What is that *thing*?" I hissed.

Wren and Kraster were looking at me in surprise.

"I am Puvva of the Pot," the creature said, its voice harsh. "What does Master wish?"

"Don't worry. She's not dangerous; she's a genie," Wren explained to me.

I blinked, and suddenly the being in front of me didn't look nearly as threatening as before. Her eyes were the same green as her hair, and what I had mistaken for claws were simply the nails of her long fingers.

Slightly embarrassed, I sank back down onto the log where I'd been sitting.

"Sorry," I muttered. "You startled me."

"I've never seen you so jumpy," Kraster laughed.

I made a face at him.

"She was a good friend of The Great Shal'eth," Wren told us, then sorrow filled her eyes. "He must have sent her away to keep her safe."

Puvva blinked at Wren. "He was not my friend, but my master, as you are now." Her words were factual, holding no emotion. They also bore a strange accent I didn't think I'd ever heard before.

"No! That can't be true!" Wren gasped. "The Great Shal'eth would never keep a slave, nor would I! My people believe that everyone should be free!"

Puvva remained completely calm and eerily still during Wren's outburst.

"What do you mean he was your master?" Kraster asked. "How did you serve him?"

Puvva turned to Kraster and studied him with unblinking eyes. "The one you call The Great Shal'eth created the four vessels long ago. I do not know what became of the other three, but he

42

retained possession of my pot. As with any I would call my master, he had the right to ask three wishes of me."

"Any three wishes?" Kraster asked in awe.

Puvva snapped her fingers, and an extremely large scroll of paper appeared in her hand.

"Any three wishes so long as they adhere to the contract of the pot." Puvva allowed the scroll to begin unraveling while she held the top, from which she began reading.

"Article one: Terms and definitions.

"One. The Pot: The dwelling place of Puvva when the master does not have need of her for wishes or information regarding wishes.

"Two. Wish: A command given to Puvva by the master of the pot using the specific phrase. Formal: 'Puvva of the Pot, I use a wish to command thee to...' Informal: 'Puvva, I wish you...'

"Three. Null wish: A wish made by the master using the proper phrasing, but that goes against the fundamentals of the contract between the master and genie. As it cannot be completed, a null wish does not count against the total three wishes per master.

"Injunction one: If only part of the wish goes against the fundamentals, only part of the wish shall be considered null, and the rest shall be carried out to the fullest extent possible.

"Injunction two: A partially null wish does count against the total three wishes per master.

"Injunction three: There is a time constraint of six hours for partially null wishes. As partially null wishes may only be partially possible. A maximum time of six hours is allotted for their achievement, during which any additional wishes made will be considered a null wish by default.

"Injunction four: A valid wish may become a null or partially null wish if conditions change in an unfavorable way while the wish is ongoing.

"Example: While I, Puvva, am able to heal wounds, I am unable to recall those claimed by death. If the wish is made that I will heal someone while they are still alive, but they perish before my power can take effect, this renders the wish null.

"Four. The wish bracele–"

"So she gets three reasonable wishes?" I interrupted. The print on the scroll was tiny, and Puvva had miles to go before even reaching the second section.

The genie glanced at me out of the corner of her eye. "If that is how you would choose to understand my words," she said condescendingly.

"Can I have three wishes next?" Kraster asked.

Puvva looked down her nose at him. "Only if the current master performs the proper ceremony to transfer ownership of the pot to you."

Kraster looked at Wren hopefully, but Wren shook her head.

"I don't know how to do that," she told him. "All I know how to do is summon her. I didn't know anything about wishes." The confusion in her eyes made it clear to me that she still wasn't comfortable with the whole complicated wish business.

"What kind of things did Shal'eth wish for?" I asked curiously.

In response, I received another side-eyed look from Puvva. She did not answer me but turned to Wren instead.

"You can tell her," Wren said.

"Is that one of your wishes?" Puvva asked eagerly.

"Don't waste a wish on that!" Kraster exclaimed.

"I won't," Wren assured him. "I don't want to use my wishes at all. It doesn't seem fair that this poor creature is forced into a life of servitude."

"Okay…" I said uncertainly. "But why else would Shal'eth have transferred ownership of the teapot to you. He must have meant for you to use the wishes."

Wren's brows knit together.

I turned back to Puvva. "So, what did Shal'eth wish for?"

I doubted the genie would answer, but, after a moment, she did. "I will tell you in the hopes that it will inspire my new master to make her own wishes so that I will be dismissed to my pot once more.

"The first wish I will not speak of."

"Could Wren wish for you to tell her?" Kraster cut in.

"She could try," Puvva said, giving him a soul-crushing look before continuing. "However, it would be a null wish as Shal'eth's second command was to never speak of the first wish, among other things."

There was a moment of silence.

"And the third wish?" I prompted.

"The third wish was that I undo the first wish," Puvva told me. Her tone made it clear she would say no more on the matter, despite the fact that she had said basically nothing.

"Do you know why The Great Shal'eth made me your new master?" Wren asked the genie.

"I do not," Puvva answered.

"It must have something to do with the stone. Show it to her," I suggested.

Reluctantly, Wren held up the stone. Puvva's eyes locked onto it.

"Do you know what it is?" I asked the genie.

"Something very old and powerful," Puvva answered, without looking at me.

"Clearly, this Shal'eth bloke gave you the stone and the teapot because he wants you to do something important for him," Kraster interjected. "I'm just not sure how we got mixed up in it."

Kraster glanced at me with a look that made it clear he was, yet again, wondering what exactly we had gotten ourselves into.

"We're going to see what The Oracle says," I reminded him. "Something bigger than what we understand is clearly going on, and the more we know, the better."

Kraster didn't argue, but I could tell he wasn't pleased with the situation.

Puvva retreated into her teapot as soon as Wren dismissed her, and, after much discussion, I got stuck with the last watch.

As I lay down on my bedroll, I tried to think of something besides the bottles of wine in my saddlebags. Wren had first watch. I might be able to sneak a few mouthfuls of the delectable beverage without her noticing. I was in the middle of making a plan when I fell asleep.

A scream from Wren woke me. I jerked awake and drew my swords as I scrambled to my feet. Spinning around, I searched the dark forest for foes, but there were none.

In the dim light of the campfire, I saw Kraster kneeling beside Wren. I joined him instantly.

"What happened?" I demanded, adrenaline coursing through my system.

Wren's eyes were huge. "I had a– a nightmare."

I lowered my weapons slowly. The two swords were long and slender, perfect for sliding between the ribs of my enemies. I resheathed them and looked down at Wren, who was still trying to catch her breath.

"What happened in your dream that scared you so badly?" Kraster asked.

"I was underground somewhere," Wren started. "I think it was a tunnel because the walls were very smooth. It was completely dark, but then there was a loud noise and flashing lights. Dozens of faces were flying past me, and I– I saw–"

Wren broke off, features contorting as if saying the next word would cause her physical pain.

"What did you see?" Kraster coaxed gently.

"Spiders," Wren whispered.

"Spiders?" I asked, unsure if that was what she had really said.

"Yes," Wren nodded. "Big ones. Blue and silver. The size of horses. And there were other creatures too, with the same legs and bodies, but human faces."

"I'm sure it was terrifying," Kraster told her. "But it was just a dream."

"It felt so real!" Wren protested.

"Dreams can be like that," I said. "However, it's just your imagination running away with you. This is your first time spending a night in the open, so it's not really a surprise."

Wren looked like she wanted to believe me.

"Candra's right," Kraster spoke up quickly. "This place is new and kind of scary. Your mind is just feeding off of your anxiety."

Wren considered for a moment, then nodded slowly. "I'm sorry," she murmured.

"It's nothing to be embarrassed about," Kraster comforted her quickly. "Everyone has nightmares from time to time."

Chapter 6
The Oracle

By the time Kraster and I succeeded in calming Wren, my brother's watch was over. I took my place by the fire while he happily sprawled himself on his bedroll. A few minutes later, he was snoring. Wren, on the other hand, tossed and turned for the next three hours. She jumped at every sound, or if I even shifted slightly.

Just before dawn, Wren's breathing grew even. Sadly, I had to rouse her half an hour later so we could strike camp. I wouldn't have minded letting her sleep in, but there was no telling what Kraster would do if we didn't reach The Oracle before nightfall.

The northern road was completely empty as we drew near the base of the three mountains. From there, a trail to the summit wound upward. The sun was almost directly overhead when the dusty path finally opened onto a broad clifftop. At the far end, a steep passage continued upward to where the three mountains separated into their respective peaks.

Beside the trailhead was a wooden building, the doors of which were thrown open to reveal stalls. Inside, a pair of donkeys were calmly munching hay out of a manger.

A gnome boy with shaggy, blond hair sat outside the building on a three-legged stool. He popped up as soon as he saw our horses step onto the plateau.

"I'm Gnob," the gnome introduced himself once he reached us. "I can take your horses while you wait to speak to The Oracle."

"Thank you, Nob," Kraster said as he dismounted.

"It's Gnob," the boy corrected him.

"That's what I said. Nob," Kraster replied in confusion.

"No, Gnob," the gnome persisted. "There's a silent G at the front."

Kraster stared at him in confusion.

"If it's silent, then how do you know he didn't say it?" Wren wondered.

Gnob shrugged. "I can just tell."

"Ok…" Kraster still seemed mystified. "Thank you, Gnob…"

Gnob beamed. "You're welcome!"

I tried not to laugh at the unusual exchange. There weren't many gnomes around Kempt and even fewer in the outlying towns. As a result, I didn't have many dealings with them and doubted Kraster did either.

"How long do you think the wait will be?" I asked Gnob. He had taken the reins of all three of our horses and was leading them away with surprising confidence despite the fact that he barely came up to their knees. Just one of those massive hooves could have easily crushed him.

"I don't know," Gnob replied. His voice was high-pitched and his words rapid. "There are three of you, so you won't have to wait for others or take turns. The last group went up half an hour ago, which means it should be soon."

"Only our friend, Wren, has questions for The Oracle," Kraster interjected, easily keeping pace beside the gnome.

"Nope," Gnob said. "It doesn't work like that."

"What do you mean?" I asked, trailing behind my brother.

"People go up in groups of three. You each ask a question, which may or may not be answered to your satisfaction. But don't worry, The Oracle knows what to say, even if you don't know it's what you're supposed to hear," Gnob explained as he settled our horses into the open-air stalls.

Wren furrowed her brow. "It's very important that my question be answered. I've been tasked by The Great–"

"The Oracle will tell you what you need to hear," Gnob reiterated, cutting Wren off. "No more, no less."

I exchanged glances with my companions.

"This sounds like a waste of time," Kraster muttered.

"But this is where we were sent," protested Wren.

"We're already here." I shrugged, trying to appear less desperate than I felt. "Might as well see what The Oracle has to say."

I could tell Kraster wasn't convinced and wondered if he'd heard from Greyward this morning. Unfortunately, I couldn't ask with Wren standing just a few feet away.

It wasn't long before a group of three persons, two humans and a dwarf, came down the trail. The two humans were talking to each other conspiratorially. They stopped to thank Gnob as he brought them their donkeys. The dwarf kept on walking without a word.

Gnob waved goodbye to the two donkeys and their riders, then turned to us. "The Oracle will see you now," he announced with a little bow, hand extended toward the upward path.

Wren started forward immediately. Kraster and I hurried after her. The trail was steep and narrow but not too much of a struggle, at least not at first. Ten minutes later, we were all panting and gasping for air.

We kept going until the land before us leveled off at the mouth of a cave. It was set in the exact spot where all three of the mountains met before separating and rising into their own peaks. As Wren had told us, the one on the right pointed east, the one on the left pointed west, and the one in the middle stood perfectly straight.

"I guess we should go in," Wren said, stepping through the cave's entrance. I laid a hand on the hilt of one of my swords and kept close behind her.

From outside, the cave looked pitch black, but as soon as I crossed the threshold, I blinked in surprise. The interior was a perfect circle, quartered into four sections. Our section was barren, but the others each held the contents of a one-room cottage with a bed, a table, a stove, and a wash basin. Those three sections were all laid out exactly the same way. The items in each appeared identical, save for the fact that in the section to our right they were new and in perfect condition, while in the section across from us they looked well-worn. The items in the space to our left were old and tattered.

Each quarter also had an entrance at the back shaped exactly like the cave mouth behind us. Through the openings on the right and left, a sun could be seen. On our right was a radiant, yellow sun. It seemed to be just rising into the sky and lit its quadrant with warmth and color. In contrast, the sun on the left was red, like the normal sun, but even darker. It appeared ready to set and seemed to produce little light or warmth.

The opening in the section straight ahead mirrored our own, showing nothing except the sky, but giving plenty of light.

"Greetings," said three voices.

I jumped, and my jaw dropped open. Standing before us, each in one of the other sections, were three identical women. Their brown, curly hair was pulled back from their faces in matching ponytails. All three had brilliant blue eyes, which stared straight ahead, expressionless.

I nudged Wren from behind. She took a step forward, standing at the point where our section met the others.

"Please, wise Oracle," Wren began. "We have been sent here by The Great Shal'eth on an errand of the utmost importance."

None of the women moved as Wren pulled out The Scrying Stone and continued. "I was instructed to bring this to you so you could tell me what to do with it."

For a moment, the entire cave was still, then the woman in the right quarter, where the sun was brightest, snapped her attention to Wren and the stone.

The sunlight streaming into the cave intensified until it was almost too brilliant to see. I felt a warm, pleasant breeze brush my cheek, the kind we only had in the very middle of summer.

"This stone was a great gift, given long ago to one who betrayed the giver," said the woman in a voice as thin and fine as morning mist. "Eight stones there were, all bestowed freely on those who became traitors, save one. The stones have since been

51

strewn far and wide across the land. One has passed into shadow and one is no more."

The speaker froze as the room returned to normal. Instantly, I missed the light and warmth.

Next, the woman in the middle turned her head to Wren. "The stone you hold is the gift of the future," she said. Her voice wasn't nearly as high as the first woman's.

"Through peaceful meditation," she continued, "it can be used to seek the others. They go by many names now and are used for many things: Azazoth's Wand, The Gem of Aero, Dimble's Legacy, The Heart of Jong, Baarthagon's Collar.

"But I offer you fair warning that such stones were not meant for mortals. Be careful when you delve into powers you do not understand or your life will be forfeit."

The silence following her words was ominous, made all the more so when darkness began to fill the cave, leaving it all the same, muted color as the left quadrant. The temperature dropped, and I felt a cold chill creep down my spine.

"The eight stones will be a beginning as they have been an end," the last woman stated. Her voice was deeper than expected and held a note of mystery. While her eyes were locked on Wren, I didn't think she was actually seeing her. "The stones will soon be united. What matters most is who holds them, for they alone contain the power to save the world from the void. Only all eight stones, coupled with the ninth gift, can free what has been bound and redeem the fallen."

The ninth gift? I thought. *What the heck is that?*

The speaker froze as light and warmth returned to the cave.

"Well, I guess that is what we came for," Kraster said quietly, inching toward the cave opening.

"Wait–" I started but cut off abruptly as the light grew stronger and stronger.

The first woman stirred again, looking directly at Kraster. No one moved, and the woman continued to stare.

"Ask something," I hissed.

"I– I–" Kraster stuttered then blurted out, "why did Greyward attack the shrine?"

"The one you call Greyward has found that which his heart most desires: great power. He has sought this power for many years. Ever since he met you."

I blinked. What was she talking about? What did Kraster have to do with Greyward's ambition?

The room's light returned to normal as we looked at the middle woman. "He is changed by shadow and is no longer the man you knew," she told Kraster. "He hunts the stones, desiring the gifts they possess."

"Can he be changed back to normal?" Kraster asked desperately while the room grew dark and cold.

"The future is not always absolute," the third woman replied, eyes and voice distant and unfocused. "But he will betray you if you give him the chance."

A shadow crossed Kraster's face, and he turned away. My heart broke for my brother. He was so loyal, and hearing these things had to be tearing him apart.

Once again, the room grew deliciously warm. The light that filled it was liquid gold as it poured into the stone cave. I took a deep breath and tried to think of a question. It didn't really matter what I asked. I'd already made my choice.

Before I managed to come up with a question, the first woman spoke. Her voice was still light and breezy, but tinged with sorrow, the first emotion I'd heard any of the three use. "You were cursed long ago," she said.

"What?! I was cursed?" I gasped. "But why?"

"Jealousy."

My mind instantly jumped to Kraster's mother. She'd been furious when she found out I was going to be born. In fact, I was pretty sure she had single-handedly turned the entire human population of Owen's Falls against me.

"Who did this to me?" I asked, not looking at Kraster.

"They are trapped, scattered, lost, hidden in shadow." The answer came as a whisper.

Before I could ask more, the light changed. I whipped my head toward the next woman, meeting her blue eyes with my strange brown ones.

"You are cursed," she began. "Others sense it, but no one understands. You are disliked and distrusted, hated and scorned."

My mouth dropped open at her bluntness.

"Now you know why," she concluded.

"How do I break my curse?" I all but shouted at her. My question came too late; the cave was growing dark. Very dark. Had it gotten this dark the last two times?

The third woman turned to me, and our eyes met. She looked at me as she had not looked at Kraster or Wren.

"You will be cursed for the rest of your life, until you take your final breath."

There didn't seem to be any air in my lungs, and my entire body felt like ice, even as the room around me warmed. I remained where I was, eyes locked on the third woman. She was still for a few seconds, then slowly faded away to nothing.

I turned to see that the other women were gone too. My mind felt blank, but, slowly, I started having memories of all the times rotten things had happened to me, when people had been cruel, and when I'd tried my best only to see it all fail.

I didn't even realize I was the one laughing until both Kraster and Wren turned to stare at me. Quickly, I raised my hand to cover my mouth, but it wasn't enough. I couldn't stop.

Of course I was cursed. I mean, why not? Everything in my life had gone wrong, so throwing a curse on top of it all like a little bow was really appropriate. Or, maybe, the curse was the reason I was so unlucky.

"Are you okay?" Kraster asked, putting a hand on my shoulder.

"I'm fine," I gasped, finally getting my mirth under control.

Kraster's brow furrowed. "You're not upset?"

"Why would I be?" I asked. "I'm the same ornery, unlikable person I was ten minutes ago. Now I know why."

Kraster's expression didn't lighten.

"I need a drink," I announced, heading for the cave opening. The others followed me down the winding path without speaking.

At the bottom, Gnob was talking to a few travelers waiting to see The Oracle.

I went straight to Tempest, who was still saddled and standing in one of the stalls. I reached into the nearest of his saddlebags and groped around until my fingers touched cool glass. I pulled out the bottle, uncorked it, and took a swig. It was good. Exactly what I needed. I took another long pull and turned to find Kraster and Wren still right behind me wearing expressions fit for a funeral.

Chapter 7
The Past

"Want some?" I asked, holding out the bottle. They both shook their heads.

I took one more long drink before recorking and stowing the wine. My head felt lighter, and there was a burning warmth in my cheeks. It helped to chase away the chill I still felt clinging to my bones.

"Why are you looking at me like that?" I demanded of my brother. Then another thought occurred to me. "Did you know?"

Kraster shook his head quickly. "No! Of course not!"

"Good," I said. "Now, let's just forget about it."

"How can you say that?" Wren demanded. "Don't you want to break your curse?"

I gave her a long look. "You seem to have forgotten that my curse will only be broken by my death..."

Wren blinked at me.

"I wasn't cursed up there today. I just found out about it is all. Nothing has changed, so it doesn't matter," I insisted. "Plus, don't we have more important things to be worrying about?"

Wren nodded slowly, but Kraster folded his arms across his chest.

"What do we do now?" Wren asked.

"She's in denial," Kraster told her. "I think we need to wait until it wears off."

I rolled my eyes.

"No, I meant about the stones," Wren clarified.

"Oh, I'm not sure," Kraster admitted, furrowing his brow.

"It seems like a lot of people are going to be looking for the stones for bad reasons," I spoke up, happy with the subject change.

"But you can use yours to find the others," Kraster recalled, turning to Wren. "That way we can get them first and keep them hidden."

Wren bit her lip. "The Oracle warned me that it would be very dangerous, so I'd rather use that as a last resort. I mean, as long as we keep The Scrying Stone safe, isn't that enough, since then no one else will be able to get all eight?"

I shook my head slowly. "I don't think that's going to work. The Oracle said we'd need all the stones to save the world."

Kraster nodded uncertainly. "That's what I understood too. I think we should gather them. What were the others' names? Aza-somebody's wand, a gem of something, and then that other one. Oh, and wasn't there something about a collar…?"

"It was Azazoth's Wand, The Gem of Aero, Dimble's Legacy, The Heart of Jong, and Baarthagon's Collar," Wren recited. "I've never heard of any of them."

"Plus the one that is no more and the one in the shadows," I added. "The fact that even The Oracle can't see them makes me think finding those two will be pretty difficult."

"Did I hear you say something about Dimble's Legacy?" Gnob piped up.

Kraster and Wren both jumped and turned around.

I couldn't see the gnome because the half-stable door was closed, concealing him completely. I moved closer until Gnob came into view.

"And you said you'd never heard of it? I say, you tall folk are all the same, paying no attention to your betters."

"Excuse me?" Kraster gasped.

"You know what Dimble's Legacy is?" Wren jumped in eagerly.

"I sure do," Gnob replied, ignoring Kraster. "It's a magic codex created by the greatest inventor of my people, Dimble."

"And where does Dimble live?" Wren asked.

"Don't you know nothing?" Gnob demanded scornfully. "Dimble died and was buried nearly nine centuries ago."

Wren's face fell.

"But we still use the codex to this day," Gnob went on proudly. "That's why it's called his legacy. Crackle Hoppindinger is the current head engineer. He uses the codex to create machines to protect our people from *outsiders*." The gnome said "outsiders" like it was a dirty word.

"How wonderful!" Wren beamed. "Do you know where we might be able to find it?"

Gnob gave her a strange look. "Find it? Why would you want to find it? Can't imagine it would do you much good."

"It's something that The Oracle told us to seek out," Kraster put in quickly.

Gnob hesitated. "The Oracle wants you to go and visit a gnomish artifact?"

"So it would seem," Kraster said as casually as he could.

"Hmmm…" Gnob didn't appear convinced.

"I don't think you know," I told Gnob. "All that showing off, and you have no clue what you're talking about."

Gnob turned on me quickly. "Of course I know where it is! The codex is only my people's most sacred treasure! Even the smallest gnome child knows it's kept in the capital city of Gnomania."

Gnob eyed me with dislike, and I caught myself wondering if it was because I'd heckled him or because I was cursed. I shrugged. Honestly, it was probably a bit of both.

"Forgive me for doubting." I tried to keep my apology sincere, but I don't think I did a very good job.

Gnob gave me a scathing look. "And don't trust everything The Oracle tells you," he started again, speaking quickly. "She prophesied that I'd be dead in a year. Incurable disease or something like that. It's been eight months and I still feel fit as a fiddle." The gnome turned on his heel and stalked away.

We all blinked after him for a moment.

"Gnomania isn't too far away," Kraster broke the silence. "Only a few days' ride to the north."

"What about the other stones?" Wren fretted.

"We can figure that out on the way," I told her as I opened the stall door and led Tempest out of the small stable.

"Should she really be riding in that state?" Wren whispered to Kraster.

"I'm barely buzzed," I called over my shoulder to her. "Get your horses, and let's go!"

We reached the bottom of The Three Sisters by mid-afternoon and struck off north. The Gnome Plateau, where the majority of the gnomes in Planosia lived, wasn't yet visible. Supposedly, it was so massive that you could see it for days before reaching it.

I'd always heard that gnomes were rather stuck-up. Not that elves or even humans were much better, but few races were as cloistered as the gnomes. Naturally, they'd chosen the highest place they could find to live so as to finally be able to look down on the other races.

Past The Three Sisters, the land was a wide open plain of grass and tumbleweeds. We traveled until the sun was touching the horizon. Half of the brush was dead, so the horses had to forage a bit to find anything to graze on, but they managed.

As we sat around the fire that night, Wren insisted on summoning Puvva from the teapot.

"It can't be good for her to be cooped up all the time," Wren explained as the genie formed from the mist.

"I do not mind," Puvva told her decisively, but Wren still insisted she remain with us for the evening.

The genie didn't eat anything. Even when Wren offered her a bite of the pheasant I'd shot, she turned up her nose. In fact, the only thing that seemed to interest Puvva was water. We'd camped next to a stream, and Puvva stared at it all throughout the meal.

Kraster and I were packing up our cooking gear when I heard a sudden splash. I froze, terror paralyzing me, but when I turned to the stream, Puvva was floating tranquilly in the middle. She didn't seem to be swimming, just kind of hovering in the water as if she were liquid herself.

Wren hurried over in concern, but I didn't take even one step closer to the water's edge. There were some things I wasn't brave enough to face.

I laid out my bedroll then retrieved the bottle of wine I'd started earlier.

"No, you don't," Kraster called from across the clearing.

I gave him a wicked smile and went to take a drink, but the bottle was suddenly plucked from my hand by an invisible force. It levitated several feet above my head as I glared at my brother.

"Give it back," I demanded.

"You've already had some today," he replied.

"That was hours ago," I protested.

"Still counts," Kraster said as the bottle rose another two feet and started to drift toward him.

I narrowed my eyes, trying to decide if I should attack. I could easily take Kraster in a fight if not for his darn magic. He had a limited reserve and didn't usually waste it like this. I guess he figured he had some energy to spare after doing basically nothing with it the past few days.

My decision was still unmade when Wren returned from the stream, forehead puckered. She glanced at the floating bottle, and her jaw dropped open.

"You can do magic?" she gasped, looking at me.

With a sigh, I raised a finger and pointed it at Kraster. "Not me, him."

"But you're related," she said. "I thought magic was something inherited through the ancient bloodlines."

"Sometimes," Kraster clarified, taking the bottle from the air and tucking it under his arm. He approached us warily, keeping a close eye on me.

"It can also be the result of years of study, use of a magical object, making an oath to a patron, or sometimes it just shows up with little to no explanation."

I cringed internally at the memory my brother's words dredged up.

"What is your source?" Wren's voice was filled with curiosity.

Kraster and I exchanged a lightning-fast glance.

"It's a long story," he began, taking a seat on a nearby stump. I settled onto my bedroll, and Wren perched on the edge of a stone. She was leaning forward, intent on Kraster's words.

"I was normal as a child, but something happened, and things changed. Our hometown, Owen's Falls, is named for the giant waterfall that can be found half a mile up in the hills. My siblings and I liked to go there and swim on the warmest summer days."

My palms started to sweat as I wondered how much of the story he was going to relay.

"One day, while we were up there, I decided to climb to the top of the falls. I slipped and fell into the water. On the way down, I hit my head on a rock."

Kraster paused for a moment, and relief washed over me. He'd left out my part in the story. It wasn't something I wanted anyone to know. I'd tried so hard to forget it but never could.

"I don't remember anything that happened after that until I woke up two weeks later.

"From what my siblings have said, I landed in the water and sank out of sight. Half the town came running to help search for me, but they didn't find me for two days. Somehow, I was still alive. When they pulled back my eyelids, my eyes were as black as night, and I was muttering strange, dark words in my sleep. The town doctor had no idea what was wrong with me and didn't think I'd ever wake up.

"My mother was beside herself since I've always been her favorite. Once I was mostly recovered, she sent me to live in the city of Kempt with my older sister, Noral, whose husband is a successful merchant. Guess, she thought I'd be safer there."

"And while you were in the city, you learned to use magic from a mage?" Wren surmised.

"No," Kraster shook his head. "But I learned a lot about trading, buying, and selling, so it wasn't a total waste."

61

"I'm confused about how this leads to you using magic," Wren told him, then turned to me. "And what were you doing during all this time? Did you guys know each other growing up?"

"Oh, yes," I replied. "We knew *all* about each other. The whole town did, and they took his mother's side. So I was mostly trying to be invisible and forgotten.

"As soon as I was old enough, I left everything behind and joined up with the military in Kempt. After several months of training, I got my commission, and do you know who else was assigned to that very same squad? My dear half-brother, who I'd been planning to never think of again."

I tried not to let too much disdain color my words. I'd been furious at the time but, as it turned out, being assigned to the same squad as Kraster had been the best thing that ever happened to me. Of all my siblings, he'd been the only one to try and get to know me when we were children. That effort was redoubled during our time in the army.

"I'm still waiting for the magic part," Wren reminded us.

"Well, that happened about a year later," Kraster went on, taking back over the telling of the tale. I was glad he did, since the next part wasn't pleasant.

"There was a band of mercenaries that had robbed a large caravan and then holed up in a nearby village. All the townsfolk had fled, and our squad was dispatched to deal with them.

"Greyward," Kraster spoke the name hesitantly, "didn't realize how many mercenaries there were or that they had several strong magic users.

"We marched into the village completely unprepared and took heavy losses. Our commander signaled the retreat, but the mercenaries cut us off. There were arrows and missiles flying everywhere."

Kraster glanced in my direction. "Candra pulled me off the street and into a building for cover. A moment later, one of the mages struck the place where we'd been standing with a fireball. The inferno it created killed the rest of our company. Unfortunately, the enemy had seen us escape. A second fireball hit the building we were in, knocking off half the roof and setting the rest on fire.

"The moment I knew we were going to die, a memory came to me of the days I'd spent in the lake. It was dark under the water, and I remembered thinking the same thing I did then, that this was the end. Then an eye opened in front of me. And not just one but hundreds, all of them singular and not human. They watched me for what felt more like forever than just the two days I was missing.

"As these memories came rushing back, I felt a surge of energy burst out of me. I didn't even mean to do it, it just happened."

Kraster turned to me. "Your turn."

I nodded. "Like he said, we were trapped. All hope was lost, then, suddenly, my brother's eyes turned completely black, and he started saying strange words. A moment later, everything, except the ground beneath our feet, exploded. The noise was followed by an eerie silence. The mercenaries were all dead, and every building for a quarter of a mile had been flattened."

"Needless to say," Kraster cut in. "We had some explaining to do when Greyward showed up."

"I'm still surprised he believed us," I said.

"What other explanation was there?" Kraster asked.

I shrugged. "You sounded more than a little crazy when you told the general about the eyes and being underwater."

"But that was important to the story," Kraster defended himself.

"Because that's where you think your magical powers came from?" Wren guessed.

"I do," Kraster told her. "Something happened to me in the water; a seed of power was planted. It woke up that day on the battlefield. I've been able to use magic ever since. It's never been quite as strong, and my eyes have never turned black again, but I've done a lot of training with the other mages in the army. I'm more powerful than most, which led to early promotion."

I snorted.

"Try not to be so jealous, Candra," Kraster chided me. "I always insisted you be part of my squad and included for special assignments, didn't I?"

"Much to Greyward's dislike," I pointed out.

"But I still did," he argued.

"Fine," I admitted grudgingly. "But you never would have learned about your powers if I hadn't saved your life from the first fireball. So, you're welcome."

"Well, you're welcome for me saving your life right after," Kraster shot back.

"I saved you first; you owed me," I reminded him smugly.

"That's so strange," Wren said, ignoring our banter. "Aren't you curious about what happened to you in the lake? I mean, you said you guys used to swim there all the time, and no one else saw the eyes or got magical powers, right?"

"*They* used to swim in the lake," I clarified quickly. "Kraster and his siblings. His full siblings."

There was an awkward pause.

"No, no one else ever got powers," Kraster said at last.

"That's amazing," Wren breathed, looking at him in awe.

I rolled my eyes. "Yes, *amazing*," I mocked. "It's all so fitting. He's blessed with magical abilities, and, apparently, I'm going to be cursed forever. Which is why I need this."

With deft fingers, I slipped the wine bottle out of Kraster's hand.

"Candra–" he started, but I'd already taken a swig.

I recorked the bottle and gave him a challenging look. In response, Kraster just shook his head and sighed.

Was he sorry he'd saved me? I wondered that sometimes, but there had been plenty of opportunities for him to get rid of me throughout the years, and he'd never done anything but try to pull me closer. He was such a singular person. No matter how cursed I was, I was lucky to have him.

Chapter 8

The Constellation

When morning light woke me, I saw Kraster half sitting, half leaning on the stump once more. He was deep in thought and didn't notice my approach as I came to stand right in front of him.

"I'm sure glad no one snuck up on us during the night," I teased lightly.

He looked up quickly, eyes chagrined, but there was something more.

"What's wrong?" I asked, voice quiet to keep from waking Wren.

In response, Kraster took out his communication charm.

"I thought you weren't going to send Greyward any more messages," I murmured.

"I didn't," he replied. "But he sent me one."

"And?" I asked.

"He wants to know where we are and why I haven't provided an update."

"I think you need to throw that thing away," I told my brother firmly. "After what we heard from The Oracle, how can you still trust him? She predicted he was going to betray us!"

"The Oracle said the future wasn't set in stone, so maybe that doesn't have to happen," Kraster protested. "All she could really tell us was that Greyward had found the power he was seeking, which changed him in some way."

"And that doesn't sound unsettling to you? How often does someone go looking for great power, and it turns out to be a good thing when they find it?" I countered.

"Isn't that what we're doing? Trying to track down a bunch of magical stones. We plan to use them to fix things, maybe Greyward wants to do the same," my brother challenged.

"No," I said with a shake of my head. "We aren't seeking any kind of power. We've been sent to find the stones to keep them safe."

"You say that now, until they are in our hands and their power is ours," Kraster scoffed.

"I have no plans to use the stones or even to unite them," I snapped at him. "We're going to gather them, each of us holding a few, then we can take them back to Shal'eth. He'll know what to do."

"Why do you trust this Shal'eth so much?" Kraster demanded. "You had one conversation with him, and it's like you're a different person, like you're the one who's changed."

"It's... I... Because..." My words came out haltingly. "He trusted me, Kraster," I finally managed to get out.

"He looked right at me, and he saw the real me and liked what he saw. Aside from you, no one does that. As The Oracle said, I'm distrusted and hated by nearly everyone, but not him.

"Maybe I'm doing all of this because, for once, I was chosen. For once, someone thought I was good enough and up to the task. I know that doesn't mean much to you. With your perfect family and magical abilities, you've always been picked first for every team and every assignment, but to me, this seems like my only chance."

"Your only chance at what?" Kraster asked.

I shook my head slowly. "At doing something right and becoming a better person. The kind of person who doesn't give up and doesn't let everyone down."

I trailed off, and we were both still for a moment.

"Are you going to throw the charm away?" I asked quietly.

This time, the silence between us was far longer. I was on the verge of breaking it to beg my brother to sever the connection between himself and Greyward, but I held my tongue. Kraster needed to make this choice for himself.

"I will," he finally agreed.

"Promise?" I pressed.

He nodded. "I promise."

"Good," I said with a sigh of relief.

Wren was stirring, so I moved to build up the fire and get breakfast started.

Instead of helping, Kraster wandered away from camp. I hoped he was taking the opportunity to dispose of the charm.

I sliced six pieces from a loaf of bread and started toasting them near the fire.

"Sleep okay?" I asked Wren as she came to join me. While I tended the bread, Wren took the package of salted pork from our supplies and set several strips on each piece of toast.

"Not really," she admitted.

"Another bad dream?" I guessed.

"Sort of," Wren answered. "It wasn't quite the same, but it was still horrifying."

"What do you mean?" I asked in concern.

"Just what I said," Wren replied. "Everything started out really nice. I was standing in the most lovely forest of silver trees. The sun was shining and the breeze was gentle. I know I've never been there, but something about it felt like home, then it all went wrong.

"The trees swelled into hideously deformed shapes, and there were tendrils of darkness coming out of them. It gathered into a cloud all around me, which filled my lungs with burning air. I couldn't breathe or call for help."

Like drowning, a voice in my head whispered. A shiver ran down my spine at the thought.

Just then, the pork began to hiss and pop, pulling me back to the present.

"I'm sure Kraster's story about seeing all those eyes stirred up your imagination," I told Wren. "At least you didn't start screaming this time."

Instead of lightening her mood, my comment only made her forehead pucker. "I wanted to scream. I tried to scream, but couldn't. There was no air. I couldn't force it into my lungs. I was dying, and it was horrible, and painful, and–"

The words were pouring out of Wren now, but she stopped herself as Kraster came back into sight.

"Sorry," she told me quietly. "I think you're right, and my imagination is getting the better of me."

I nodded and didn't say anything else, but turned her words over in my head as we ate breakfast and departed. Around midday, my mind shifted to other things. The land had grown barren, revealing large patches of reddish colored earth. The few bushes that managed to push up through the cracks in the dry ground grew nothing but a handful of scraggly leaves.

The air was dry and dusty. Despite the fact that the sun was bright in the sky, shining like a ruby in a blue sea, it provided little warmth.

As evening drew near, the plateau came into view on the horizon. It was nothing more than a tiny rise at the moment, but I knew that once we got closer, it would grow into a vast mountain.

We would have made camp before nightfall, but Kraster insisted that there was one last human town between us and the plateau, so we pressed on. Half an hour after sunset, in the last light of dusk, we found it.

The common room of the tavern was about half full. Instead of the cheerful sounds of drinking and fellowship, our entrance was met with hard stares and quiet whispers.

We approached the barkeep, who was probably also the owner. Even he gave us a distrustful glance, his eyebrows drawn low over his small, pig-like eyes.

"Has someone died?" I asked the man, who was short and very squat.

"Lots of someones," he growled. "The army of Kempt seems to have gone mad."

"What?" Kraster and I both gasped at the same time.

"Not surprised you haven't heard," the barkeep went on. "We only received news of it today. Seems they're headed for Bennton, burning and looting as they go."

He leaned toward us, eyes narrowed. "You're not from Kempt, are you?"

"No," Kraster spoke up quickly. "The Coral City."

The man grunted, but didn't challenge Kraster's claim and gave us two rooms. There was only a corral for the horses. After seeing to them, we all got drinks. Wren's was just hot water, in which she put a teabag from her pack.

Those in the common room didn't warm to us. Throughout our entire meal, I could feel their hostile glares on me and my companions. We retired as soon as we finished eating. Even I didn't want to linger for an extra drink with so many distrustful eyes watching my every move.

Wren passed another restless night.

In the morning, I left her sleeping as I slipped out to the common room for breakfast. Once again, menacing looks and angry murmurs greeted my arrival. However, I was quite used to people not being happy to see me, and I ignored them.

As I glanced around, I spotted Kraster sitting at a table with a golden-haired young man, who seemed only a little older than Wren. He alone of all the strangers appeared to be in a decent mood as he laughed at whatever my brother was saying to him.

I approached them, a plate of food in one hand.

"Is this seat taken?" I asked, nodding to one of the open chairs.

The youth looked up, his green eyes rimmed with gold.

"No, please join us," the young man said, scrambling to get up and pull the chair out for me. No one had ever done that before, so it took me a moment to realize what was happening.

"Thank you," I told him, trying to hide my surprise.

"James Trenton Bartholomew Apricot the Eighth, at your service," he said with the slightest of bows. "But please, call me Apricot. Everyone does."

"This is Candra, my companion," Kraster told Apricot. It was usually easier when he introduced me as such, so we didn't have to explain away my pointed ears.

"Now, as I was saying," Kraster went on. "You've got your whole life to learn farming. If you feel the desire to travel while you're young, do it. There's much to learn wandering on the road that you'll never discover toiling in a field."

Apricot nodded his golden head slowly, eyes locked on Kraster's face. "I've always wanted to go south, stopping at every village along the way to hear their stories and observe their customs."

"Then go!" Kraster exclaimed.

"You're right." Apricot stood, eyes glowing with excitement. "I think I will!" He darted out of the common room.

"What was that all about?" I wondered, taking a bite of bacon.

Kraster grinned at me. "He's a good lad. Wants to see the world, but feels like he should settle down and take up farming or some such with his uncle."

"And you told him to flagrantly disregard his responsibilities?" I cocked an eyebrow at my brother.

"Come on, Candra. He's only going to be young once. Might as well make the most of it."

I snorted softly before giving my breakfast the attention it deserved. Wren joined us a short time later. She looked exhausted.

I decided not to press her with questions. The less she focused on the bad dreams, the better.

Despite our late start, we made good time throughout the day, and The Gnome Plateau grew closer and closer. We knew we wouldn't reach it until at least tomorrow but were still determined to remove as many miles between us and it as we could.

Finally, when the horses were stumbling from exhaustion, we came to a halt. Wren and I gave the beasts a well-deserved rub down while Kraster went to look for wood in the barren landscape. He returned with only a few sticks, so we barely had a fire going long enough to warm a simple supper.

The weather turned windy the following day. I wore my cloak to defend against the chilly air. Conversation was impossible, and we were forced to stop a few times when dust clouds threatened to engulf us.

In the late afternoon, we found a sheltered spot with a stream. Due to the delays, we wouldn't be able to reach the plateau before sunset and decided to remain by the water for the evening. I stayed far away from the edge, letting Kraster fill the empty canteens.

There wasn't any wood for a fire and no moon to be seen. When night fell, we were left in darkness until Wren took out the teapot, which glimmered with minty green light. She summoned Puvva. After giving her normal greeting, the genie promptly walked into the stream and sat down.

The sky was clear, and the glow of the teapot wasn't enough to impair our view of the stars. I lay down on my back, looking up at them happily. It wasn't often that I had time or opportunity to admire their beauty.

"Do you know any of the constellations?" Wren asked Kraster as the pair returned from the stream.

"Sure, I guess," he told her and raised his hand skyward toward the points of light that made up The Constellation of the Great Dragons. "That group of bright stars is Morazz the Fire Drake. Beside him are the twins, Zaydia and Camroc. Their stars have faded a bit, so you can't see all of them now. Below them is the great void."

"You are incorrect," Puvva's voice said from her place in the middle of the stream. She wasn't looking up, but down at the water. Her wet hair was hanging like a curtain around her head, almost completely hiding her face.

"What do you mean?" Kraster asked the genie.

"That is Char." Puvva pointed up without lifting her eyes.

I felt a shudder pass through me as I gazed into the patch of sky that was blacker than all the rest. If there had ever been stars there, they were gone now, replaced with a darkness unpierced by light.

"But there's nothing there. That's why it's the void," Kraster told her.

"No," Puvva responded abruptly. "That is Char the Corrupter."

71

Kraster opened his mouth, but I cut him off. "Is there any point in arguing with her?" I asked.

"No," Puvva answered firmly. Kraster rolled his eyes and shook his head slightly.

"I knew about Morazz but have never heard the names of the twins before," Wren put in, tactfully changing the subject.

"They died a long time ago, and people are starting to forget them," Kraster told her. "Legend says that's why their part of the constellation is beginning to fade."

"That's so sad," Wren lamented. "The Queen of the Dragons, Asteropaios, and The Great Shal'eth are up there as well," she added.

"Really?" I asked. "I don't think that's right."

"Well, there's Asteropaios," Wren gestured at a large grouping of the brightest stars in the heavens.

"I didn't mean that one," I chuckled. "That's the most well-known constellation in the world because Asteropaios is the only one of the great dragons who's still alive."

"Wrong again," Puvva muttered. She had one of our canteens and was dunking it under the water to fill it, then emptying it over her head repeatedly.

"How can you say that when The Great Shal'eth is right beside her?" Wren teased me, pointing back up at the stars of Asteropaios's constellation.

I squinted. The stars weren't too bright, but I could sort of see the shape of a long, thin dragon's body.

"When I saw Shal'eth," I started. "He wasn't exactly a dragon..." I trailed off, not sure how to phrase the question I wanted to ask without offending her.

"All dragons have mortal forms too," Wren told me.

"I am aware of that, but– Shal'eth wasn't exactly human either..."

There was a moment of silence.

"He is stuck," Puvva told us.

"What do you mean?" Wren asked uncertainly, and I instantly regretted bringing up this topic. The last thing I wanted was for Wren to experience a crisis of belief right now.

"He cannot turn fully into a human or a dragon," Puvva explained, still playing with the canteen. "He is stuck, and in more ways than one."

Before Wren could ask for further clarification, I changed the subject. "Does anyone know the names of the last two dragons? The ones whose stars are almost too dim now to be seen at all?"

"Of course." Puvva's voice was as factual as ever. "There's Karradin the Wise and Lathaan Great Wing."

I nodded slowly. Puvva did seem to know a lot about the great dragons, and those names sounded right, but I wasn't sure where I'd heard them before.

"I'm surprised you didn't learn more about the constellations," Kraster told Wren. "Especially if Shal'eth is really up there."

Wren shrugged. "I guess he didn't think it was important."

"That's odd," I put in. "Even my mother tried to teach me something about the stars. She said they were a portrait of the past."

"Your mother said something so poetic?" Kraster gasped with exaggerated surprise.

I made a face at him. "She did. But she seemed kind of bitter when she said it."

"And that's unusual because?" he asked.

I gave my brother a kick that was only half playful, causing him to groan dramatically.

We looked at the stars for a little longer. Eventually, Puvva returned to her pot, and the other two drifted off to sleep while I took the first watch.

Chapter 9
The Plateau

After sleeping for only an hour, Wren jerked awake.

"Are you all right?" I whispered, moving to her side.

She nodded. I could see in the starlight that, while her face was grave, it didn't hold the traces of fear that her nightmares often brought.

"I dreamed again," she murmured.

"That's what happens at night when you sleep," I said lightly. "Not a bad one this time, I hope?"

Wren shook her head. "No, I saw– I saw a lion made of fire."

"Like the lion statue at Lion's Hill?" I asked. "I've heard it glows with inner light when the sun touches–"

"No," Wren interrupted. "An actual lion made of fire with wings of flame."

"That sounds pretty amazing," I told her.

"The creature was majestic! Someone was riding it. A young man who had golden hair and carried a sword. There was a group of others with the man and the lion. They were strong warriors of the light!"

Wren's face grew somber suddenly. "Except for one of them. He was going to betray the others. I felt his evil thoughts and his great malice. He had terrible things planned for each of them!"

An expression of anguish contorted Wren's features.

"It was just a dream," I assured her. "Focus on the parts of it that you liked, and you'll soon forget the rest."

Wren nodded slowly. We talked a bit longer, then she drifted off to sleep again. I went to get a wine bottle. It was about half empty, and I only had one more left after this. Hopefully, the gnomes would have something I could use to replenish my supplies.

I drank slowly for a change, savoring the taste while looking up at the sky. If I concentrated really hard, I could almost make out the shapes of the great dragons in the stars above. They were from an age long passed and most had faded into myth just as they were fading from the heavens.

I hid my nearly empty bottle before waking Kraster. Once he'd taken over on watch, I settled myself and slept until Wren roused me in the morning.

We rode north all day, through vast, windswept plains, speckled with scrub. At last, as the shadows were growing long and the afternoon turning into evening, we reached the bottom of the plateau. A lift had been fashioned there by gnomish engineers, who were the best in the world. It was currently in high demand, with a long line of those waiting for a ride to the top. An earthen ramp to the right was the only other way to reach the plateau above.

We dismounted and got in the back of the line. The area was bustling with travelers and their carts, all of whom seemed to be coming and none going.

When we reached the front, the gnome accepting payment narrowed his eyes at us. He had thick, bristly eyebrows that drew together in a scowl as he looked me up and down.

"What are you tall folk doing here?" he demanded. His voice was unusually deep for a gnome.

"We'd like to visit the plateau, please," Wren told him innocently.

"Are you spies?" the gnome demanded.

"Of course not," Wren replied indignantly.

"There's a war starting out there," the gnome went on. "A war of the tall folk, and we don't trust your kind no more."

"My dear fellow," Kraster began. "We have no desire to cause any trouble. My brother-in-law is a well-known merchant. He has asked me to check on one of his suppliers who is based on your lovely plateau."

"Name of the supplier?" the gnome challenged suspiciously.

"Gnorman of Gnorman & Sons," Kraster replied.

The bristly eyebrowed gnome considered Kraster for a moment. "Fine, but it'll be five gold pieces for you, ten for your horse, and double that for your half-breed companions."

"Excuse me?" I demanded.

"Elves never been good trading partners," the gnomes sneered. "They are not worth the air they breathe on our plateau."

Kraster grabbed my wrist as I started to draw one of my swords.

"It's fine," he told me quietly.

"It's not fine," Wren exclaimed, seeming nearly as furious as I was.

The gnome was smiling nastily at us.

"I'll walk before I give you so much as a copper!" I spat over my shoulder, leading Tempest toward the steep path, which zigzagged to the top of the plateau. Wren followed behind me with Valor. When I glanced back to see where Kraster was, I spotted him with Raspberry halfway up the cliffside on the lift.

"I'm going to kill him," I swore, imagining it for the next fifteen minutes as we toiled up the sharp incline leading our horses.

"Maybe we overreacted," Wren panted by my side.

I was breathing hard myself, but shook my head. "No. The only thing I did wrong was not skewering that little pipsqueak."

The climb was as miserable as it had looked. I was dusty and drenched in sweat when I reached the top nearly an hour and a half later. My mood didn't improve at all when I saw Kraster waiting for us at the top, looking as fresh as a daisy.

"Thanks for the solidarity," I grumbled as I stalked past him.

"Don't be too upset, Candra," he pleaded. "I used the extra time to get us lodgings."

I ignored him as I headed for the cluster of buildings located close to the top of the lift.

"How long will it take us to get to Gnomania?" I heard Wren ask Kraster behind me.

"There's a bit of a hiccup with that," Kraster admitted.

"And what would that be?" I demanded, turning back to face them.

"Well, I've been asking around," Kraster told us. "As you can see, the plateau is experiencing an influx of refugees trying to escape the war."

"What war?" I asked.

Kraster hesitated before replying. "Greyward has continued to sack towns and seems to be making his way toward The Coral City. He is also putting to death all those he finds who aren't human."

A coldness gripped my stomach. Would Greyward have had me killed if I'd stayed?

"Understandably," my brother went on, "it's caused a lot of panic. All of the other races are trying to put as much distance between themselves and Greyward's army as possible. That's why only gnomes are being allowed into the capital city of Gnomania right now, unless you have official papers naming you as a friend and ally."

"Can't we find a way to sneak in?" Wren asked.

"If it was a human city, maybe," I told her. "But here, we're all going to stick out like sore thumbs."

"Then how will we find the stone?" Wren wondered.

"Simple," Kraster told her. "We just need to get official papers."

"And how is that going to be simple?" I scoffed.

"We're going to see Gnorman, of course," Kraster replied.

I blinked at him. "I thought you made that name up," I admitted.

"No, he's real and has been working with our brother-in-law for many years. I've even met him a few times," Kraster explained.

"Is he here?" Wren asked eagerly.

Kraster shook his head.

"The plateau has four major towns along its edges, and Gnomania is in the center. Gnorman lives in the town of Gnomonly on the eastern side. We go there, get our paperwork, then head west to Gnomania." Kraster seemed very pleased with himself as he explained.

"It's a good plan," I admitted, causing my brother to smile brightly. "But I'm still mad at you for ditching us."

I pushed past him and headed for the small town. It was uncreatively called Liftton.

Gnomes have such strange ways of naming things, I thought.

The accommodations Kraster had found for us were actually pretty decent considering how full the town was. There were hundreds of gnomes, lots of dwarves and halflings, and even a few groups of humans, but no other elves. Both Wren and I let our hair cover our pointed ears, but anyone who knew anything about elves or half-elves would easily identify my slanted eyes and Wren's perfect nose.

However, it seemed that most people were too busy to hassle us, and we arrived at our destination without incident. The place was called The Big Inning. As the name implied, it was one of a few establishments built to cater to the tall folk who visited the plateau. Even still, Kraster's head brushed the ceiling in a few places, and we all had to duck to make it through the doorways.

When I walked into the common room, I did a double take. The bar opposite the door was over a yard tall, and yet, there was a gnome working behind it. Instantly, I assumed he was standing on a crate or something, but then I saw him walk out from behind the bar to greet us. Strapped to his legs were a pair of stilts. He wasn't quite as tall as Wren and me, but he came close.

"Welcome! My name is Gned, and I will be happy to make your stay as pleasant as possible!" he said, shaking each of us by the hand before taking our food and drink orders. Unlike the gnome working the lift, Gned was very friendly to all the tall folk and joked incessantly about his own shortness.

"I've owned this place for fifteen years," he said, setting plates of food before us. "And I've never seen it as busy as it is now. Why, at the beginning of the week, I was a bit taller. Yes, siree, in just a few days I've worn through an inch of wood."

I tuned the gnome's shrill voice out and tucked into the best meal I'd eaten in ages, washing it down with mugs of ale. I drank and drank, until I felt better about the gnome at the lift and the grueling climb to the top of the plateau.

Chapter 10
The Courage

After sleeping in a bed that was literally the same length as I was and only a few inches wider, I came down for breakfast expecting more of Gned's chatter. Instead, I saw a second gnome serving the room in his place. At least, I thought he was a gnome until I realized he wasn't wearing stilts.

"I'm Devin," he introduced himself shyly. "Would you like some breakfast?"

I nodded and couldn't help glancing at his feet to make sure he wasn't standing on something. Devin wasn't as tall as Gned with his stilts but was definitely taller than any gnome I'd ever met, which in fairness wasn't a lot.

Devin shifted uncomfortably, and I forced my eyes away. "I'll take whatever you have," I told him. He bobbed his head and hurried away at an uneven gait.

Before Devin returned, Kraster came to join me at my table. He didn't bother to ask how I'd slept. We'd all been in the same room because of the limited accommodations for us tall folk. Kraster had ended up on the floor since none of the room's four beds were suitable for his height.

"Wren up yet?" I asked.

Kraster shook his head.

With my brother blocking my view, I didn't see what happened, but there was a sudden thud. I sprang to my feet. Devin was sprawled on the floor along with what appeared to be my breakfast. The table next to him let out howls of mirth at the accident.

Eyes fixed on the ground, Devin got to his knees and quickly scooped the food back onto the wooden plate, then retreated to the kitchen.

I sank back into my seat.

"Wonder if he'll throw it away or try to pick out some of the dirt and serve it," a heavyset man with greasy, dark hair mused loudly. He was one of those who had laughed loudest at poor Devin's misfortune. The smirk on his scruffy face instantly irritated me. Some girls might have thought his smile rakish, but all I wanted was to knock out a few of his crooked teeth.

"Clumsy half-breed," spat one of the man's companions, a dwarf. I felt heat rise to my face at the insult, even though it was not directed at me for a change.

"Good job tripping him." Their gnome companion congratulated a second man, this one with dirty blond hair and a slighter build.

"Nothing with dwarf blood should be that ugly and unable to grow a beard to cover it," the dwarf laughed.

The gnome grinned in a nasty way. "And nothing with gnome blood should be that tall."

The four laughed rancorously, and my temper flared.

"Excuse me for a moment," I said to Kraster, rising once more.

"Candra, wait–" he started, reaching for my hand.

He was too slow. I walked five paces across the room, then my fist was buried in the face of the blond man who'd tripped Devin.

The man's companions were slow to react, giving me time to kick his chair out from under him as well. Since he was off balance from my blow, the blond man fell and landed on the floor in a heap.

The other human and the gnome jumped to their feet. The dwarf seemed unsure if he wanted to get involved.

I whipped my head toward the trio.

"Why aren't you laughing?" I snarled. "Isn't it funny when people fall down?"

As the dark-haired man rushed me, I knocked him away with a kick to the side of the head. The blond man I'd sucker punched clambered to his feet. He lunged for me, but it was a clumsy attack, and I easily dodged away. Without a moment's hesitation, I crashed into the dark-haired man's side, elbow out, catching him sharply in the ribs. He tottered and went to his knees.

A wooden plate clipped my left shoulder, sending a jolt of pain through my body. I spun around, but not quickly enough to avoid a second plate thrown by the gnome. He had climbed onto a chair and was picking the plates up off the table and sending them toward my head as fast as he could. His aim was poor, and the second missile struck my left hip.

Reflexively, I ducked to the side as the blond man swung his fist in my direction. This motion brought me close enough to the table to shove the chair the gnome was balanced on. He toppled over, a full plate of food in his hands. Unfortunately, the gnome landed on the head of the dwarf who had, thus far, only been an observer.

An angry light ignited in the dwarf's eyes as he brushed bits of syrupy flat cakes out of his graying beard. He rose, lifting his battleaxe from the floor beside his chair. The gnome scrambled to his feet and pulled out a knife the size of a toothpick. Behind me, I sensed the dark-haired man closing in, brandishing a weapon of his own.

In one fluid motion, my long swords were in my hands. I gave them an expert spin, causing the man behind me to take a step backward.

The dwarf hefted his axe. As I prepared to strike, the blond man I'd lost track of lunged for me from the opposite side.

"That's ENOUGH!" Kraster boomed louder than was humanly possible. At least, humanly possible without the use of magic.

Everyone in the room froze as my brother walked forward, making a show of holding a dark purple ball of magical energy in his hand. He grabbed me by my shoulder and pulled me out of the circle of foes like I was a naughty child.

"Lucky for you all, we have more important things to take care of than gutter trash!" I spat at them as Kraster shoved me back into my seat and took his own.

"I could have taken them," I grumbled to my brother.

"Probably," Kraster agreed. "But I don't want you to destroy this establishment while doing it." He looked pointedly at the spilled food and the chair that the gnome was trying to perch on despite its broken leg. He and his companions were all glaring daggers at me. I gave them an impish sneer.

"Fine," I sulked. "But if I see them outside, no promises."

Kraster sighed. "Candra, why do you have to be at war with the whole world?"

"Because the whole world seems to be at war with me!" I snapped at him.

That put an end to the conversation. After five minutes of steely silence, those from the other table headed out of the inn. I was pleased to see that one of the men was cradling his arm, the other human and the gnome were limping, and the dwarf still looked sticky.

Only after they were gone did Devin appear again. His eyes were fixed on the ground as he trailed along behind Gned, who was in his nightshirt and without his stilts. I tried not to cringe as Gned marched right up to our table. He seized Kraster's large hand and started shaking it vigorously.

"Thank you so much, my good sir, for standing up for my nephew against those hooligans!" Gned continued to pump Kraster's hand. "I can't tell you how grateful I am! Don't know why folks can't leave poor Devin alone and mind their own business. It ain't his fault what that crazy sister of mine did, but he's the one they blame for it. I had to take him off night shifts completely because there was no end to the trouble it caused. Now it seems trouble has found him in the mornings as well, but what can I do? No one else will hire him, and he's family."

Despite his kind tone and seemingly good intentions, I found myself wanting to punch Gned too. Devin was staring at the floor so hard I'm pretty sure he was mentally begging it to open and swallow him whole.

"It actually wasn't–" Kraster started.

"Of course it was some trouble!" Gned interrupted him. "But you bravely stood your ground! Consider breakfast for you and your companions on the house! And it will be a stellar breakfast indeed! I'll see to it right away and have your horses prepared for you immediately after."

I shook my head ever so slightly at Kraster, hoping he would keep his mouth shut. Such was my luck that if Gned found out I was the one who had started the fight, I was sure breakfast would be off the table completely, and we'd have to pay to clean up the mess.

Kraster pursed his lips but didn't say anything as Gned spent the next ten minutes gushing about his bravery and prowess, before returning to the kitchen, promising great things.

He was true to his word. By the time Wren joined us, our table was overflowing with plates of toast, flat cakes, bacon, and scones, along with pots of honey and jam. We ate our fill and headed to the stable to fetch our horses.

Devin was there, clearly trying to stay out of the way. As we were leaving, our eyes met. I gave him a nod before he turned away. I hoped someday he would find the courage to make his own way in the world.

Despite not having set foot on the plateau before yesterday, Kraster confidently took the lead. All morning, I kept expecting the day to grow warmer, but it never did. The air didn't feel too thin even though the plateau was about a thousand feet higher than the rest of Planosia.

For a while, the road took us along the cliff's edge. I had a good head for heights and nudged Tempest close to the side, so I could see the dizzying drop below.

"Don't do that," Kraster called.

I grinned at him, but guided my horse back to the others who were staying as far from the edge as possible. Less than an hour later, our path turned slightly to the left, and we entered a forest of stunted, evergreen trees. The edge of the plateau was still close by and, every so often, I'd catch a glimpse of the dizzying drop.

"How come there aren't any other travelers?" Wren asked. Her voice sounded loud since none of us had broken the silence for nearly an hour.

"I guess everyone else is going to the capital," Kraster replied.

"But there were so many at the lift. Surely, a few of them were heading this way," Wren protested.

"I'm not sure," Kraster shrugged. "Maybe we'll bump into some other travelers soon."

His words turned out to be prophetic. Not even twenty minutes later, we drew our horses to a halt when we turned a corner and came upon a trio of gnomes standing in the road.

"Halt!" squeaked the first one, even though our horses had already stopped moving. "We must insist that you hand over all of your valuables immediately!"

The two gnomes beside the speaker brandished swords as each took a step forward. I think it was supposed to be threatening, but it just made me want to laugh.

"Listen," Kraster started. "I think you've got the wrong idea about how this is going to go–"

Before he finished speaking, an arrow came out of nowhere and whizzed by my brother's head.

"Last chance!" the gnome cried.

"No, you're out of chances," Kraster said darkly. Light flashed from his hand and collided with the speaker. The gnome let out a squeal as he was flung backward. His two companions rushed us, and another arrow flew straight for Kraster. This time, I'd seen where it came from and directed Tempest toward the undergrowth to our right.

Out of the corner of my eye, I saw the arrow strike Raspberry's flank. The horse bolted forward, running straight at the advancing gnomes, who scattered.

In front of me, a pair of gnomes with bows broke cover and sprinted in opposite directions. I swung off Tempest and reached for the nearest one; he was little more than a child. I caught him by his collar, causing him to drop his bow.

"Let me go!" he screeched, struggling like mad, but I didn't. Instead, I lifted him from the ground and hauled him back to the others.

The young gnome went still, then tried to bite me. I slapped him across the face. His eyes widened and filled with tears as his bottom lip started to quiver.

He must be even younger than I thought, I realized. It was so hard to tell with gnomes. They were all so short and squeaky.

When I reached the others, I saw Kraster, one side of his body covered in dirt, glaring at the retreating figures of the other gnomes.

"Take a tumble?" I asked playfully.

"Yes," he snapped.

Wren was walking toward us leading Valor and the injured Raspberry. There was a sorrowful expression on her face.

Without speaking, Kraster touched Raspberry's head. Instantly, the beast's eyelids drooped, and his breathing deepened. My brother moved to the horse's side and pulled the arrow out of Raspberry's flank. The animal flinched, but didn't wake from his magical slumber. Wren brought out a little pot of healing salve and applied it to the wound.

"It's not deep," she assured Kraster.

He nodded but still wore a grim scowl.

"What are you planning to do with that one?" Kraster asked, causing the young gnome in my arms to start struggling wildly.

"Oh, he's so cute!" Wren exclaimed, noticing the child for the first time.

"No! I'm not cute!" the gnome cried. "I'm part of the infamous gang Agnomonymous! We are mighty!"

"*So mighty,*" I said sarcastically as I dropped the gnome to the ground between the three of us. "Why did your 'gang' attack us?"

The young gnome blinked at me. "To steal your money. This road is ours, and all who trespass must pay!"

"Guess that explains why we seem to be the only ones out here," Kraster said to Wren, who nodded vigorously.

"So what do we do with the petty thief?" Kraster asked, turning to me.

I considered for a moment. "What's your name, kid?" I asked, looking down.

"Gizzi," the gnome answered.

"Where are your parents? Do they know you're out here?" I questioned him.

"They're dead," Gizzi retorted. "But they would be proud of me. I'm making a name for myself!"

"Really?" I wondered. "What skills do you have?"

"I'm a good shot," Gizzi spat, pointing at Raspberry. Kraster stiffened, and his expression darkened. "And I'm small and can squeeze through bars. I pick pockets and hide really well."

"He might be useful to have around, " I said with a glance at my companions.

"We are not keeping him!" Kraster almost shouted.

"Think about it," I went on. "He knows his way around and is familiar with the customs; he could be a big asset."

"I'm not going to help you with anything!" yelled Gizzi shrilly.

I turned my gaze on him. "Then we are going to turn you into the magistrate at the next town, and we'll see what they do to little thieves."

"Fine," he snapped. "Anything is better than being around you tall folk."

I rolled my eyes and hoisted Gizzi from the ground, then shoved him toward Kraster. "Hold him for a second," I said as I went to get Tempest. On my way back, I also spotted two swords dropped by the gnome assailants. I collected them and stowed them in my pack.

I mounted Tempest, and Kraster handed Gizzi up to ride in front of me. The gnome squirmed at first until I threatened to drop him under my horse's feet. He was still after that.

Early in the afternoon, we came to a little town, which was really more of an outpost.

"This isn't Gnomonly, is it?" Wren asked.

Kraster shook his head. "It's too small, I think."

"No, Gnomonly is still miles away," piped up Gizzi scornfully.

I dismounted quickly, pulling the gnome off with me. He squeaked in surprise.

"Last chance," I told him. "You can help us, or I'm turning you in."

The gnome child set his features stubbornly. I sighed and dragged him off toward the most official-looking building in sight. My instincts were correct, and I found the mayor himself manning the front desk.

"Welcome," he greeted me, popping up from his seat as I ducked through the door. "I'm Mayor Lingilton. Welcome to our humble town. My secretary is out to lunch, so what can I assist you with?"

The mayor wore a purple jacket and a large top hat, which he tipped to me. He listened as I explained what happened on the road and Gizzi's part in it.

"Such a shame," the mayor said. "It's no wonder we don't get many travelers these days. Thank you for scaring off the ruffians and apprehending this one. We will certainly take great pains to see that he's taught the error of his ways." With that, the mayor seized Gizzi by the arm and started leading him away.

I headed back outside, then had to track down the others. They were at the only inn, which was behind the town hall where I'd met the mayor.

"Are we getting drinks?" I asked eagerly.

"Not a chance," Kraster told me. "They don't serve tall folk, not even in their common room."

"Drat," I growled. "I don't suppose they'll sell me a small barrel for the road?"

"Come on, we're leaving." Kraster grabbed my arm and towed me back the way I'd come.

As we reached the main street, I glanced at the town hall and saw the mayor in his purple suit outside talking to a gnome child who looked suspiciously like Gizzi. The mayor patted him on the head, and Gizzi darted off.

Unbelievable, I thought with an internal sigh. *Oh well, how much trouble can one child cause?*

Chapter 11
The Ambush

We camped a little way off the road that night, in a dense clump of foliage.

I took the two gnomish swords out of my pack to inspect them. They were hardly longer than a common dagger, and each of their hilts had some sort of lever crafted into it. There was a tiny arrow painted on the end of the lever, which pointed at the blade. Slowly, I turned the lever to the left on one of the swords making the arrow move ninety degrees. When I glanced down at the second one, I saw that the lever on its hilt had also moved and was in the same position as the sword I held.

I set the weapons beside each other so I could look at them together. Suddenly, the levers on both swords began to move on their own. In perfect synchronization, they rapidly dipped up and down several times before returning to the original position.

Quickly, I called my brother over.

"Do you sense any magic on these?" I asked him.

He contemplated the two swords for a moment, then nodded. "Yes."

"What can they do?" I inquired eagerly.

"No idea," he replied.

"Some mage you are," I grumbled.

He shrugged. "I don't recall you saying that any of the hundred times I've saved your life."

I glowered at his cheeky grin and put the swords back in my pack before settling down to sleep.

In the predawn hours, I woke to a horrible gale of cold wind.

"Lovely," I growled, tucking my cloak tighter around my body and pulling my hood low over my face.

"Should we set up the tent?" Wren, who was on watch, wondered.

"Too late now," I muttered. "As soon as we got it up, it'd be time to take it down again."

I tossed and turned for nearly an hour before admitting defeat. Somehow, Kraster had managed to remain asleep despite the weather. I left him to slumber and went to sit with Wren by the rock she was using as a windbreak.

"Any more dreams?" I asked.

"Yes," she replied.

I waited for her to go on, glad for any distraction.

"I dreamed I was climbing down a mountain when the path gave way underneath me, and I nearly fell to my death. Then all these giant bird things were clawing at me with their talons and– and something was burning on the mountain top, blotting out the sun with black smoke."

"That doesn't sound fun," I told her. "Still, it's much better than darkness and spiders."

She nodded her agreement but didn't speak again.

A few hours later, we had a cold breakfast, since the fire wouldn't stay lit for more than a minute before getting blown out. The dismal weather continued for the next few hours, making the horses twitchy and nervous. It finally let up, leaving us chilled to the bone.

What a rotten summer we're having, I thought.

Half an hour later, I pulled Tempest to a halt and dismounted.

"What's wrong?" Wren asked, stopping Valor just behind us.

"Look at those." I pointed to several hoof marks in the loose dust. They weren't made by a horse, but by something large, with a split hoof.

Kraster brought Raspberry up beside me. He studied the fresh tracks for a moment, then gave me a questioning look.

91

"They are probably from deer or something that lives around here," Kraster suggested. I didn't think he was right but couldn't offer a better explanation.

As we continued forward, the land grew hilly. A wall of rock rose to our left. On the right, the trees continued to grow denser. Due to a lack of good campsites, we rode until dusk before finding a place where the trees thinned out a bit, and the ground was level. It was also covered in stones, but asking for a comfortable resting place would have been too much.

I had the second watch and woke easily when Wren touched my shoulder. She moved to her bedroll and lay down.

After gathering a few armloads of wood, I settled beside the fire and started feeding it twigs. Something vibrated close by, making me jump to my feet. There was another rattle, and I realized it was coming from my pack.

Quickly, I opened it and found the levers on the two gnomish swords were moving again. I watched in fascination as they turned several times, then went still, then turned again.

Realization dawned on me in a moment. There were more than just two swords connected by magic. I didn't know if the pair I had could be tracked or if they were only used for communication, but it was stupid to have kept them. Immediately, I hurled both blades into the trees on the far side of the road.

I tilted my head and strained to catch any sound of pursuers. In the distance, I thought I could hear a dull thud. A moment later, it came again, louder and clearer. Something, or a group of somethings, was coming after us along the path we had traveled that day.

I shook the others and motioned for their silence. Both listened for a moment. Wren heard it too, but the noise wasn't loud enough for Kraster's human ears. I quickly started saddling Tempest. The others followed my lead.

It took us only a few minutes, but the thudding was close enough that even Kraster could make it out as we mounted and set off at a brisk pace. I gestured for Wren to take the lead, so Kraster, whose sight was limited in the dark, could be in the middle, while I brought up the rear.

Bow clenched in my hand, I twisted around, trying to see if I could make out anything in the darkness. I had no idea what was following us, but it was large and heavy.

Because I was so focused on the road behind us, I didn't notice that the others had stopped until Tempest bumped into Raspberry.

Whipping my head around, I saw a freshly felled tree lying across the path. I knew this tactic all too well. Kraster and I had used it on more than one occasion. Quickly, I directed my horse to the front and motioned Wren to fall back.

"They're already here," I whispered as I passed Kraster. "Why don't you let them know who they are dealing with?"

Instantly, Kraster raised his hand, and a burst of light streamed into the sky above his head. It separated into four spheres, which spread out and began slowly rotating in the air.

"We have no wish to fight," Kraster announced loudly.

After a moment, nearly a dozen gnomes moved into view. Some were crouched behind the fallen tree, others had been concealed in the woods. Three were mounted on large war rams. All of them held weapons.

"We will defend ourselves with lethal force," I warned.

I expected the gnomes to demand our surrender or, at least, try to intimidate us. Instead, one of the mounted gnomes spurred his steed forward. It leapt the fallen tree and charged our horses, horns lowered.

I fired an arrow but missed as Tempest lurched away from the charging ram. My shaft thunked uselessly into the fallen tree. All of the gnomes sprang to life, leaping forward to attack.

As I scrambled from my horse's back, I saw Valor rearing up over the ram's head, causing the animal to come to a skidding halt. Then I was on the ground, drawing my swords and striding toward my foes who were now within reach.

The first two gnomes rushed me. I was able to parry both blows, throwing them back. As I did, an arrow embedded itself in the leather armor covering my chest. I looked up and spotted the archer perched in a tree.

"There, Kraster!" I pointed as a second arrow struck me, this one in the shoulder. My armor didn't stop it completely, and I could feel hot blood running down my right arm.

With a snarl, I charged the nearest group of gnomes, slashing with wide strokes, while being careful not to let them inside my guard. That was the only advantage they'd be able to get over me, and they knew it.

One gnome lunged with a long spear. It raked across the armor on my side. While I was sure it would leave a nasty bruise, it didn't pierce my skin.

Kraster was throwing fire this way and that. He'd taken out the first archer as well as a few others in the branches above and on the ground below. Several trees were burning now, giving an abundance of light.

As quickly as the fighting started, it seemed to end. Wren had just sent the final attacker crashing into the undergrowth with a perfectly aimed roundhouse kick.

A few gnomes lay groaning on the ground; the rest were still. All three rams were riderless and had taken to cropping grass with Valor and Tempest. Raspberry, who still bore Kraster, was tugging at the reins to join them.

"Anyone hurt?" Wren asked.

"A few scratches," I replied. "Nothing that won't hea–"

A jarring impact from behind knocked the breath out of me as I hit my knees.

Wren screamed, and Kraster stared at me wide-eyed as I scrambled to regain my feet. Something fell from my back and hit the ground behind me. I spun and saw that it was a spear thrown by one of nearly a dozen gnomes closing in on us from the opposite direction. Clearly, they'd meant to cut off our retreat while their friends ambushed us from the front.

The impact of the weapon had knocked the breath out of me. I coughed, trying to force air back into my lungs. Kraster spurred Raspberry past me with a battle cry, another ball of fire flying from his hand.

Wren was at my side a moment later.

"Are you okay?" she asked.

"No clue," I panted. "I'll check later."

I turned toward the battle. Kraster was surrounded by two mounted gnomes and many more on foot. My eyes narrowed as one of the archers took aim at my brother. With a scream tearing from my throat, I rushed after Kraster. The blood roared in my ears as the gnomes turned to look at me. There was fear in their eyes, and I relished it. Fighting was something I was good at. It made me feel warm and alive. It was almost better than drinking.

My first target, the closest gnome holding a bow, was easily dispatched with a single twist of my wrist. I continued to cut through his companions, ignoring the warm liquid oozing down my arm and the pain in my chest, back, and side. Before my adrenaline ran out, the remaining bandits had fled the scene.

Slowly, I lowered my blades. Kraster was no longer mounted on Raspberry but didn't appear injured. There was a nasty scratch across one of Wren's cheekbones, and she was breathing hard, but otherwise, she seemed to be uninjured.

"How many got away?" I asked, moving to my friends.

"Only a few," Kraster replied, casting a suspicious glance into the darkness behind us.

"It's probably best not to linger here," I suggested.

I went to collect our horses. The rams the gnomes had been riding were hovering close by, so I rounded them up as well.

"What are you planning to do with those?" Kraster asked when he saw the string of woolly mounts I was leading. "They are too small to ride."

"For us, sure, but maybe we can sell them when we get to the next town," I suggested. "Plus, some of them have saddlebags, and we could use the extra supplies."

Kraster nodded as Wren approached and started stroking the head of the largest ram.

"He's so cute!" she exclaimed. The ram nuzzled her gently, enjoying the attention.

"We should get going," I said, glancing around. "Did you guys get anything useful off the bodies?"

Wren sobered at the question. "They didn't have much other than their weapons."

"Where are those?" I asked.

Kraster pointed to a small pile of swords. I sorted through them quickly and found three with levers. I ignored those, instead choosing several of the others. I placed two on my belt and added one to the strap I wore on my thigh before tossing a couple more into my pack to conceal on my person later.

"Do you really need so many?" Wren asked. "Won't they weigh you down?"

"You can never have too many weapons," I told her.

"Why did they do it?" Wren asked quietly as we attached thick ropes to Valor. He was the largest and strongest of our three horses. Dawn was creeping into the sky, casting the road and the bodies on it in a ghastly sheen of red.

"Do what?" Kraster asked. Holding Valor's reins, he led the horse forward. The massive beast strained against his leather breast collar for a moment, then the fallen tree began to pivot, unblocking the road.

"Attack us," Wren clarified, voice sad. "They were clearly outmatched, so why attack us?"

One of the gnomes on the ground stirred suddenly and rolled over.

"Here's your chance to ask," Kraster said, dropping Valor's reins and lunging forward to seize the gnome by the front of his tunic.

The gnome's eyes opened as he was half lifted from the ground. He grabbed Kraster's hand and thrashed around, desperately trying to free himself, but it was useless.

"How many more of your gang are waiting to attack us?" Kraster demanded.

The gnome didn't answer, just continued to struggle.

96

My brother's hand ignited with fire. The gnome squealed in surprise and tried to kick Kraster. Almost as a reflex, he slammed the gnome's small body to the ground.

I stared at him in shock. Kraster had never pulled his punches with enemies, but this seemed extreme even for him.

"How many?" he growled, face inches from the gnome's.

"None," the gnome wheezed shakily. "That was the whole gang. Gizzi said to bring everyone, so– so we did." The gnome's words started to slur toward the end.

"Good," Kraster relaxed his grip a little. I half expected the prisoner to try and escape, but he didn't. Instead, his eyes rolled up into his head.

Wren moved a little closer. "Is he all right?" she asked, voice full of concern.

Kraster straightened and shrugged. "He'll be fine, but he'll have quite the headache when he wakes up, that's for sure."

"You didn't have to hurt him so badly," Wren chided.

My brother spun on her with anger in his eyes. "I saw you during the fight. You kicked more than one gnome in the head hard enough to knock them out, so I don't want to hear it. We need to know if we are going to get ambushed again or not."

Wren held her tongue.

"Let's go," I said, untethering Valor from the tree.

We got back on our horses, bringing the rams along on leads. Wren wore a perturbed expression. I dropped back to try and smooth things over with her. She wasn't a soldier like we were, so she couldn't understand how sometimes you had to do things you didn't want to in order to complete the mission.

"You okay?" I asked softly.

Wren didn't look at me. "I still don't understand why they attacked us."

"They probably took us for the merchants we're pretending to be," I said. "Merchants they could have intimidated or slaughtered. If they'd known that we were military and, whatever you are, they probably would have let us pass and waited for easier prey. They didn't appear to be a very well-trained or skilled lot.

97

They relied on numbers and surprise to overwhelm us, but it didn't work for them this time."

"It felt…" Wren paused, searching for the right word. "Bad to fight them. They were so small."

"They would have killed us," I reminded her, while trying to push down the surge of guilt that filled me. "As I'm sure they have killed others in the past. We weren't looking for a fight; they were, and they took on more than they could handle."

Wren nodded, then suddenly looked up at me. "We need to stop," she gasped. "You're wounded."

"I'm fine," I assured her.

"No! We need to make sure you're all right," Wren persisted.

Only once we'd put a few more miles behind us did I agree to stop.

My injuries really weren't that bad. My shoulder was almost done bleeding, and my ribs were only bruised, not broken. It was my back that Wren spent the most time fretting over. The spearhead had left a small, jagged wound in the flesh of my right shoulder blade. It didn't hurt too badly, and I was sure it would heal in a day or so, but from the way Wren acted, you'd have thought I was dying or about to lose a limb.

"Where did you learn to fight like that?" I asked as she worked.

"Everyone in Thea was trained in martial arts," she reminded me. "We believe that a strong body and a strong mind go hand-in-hand."

I nodded slowly. Somehow, Wren's quiet little village continued to surprise me.

Once she was finally done fussing, we set out again and rode in silence most of the morning. In the early afternoon, we stopped at a place where the stone wall to our left dipped inward, providing a sheltered campsite that would be easy to defend if anyone came seeking trouble or revenge.

After we settled in, Kraster and I started going through the saddlebags the rams had been carrying. Wren helped at first but was soon distracted by the big ram from before, whom she'd decided to call Ramulus. He seemed to like her just as much as she liked him, and she set about braiding the tuft of fur between his ears.

Inside the saddlebags, we found gnomish rations, which were a welcome addition to our own. There was also a map of the plateau, a few personal trinkets, some gold coins, and a pair of matching daggers. I added the daggers to the collection on my belt, knowing I had been correct earlier when I'd told Wren that you never could have too many weapons.

"Look at this," Kraster said, pointing to a spot on the map that appeared to be an inkblot.

"What about it?" I asked.

"I bet that's their hideout," he replied.

"Really? Looks like someone just spilled a little ink to me," I replied.

"That's what they want us to think," Kraster insisted. "But what better way to mark and, at the same time, conceal their hideout?"

"Fine," I rolled my eyes. "It's probably their hideout. What now?"

"Well, we'll be going right by it tomorrow. I think we should stop in for a look around," Kraster suggested.

"So we can get jumped again?" I asked sarcastically.

Kraster shook his head. "I doubt there are enough of them left for that. This road isn't well-traveled, and we've already taken out around twenty bandits. I can't imagine there are any more."

I had to admit that seemed logical.

"Plus," he went on in a teasing voice. "I bet there are more sharp pointy things for you to play with."

"I do like the sound of that," I grinned.

The next day, as we neared the spot on the map obscured by the inkblot, Kraster took the lead once more. He held the map in one hand and kept looking from it to the path in front of us. At last, he stopped Raspberry and dismounted. Wren and I followed him

99

after tying the rams to a tree trunk. We took the horses with us as we followed Kraster through the press of undergrowth.

"Are you sure this is right?" Wren asked.

"Yes," Kraster called back to her.

As the foliage grew thicker, I was starting to worry that the horses would get stuck. Just before I said something, we stepped into a clearing.

"Told you," Kraster said to both of us with a smug smile.

"You were right," I admitted, before muttering under my breath, "this time."

The clearing was oval in shape and completely empty. The earth inside was marked with the hoofprints of rams and the scorched earth of fire pits. A worn path led out of the clearing a few feet from the way we'd come in. On the opposite side was a stone cliff with a hole in the rockface just large enough for a gnome to fit through.

It was the hole that held our attention, since there was a lack of loot lying out in the open. This time, we did leave the horses behind as we ducked inside the cave one after another. Wren and I had no trouble, but it was a tight squeeze for my broad-shouldered brother. The inside was brighter than expected. The vaulted rock ceiling was cracked enough for me to see the sun through it.

"Look! A chest!" Wren exclaimed. I turned to see her pointing at a large, wooden box in the back corner of the little cave. "Does anyone know how to pick locks?" she asked.

"I do," I said, selecting a large rock from the ground and smashing it against the keyhole of the chest. Wren stared at me, and I grinned at her shocked expression as I pulled the lid open.

Inside was nothing but a small, black bag. Kraster plucked it from the chest and turned it upside down, but nothing fell out.

"It's empty?" I asked. "Then what's the point of the hideout, the cave, and the chest?" I was nearly laughing at the irony of the situation.

"Maybe it's not," Kraster said, studying a few runes embroidered near the bag's mouth. "It might be one of those bags that magically holds tons of stuff."

"I've heard of those," Wren piped up. "You just have to reach inside and think of what you're looking for, and, if it's in there, you can pull it out."

"Yes, but–" I started. It was too late. Wren had already shoved her hand into the open mouth of the bag.

"I'll start small," she said. "I'm thinking of five gold piec–" Her words were cut off by a scream of pain. The bag suddenly lurched forward, moving farther down her arm than was physically possible.

"What the–" Kraster gasped, pulling the bag in the opposite direction.

"Something's got me!" Wren cried.

"It's booby trapped!" I yelled, surging forward, then stopping, not sure how to help.

Both of them were pulling as hard as they could, but Wren's arm didn't reappear. Her face contorted in pain, and she twisted slightly, then yelped as her arm was swallowed up to the elbow.

"I can't pull it off!" Kraster snarled, teeth clenched as he tugged hard on the bottom of the sack.

His efforts only succeeded in unbalancing Wren, who stumbled and almost fell to the ground. The bag was nearing her shoulder, and she let out another screech of pain.

I drew a dagger from my belt. It was the sharpest blade in my arsenal. I knew from past experience that it could cut cleanly through muscle, tendon, and bone.

Wren's eyes widened at my approach. "Don't!" she gasped.

"The longer you wait, the more you'll lose," I warned.

"First, try cutting the bag," ordered Kraster.

"We don't know what that will do!" I protested. Meddling with magical items rarely ended well.

"Can it really be that much worse than her losing an arm?" he countered.

I stabbed forward, cutting the taut bag in two as far from Wren as possible. Both she and Kraster toppled backward. The pieces of the bag fell to the ground, and Wren's arm emerged mostly intact. There were two pieces of metal, shaped like jaws, latched onto her wrist. On the side, scrawled in barely legible handwriting, was the name "Betty".

Kraster reached out and touched the trap, making it fall away. I heaved a sigh of relief. Wren was bleeding where the iron teeth had punctured her skin, but at least her arm was still attached.

I rushed back to Tempest for a bandage, while Kraster used the remains of the sack to stanch the bleeding.

Once Wren's injuries were tended, we searched the rest of the cave and the clearing but didn't find anything to make it worth our while. However, I couldn't help but be relieved. After being hunted and attacked then stumbling into a booby trap, today could have gone very differently.

If there was a single thing I'd taken from my days of espionage, it was that a good day was a day when everyone walked away at the end. Today wasn't a great day, but it was a good day.

At least, that's what I tried to convince myself instead of focusing on the blood that had been needlessly spilled. I drank the rest of my wine that night, but there wasn't enough to make me feel any better.

Chapter 12
The Disaster

We reached Gnomonly before noon on the following day. It was a medium-sized town built on a slope. The dirt path we'd been following intersected with a broad, stone road running due west toward Gnomania. It started in Gnomonly's town square, where a beautiful fountain spouted crystal clear water.

"Do you know where Gnorman and Sons is located?" I asked Kraster.

He shook his head. "I'll have to ask around."

"Want me to go and see about selling the rams?" I suggested.

"Even Ramulus?" Wren wondered, moving Valor up to stand beside Tempest.

"We can't keep him," I told her. "He's too small for any of us to ride. Plus, he belongs up here, on the plateau. I doubt he'd do very well if we tried to take him with us after leaving."

Wren nodded sadly.

"Also, I think Valor is a bit jealous," Kraster added.

A furrow appeared on Wren's forehead, and she hurriedly gave her horse a few loving pats. Even though she seemed to agree it was for the best, I sent Wren with Kraster when we split up.

As I headed off, leading the rams, I spotted a few gnomes hastily moving crates inside one of the shops. They seemed rather annoyed when I interrupted to ask for directions but sent me to the town's only livery.

When I found it, I saw an old, gray-haired gnome perched on a barrel in the courtyard. He was smoking a pipe as long as his arm, while six much younger and more energetic gnomes carried bales of hay from the yard into one of the stalls.

"Hello," I greeted the old gnome, dismounting from Tempest.

He gave me a nod without taking the pipe from his mouth.

"I'm wondering if you would be interested in purchasing these rams," I explained, motioning to the creatures tethered behind my horse.

The old gnome cocked his head and squinted at the animals.

"Where did you get these?" he asked finally.

"My companions and I found them along the road on our way here," I told him.

The old gnome contemplated me for a moment before wondering, "And there's no owner who might come looking for these fine chaps?"

I shook my head. "No."

The old gnome nodded slowly. "How much you want for them?" he asked.

"A fair price," I replied, having no idea what that number would be.

The old gnome seemed to know that as well, because he grinned at me. "I'll give you six gold a piece," he offered.

I may not have known much about rams, but I knew enough to tell that his offer was extremely low.

"I'll pass," I scoffed. "A butcher would give me more for their carcasses." I moved to turn away.

"Wait, wait, wait," the old gnome called after me. I stopped, mostly because I knew Wren would never speak to me again if she found out I'd sold Ramulus, or any of the other rams for that matter, to a butcher.

"Yes?" I asked pleasantly.

The old gnome scowled. "Ten each," he offered.

"Fifteen," I countered. "And five extra for the big one." I nodded at Ramulus.

"Deal!" the old gnome announced so quickly I felt I still hadn't gotten a fair price. Not that it mattered. I'd rather have these beasts off my hands, and the gold would go a long way toward helping us on our mission.

"Are their saddles for sale too?" asked the old gnome.

"Yes," I told him hastily, having taken for granted that the Ram's tack was included in the sale. "I'll be happy to make a deal for those as well."

Ten minutes later, I was over a hundred pieces of gold richer and five rams poorer.

"Do you know where Gnorman and Sons is?" I asked as the rams were being led to stalls.

"Sure do," the old gnome answered. "It's just down the way."

I nodded and glanced in the direction he indicated. It seemed that the streets were now crowded with gnomes moving every loose item they could inside and strapping down those they could not.

"What's all the fuss about?" I asked.

"Big storm's a comin'," the old gnome told me, taking a puff of his pipe. "A big storm indeed."

I looked up to where the red sun was hanging high in the sky without a cloud in sight. It wasn't a hot day, but it was warm enough that I didn't need a long-sleeved tunic.

"A storm? Today?" I couldn't help asking.

"Of course," the old gnome replied knowingly. "Should be arriving before dusk. Better find cover."

"I'll do that," I said, mounting Tempest.

Despite the lovely weather, it seemed the entire town really did believe a storm was coming. I had to be careful to keep from trampling anyone as they scurried around making preparations.

It wasn't hard to find Gnorman and Sons. Raspberry and Valor were tied up outside with Wren and Puvva close by. Wren waved when she saw me, but the genie's eyes were fixed on the fountain in the middle of the town square.

"Is Kraster inside?" I asked, bringing Tempest to a halt and sliding to the ground.

"Yes," Wren answered. "There really wasn't room for me as well."

I nodded, glancing at the tiny door. I was unsure how Kraster had squeezed his shoulders through.

"What's she doing out?" I gestured at Puvva.

"We were getting some nasty looks, and Kraster thought I'd be less likely to be attacked if I wasn't alone."

"As if she'd be any help," I snorted.

"I'm sure she'd do her best," Wren said defensively.

I didn't want to argue, so I let the topic drop. "How long has he been in there?"

"A while," Wren answered.

"That's good," I said. "At least that means he didn't get turned away."

A few minutes later, Kraster emerged, carefully maneuvering himself sideways through the door frame. In his hand was a thick stack of papers. My brother was followed by a gnome who was shorter than most and had an extremely high-pitched voice.

"While it is so good to see you, Kraster, you should take care while traveling during these times. I've heard rumors of war, and there are those who are afraid we might be attacked here on the plateau!" Unbelievably, Gnorman's voice grew even more shrill at the end of his sentence.

"I have heard similar things," Kraster replied to the gnome. "But we must make the most of what we are given. I cannot thank you enough for helping me with this paperwork."

"Of course!" Gnorman exclaimed. "Do say hello to your brother-in-law for me. It's been too long since we had the chance to catch up."

"I will," promised Kraster.

"And, please, be careful," Gnorman added, glancing up. "There's going to be a storm today."

"There is?" Kraster asked, echoing my own uncertainty.

"Most definitely," Gnorman assured him. "The announcement came from Gnomania three days ago."

"I'm not sure they were right," I mumbled. No one heard me, which was probably for the best.

"I'd invite you to shelter with us," Gnorman glanced around at us and our horses. "But I'm afraid we haven't the room."

"That's quite all right," Kraster told him.

Gnorman nodded vigorously. "There is a tavern that services tall folk behind the blacksmith."

"We'll look into it. Thank you so much for everything." Kraster nodded to the short gnome. Gnorman dipped his head in return then vanished back inside. Kraster and Wren untied their horses and started leading them down the street.

"Seems like that went well," I commented.

"Indeed," Kraster replied. "I just had to convince Gnorman that it was a different one of my siblings who our brother-in-law had said joined the military."

"There are so many of you, how could anyone keep track?" I teased, thinking of the large brood Kraster came from, all of them my half-siblings and complete strangers.

"That's exactly what Gnorman said," chuckled Kraster.

"Are we going to seek shelter from the storm?" Wren asked.

"What storm?" I demanded.

"Everyone here seems to think one is coming," Wren replied.

"There will be a storm soon," Puvva announced.

We all turned to look at her.

"How do you know?" Kraster asked.

"I can feel it. The storm and the dragon will arrive in about six hours." Puvva's voice was completely self-assured.

"The dragon?" Wren gasped.

"Yes, Asteropaios, Queen of the Dragons and of Storms," Puvva replied. While she was speaking to us, her eyes were fixed on the cascading water coming out of the fountain across the square. Almost unconsciously, she took a step toward it.

"Asteropaios is coming here?" I demanded, unexpected excitement welling up in my chest.

"Yes. I can sense the storm she is bringing with her. At the moment, we will be on the very edge of it with the main force centered many miles to the west."

"Why would Asteropaios bring a storm upon the gnomes?" Kraster wondered aloud as Puvva took another step closer to the fountain. "Surely, she's not planning to attack the plateau."

"Of course not!" A squeaky voice piped up from the left. A gnome girl stood there, holding a flower pot almost as big as she was in both hands. Her large, blue eyes were the same shade as the petals of the plant she carried.

"The benevolent Asteropaios comes to our plateau six times a year to provide water and electricity to our cities," the blue-eyed child explained. "Without her, we would be unable to live here since there are few natural storms, and our city alone has its own source of water."

The child's words sounded like a recitation of something she'd learned in school.

"The fountain," Puvva murmured, and the girl nodded.

"Yes! The fountain was one of the many gifts given to our race long ago by the great dragons Camroc and Zaydia. It will provide us with water for all of eternity," the girl quoted.

"What were the other gifts?" Kraster asked her.

"The gears of ever-turning for the great lift, the cosmos tower in the north, the undying orb of light, and the stone which preserves Dimble's legacy." My pulse quickened at the mention of the last item.

"Dimble's Legacy came from a dragon?" Wren asked, cocking her head.

"No," the girl shook her head. "Camroc only provided the stone to Dimble so he could store the knowledge of his inventions. Dimble was the greatest genius our people have ever had! With the use of his legacy, the engineers in Gnomania are still able to replicate his designs even centuries after his death."

"Where in Gnomania do they keep the stone?" Kraster asked.

I cringed. The question seemed a little too direct to me.

"In the golem factory," the girl replied without hesitation, having no idea that she was being worked over for information.

Well, she is only a child, I reasoned to myself.

"You're very smart to know so much," Wren complimented her.

"Thank you!" The little gnome beamed proudly. A moment later, a woman called the girl inside and gave us a suspicious look with her beady eyes as she closed the door.

"Now what?" I asked. "Do we seek shelter or head for–" I cut off.

Puvva was no longer standing with us. I spotted her just as she stepped over the lip and put a foot into the fountain basin.

"Wren, go get your pet," I said, rolling my eyes.

Wren glanced around until she realized what I meant.

"She's not a pet!" Wren insisted. "She's not a slave or a tool. She's an independent being who deserves–"

Wren stopped, and both of us stared as Puvva reached up to the top of the fountain. A feeling of dread spread through me.

"Stop her!" I commanded.

"Puvva!" Wren called. "Please come bac–"

Puvva ignored Wren and pulled a sparkling sapphire from the place where the water spouted. For a moment, the gem continued to gush with water, then it spluttered, and the flow of water stopped completely. In a matter of seconds, all the water drained from the fountain's basin.

I quickly surveyed the square and was thankful to see that the few gnomes in sight were too occupied with storm preparations to have noticed the dry fountain yet.

"Do something!" I hissed at Kraster, who gave me a wide-eyed look full of uncertainty and confusion.

Puvva had started walking back toward us, the sapphire plain to see in her hand. Behind her, cracks started to appear in the stone of the fountain, and a few smaller pieces began to break off.

"That was their only water source," I gasped as the fountain crumpled to the ground. "If anyone finds out we ruined it, we'll never get into Gnomania!"

Kraster nodded and raised his hand into the air, then jerked it down, pointing two fingers at the pile of stones that had been the fountain. Lightning flashed from the clear sky and struck the largest remaining rock. It exploded with a sound like thunder.

The square was filled with gnomes a heartbeat later. All of them stared at what was left of the fountain in shock and dismay.

"What happened?" asked someone.

"It was lightning!" declared the same gnome child we'd been speaking to earlier. "Lightning from the sky!"

I breathed a sigh of relief.

"Asteropaios would never do such a thing!" argued a middle-aged gnome with drooping mustachios. His gaze moved from the girl to her mother who was beside her.

"I didn't see anything," the woman said. "We were busy getting the plants inside."

"It was definitely lightning," the child insisted.

"Did anyone else see the lightning?" the mustachioed gnome demanded, turning to survey the entire square. Puvva was standing close to us, the sapphire close to her face as she inspected it.

I practically jumped in front of her to shield the gem from the view of the gnomes.

"Yes," I blurted out. "It's just like she said. There was a blast of lightning that hit the fountain and destroyed it."

"I told you!" the little girl chortled smugly, drawing the gaze of the crowd once more.

"We need to get out of here," I breathed to Kraster.

The majority of the gnomes were moving away from us, closer to the fountain. A few were shifting through the broken stones, but most wore glazed expressions, wondering what had brought this woe upon them.

From somewhere behind me, I heard Wren quietly admonishing the genie. "Puvva, I wish you wouldn't have taken the stone, and the fountain was still in one piece. These people depended on–"

I turned just in time to see one of the three bangle bracelets, which always appeared on Wren's arm when she summoned Puvva, dissolve in a puff of green smoke.

"Oh no!" Wren gasped. "I didn't mean to–"

"The first part of your wish is null as I cannot reverse time," Puvva announced loudly. "Thus, I will only be able to attempt the second half."

With that, she turned and started moving quickly toward the fountain. Kraster tried to stop her, but she twisted out of his grasp easily. Wren and I hurried after the genie, who was halfway to the remains of the fountain.

"Puvva, I wish you to stop!" Wren called.

"Article one, section three, injunction three: There is a time constraint of six hours for partially null wishes. As partially null wishes may only be partially possible, a maximum time of six hours is allotted for their achievement, during which time any additional wishes made will be considered a null wish by default."

"What does that mean?" Wren asked.

"It means she's not going to stop," I explained. "Not for six hours!"

Puvva was almost to the fountain. In a moment, she would reach the group of gnomes clustered around it. They were too busy with their discussion to have noticed us yet. However, that was sure to change when Puvva began shoving or, more likely, trampling over them to reach the pile of rubble.

"It's always up to me," I muttered as I lunged forward and seized Puvva by the back of her neck. She attempted the same move that had worked on Kraster a moment ago. I was ready for it and used her own momentum to twist her around, so she was facing away from the crowd and the fountain.

"I must complete my master's wish," she told me. Her voice was firm and deceptively calm as she tried to jerk her head back into my nose. I avoided the blow by a hair then kicked one of her legs out from under her.

The genie didn't go down the way most people would, since gravity didn't seem to affect her normally. Thankfully, Kraster was there to help me get her under control.

"I must complete my master's wish," she repeated, voice slightly strained.

111

Several of the gnomes were looking in our direction now.

"Our friend is unwell," Kraster explained to the nearest one.

"I must complete my master's wish!" Puvva's voice was louder this time, and many heads turned in our direction.

Not good! Not good! I thought. *We need to leave now!*

"You should take her to the town doctor," a kindly-looking gnome woman suggested. "Phillis Nithe is the best there is outside of Gnomania."

"We will find her immediately," Kraster replied.

He and I carefully hoisted Puvva from the ground. She was struggling furiously as she screamed, "I must complete my master's wish!"

Despite the genie's size, she was incredibly strong. My brother and I almost lost our hold on her more than once. It felt like a painfully long time before we were able to haul her around the corner of the nearest building, out of the sight of the curious gnomes.

Wren joined us a moment later, leading the horses.

"Good," I said. "Wren, there's some rope in my saddlebag. Can you grab it?"

Wren furrowed her forehead. "What do you need rope for?"

"For Puvva," I replied.

"You can't tie her up!" Wren exclaimed, crossing her arms.

Almost as if on cue, a scream tore from Puvva's throat. "I must complete my master's wish!"

I raised an eyebrow at Wren.

"I'll get the rope," she sighed.

"Bring one of her shirts as well," Kraster called.

I gave him a questioning look.

"We can't have her yelling the whole way out of town," he explained.

Several minutes later, we had Puvva bound, gagged, and laid over Valor's back as we made for the western road leading to Gnomania.

"Where are you going?" a voice called behind us. We all stopped dead in our tracks. I turned back to see the kindly-looking woman from before. "The doctor lives on the other side of town. I'll show you the way."

"Please don't trouble yourself, ma'am. We can–" Kraster started to say, but was interrupted.

"My name is Peeket," the gnome told us. "It's no trouble as it's on my way home. Just follow me!"

As the gnome set off, I exchanged a quick look with Kraster and knew he was thinking the same thing I was: time to run. However, Wren was already leading Valor after Peeket, leaving Kraster and me no choice but to follow.

"If we don't get into Gnomania because of this, I will dropkick that teapot off of this plateau," I muttered under my breath.

Chapter 13
The Shadow

The doctor's house was larger than most. Even still, it felt extremely cramped with the four of us and the two gnomes stuffed into the main room. Peeket was nice enough to explain the situation to Doctor Nithe, who had honey-toned skin and a short mop of curly, golden hair. She also wore wire-rimmed spectacles, which greatly exaggerated her eyes.

After listening to Peeket's explanation, Doctor Nithe ushered us into an even smaller room. It had an exam chair and counters crowded with beakers and strange-looking equipment.

Kraster and I muscled Puvva into the chair and had to hold her down while the doctor began to look the genie over.

"How long has she been like this?" Doctor Nithe asked, peeling back one eyelid to look at Puvva's mint-colored eyes.

"About five minutes," Wren told her.

"And has this happened before?" the doctor wondered.

"Not since we've known her," Kraster said. "But that hasn't been very long."

Doctor Nithe carefully removed Puvva's gag. "Can you hear me?" she asked the genie.

"I must complete my master's wish!" Puvva bellowed.

"Does anything hurt?" the gnome doctor tried again.

"I must complete my master's wish!" the genie repeated, words tearing from her throat.

Doctor Nithe hastily replaced the gag. "I'm not sure what's wrong with her, but I don't believe it's anything that I can fix. The fit your friend is experiencing is something I believe only time will cure."

"I think what she really needs is an exorcism," Peeket announced. "I'll show you the way to Father Tinketon, but we'd better hurry because of the storm."

I was starting to think Peeket was less kindly and more of a busybody.

Kraster locked his arms around Puvva and hauled her out the door. She was shrieking through the gag the whole time. Peeket and Wren helped steer the thrashing genie out of the room. With a deep sigh, I moved to follow them.

A twinge of pain brought me up short. Gently, I braced my hand against my side where the spear had grazed me a few days ago. I hadn't even had time to see how bad the bruise was today.

"Are you injured?" Doctor Nithe inquired.

"I've had worse," I told her. "Heck, I have worse right now."

"What do you mean?" the doctor asked uncertainly.

I sighed again and sank down onto the edge of the exam chair. "You see, doctor," I started, putting on a grave air.

"You can call me Phillis," she interjected, pulling up a chair to sit beside me.

"You see, Doctor Phil–," I began again.

"Just Phillis," she corrected me.

"Okay then, Phillis. I'm cursed, my mother hates me, my father won't acknowledge me, most of my siblings are outraged that I even exist, my military career is over, I'm hated as a half-breed, and I am trying to complete an impossible task for some dragon-human hybrid that will probably result in my death."

The look on the gnome's face made me think I'd gone too far. I hadn't meant to say so much, but humor was quickly becoming my automatic coping mechanism since alcohol wasn't as readily available as I'd have liked.

"All of that is unfortunate," the doctor replied, placing a small hand on my arm. Her touch was quite warm and strangely comforting. "But I don't think it means you're cursed. It is easy to want somewhere to place the blame when it feels like nothing in life is going well."

"Oh, it's not that," I told her. "I know I'm cursed."

I started to rise, ready to escape.

"We'll see about that," the doctor replied. "Do you mind?" She held up a strange-looking set of glasses with nearly a dozen different lenses that could be put up or down.

"Sure," I said resignedly, sitting in the chair properly this time.

Doctor Nithe put on the glasses and started setting the lenses. They were all different colors, and a few appeared to have been made with slices of gemstone. After examining my hand, she moved to my face. A frown appeared on the gnome's lips, and she flipped down a few more of the lenses.

After several additional adjustments, Doctor Nithe sank back in her chair, a shocked look on her face.

"What did you see?" I couldn't help asking when several minutes had passed without her saying anything.

"You *are* cursed," the doctor replied in disbelief. "I've never– never seen anything like it. Your soul– It's–" She cut off, then cleared her throat and continued in a soothing tone. "I'm so sorry, but there isn't anything I can do to help you."

"No worries," I told her quickly. The level of concern in the doctor's voice had caught me off guard. "I've lived with this my whole life, and, according to a prophecy I recently received, I'll have it until I die."

"A prophecy?" the gnome mused, cocking her head slightly. "There is someone in Gnomania who might be able to help you," she told me.

"Really?" I asked almost eagerly.

"Not with the curse," she replied somberly. "But if you are on a quest from a dragon, then it is clearly a matter of great importance. My brother, Rakus, lives in Gnomania. He is a brilliant wizard. As I have worked to save life, he has worked to preserve knowledge."

The gnome studied me once again, using only her eyes this time. They were a vivid green. "And I know he'll be very interested in meeting you."

"Okay, I'll look him up," I said, getting to my feet. Phillis's sudden intensity made me uncomfortable. "I'd better go find my friends."

When I walked out of the doctor's house, I heard a well-known whistle to my left. Turning, I saw Kraster standing in the shadow of a narrow alleyway. He motioned for me to join him.

"What took you so long?" he whispered, leading me farther down the alley.

"I was having a heart-to-heart," I said softly, matching his tone. "Why are we sneaking?"

"Because we managed to give Peeket the slip," he explained. "Wren is waiting for us."

We found Wren with the horses on the edge of the village. Puvva was, once again, strapped to Valor's back. She was struggling like mad, and, even though her words didn't make it through the gag, there was an excessive amount of noise.

"We should have kept Ramulus," lamented Wren as I pulled her up behind me on Tempest.

"How much longer until this wears off?" Kraster gestured at Puvva.

"Five and a half hours, according to the contract," I sighed.

"Lovely," Kraster muttered.

I nudged Tempest onto the road leading to Gnomania.

"What are we going to do if someone comes along and sees us? They'll think we've kidnapped her!" Wren fretted.

"Hopefully, the storm keeps everyone inside," I replied.

"You sure there's going to be a storm?" Kraster inquired.

The sky above us was still blue, but now there were wisps of clouds streaking the horizon.

"If Asteropaios," my heart leapt when I spoke her name, "is coming to Gnomania, there is every likelihood she will be bringing a storm with her."

"Do you think it would be possible to speak with her?" Wren asked.

"Why would you want to do that?" Kraster asked aghast.

"She probably knows Shal'eth," Wren pointed out. "She might be able to help us."

"Do you think that if the literal Queen of the Dragons was available to help Shal'eth, he would have sent us to chase random stones high and low across the land?" My words were twisted with wry humor.

"We're currently doing the high part," Kraster pointed out. I rolled my eyes at him.

"I still think we should talk to her," Wren said.

"If we get the chance, and only if she's had a big meal recently," Kraster joked.

Over the next few hours, the clouds in the west thickened, nearly masking the setting sun. The gnome capital city was still far in the distance as the light faded from the sky. Puvva had stopped thrashing about half an hour ago, so I hoped that the power of Wren's wish had finally dissipated.

A short time later, Kraster turned off the road into a small clearing. "We should be able to pitch a tent here," he called.

Just before Tempest and I followed him into the trees, the clouds over Gnomania lit up with the glow of blue lightning. For a moment, I saw the shadow of a dragon outlined in the storm.

My heart froze. It was Asteropaios. I knew it was. I blinked. Suddenly, I was flying through the storm myself, on feathery wings bent to catch the wind. Air and power swirled around me, letting me soar on their currents.

The sensation ended as suddenly as it had started.

"You okay?" Wren asked from where she sat behind me.

"Yeah," I told her, trying to sound normal as I steered my horse into the clearing. "I'm fine."

It was a miserable night. The tent wasn't too leaky, but the constant explosions of thunder meant someone had to stay outside with the horses in case they broke their picket lines. Valor alone seemed unbothered by the brutal weather. The other two stood with their heads down and spooked every time lightning split the sky.

In the early hours of the morning, Kraster replaced me on watch. Much as I'd strained my eyes, I hadn't been able to catch a second glimpse of Asteropaios through the thick storm clouds.

"Didn't know she was the dragon of soggy weather," my brother muttered, pulling his cloak tighter around his body. It wouldn't do him any good. I knew from experience he would be soaked through in less than ten minutes.

"She is known for being the most powerful dragon ever to have lived," I told him. "And she breathes lightning, so I'm not sure why you're surprised…"

I didn't stick around to hear his reply. Instead, I crawled inside the tent and spent the next hour shivering. All the time I'd spent in the cold rain had left me chilled to the bone. Needless to say, I didn't get much sleep.

When morning came, there was still a steady drizzle. I felt like death itself. My clothes hadn't dried, and my skin seemed hot and feverish. I refused the breakfast of hard bread Wren offered me as I saddled Tempest.

"She gets like this in the rain," Kraster whispered to Wren. "Reminds me of a cat."

I managed not to hiss at my brother as I mentally prepared myself for a day of riding in the cold, wet weather. It was every bit as bad as I anticipated. Puvva had retreated into the teapot without a word last night, so I rode on Tempest alone.

Kraster and Wren's horses matched their strides in front of me. The pair didn't seem miserable at all. I wanted to throw things at them and have a drink, but not in that order.

Due to the overcast sky, night came early, and Gnomania was still miles away.

"Maybe we should ride through the night," I suggested. "Pretty sure all of our bedding is soaked, so I don't see any reason to stop. The tent isn't that much shelter anyway."

"What about that cave over there?" Kraster pointed into a clump of trees.

"Is it dry inside?" I asked.

"Only one way to find out," he announced.

My brother dismounted and approached the gaping entrance.

"Dry and warm!" he reported from several steps inside. "And there's enough room for the horses too!"

Slowly, I nodded. "Sounds like a good place to spend the night."

"That's exactly what I was thinking," Kraster replied, sticking his head out to give me an impish grin.

As Wren and I entered, Kraster lit a torch, which cast strange shadows. I could have seen better without it. However, my brother would have been all but blind. The walls were smoother than seemed natural, and the cave was shaped like a tunnel, the far end vanishing into darkness.

Despite the fact that it was warm inside, I felt a cold chill run up my arm as I traveled deeper inside. I pushed the feeling away and wrapped my cloak tighter around my body.

"This is nice," Kraster said, strolling around and using the lit torch to look at the walls.

"Do you hear–" Wren started, but I cut her off.

"Something's moving back there!" I warned, drawing both my swords and stepping forward. I wanted to put my steel between my companions and whatever lay concealed in the blackness.

"Fall back!" I ordered as the sound of scuttling echoed along the stone walls. "We need to get–"

Before I could say anything else, the largest spider I had ever seen charged forward, flanked by two others. The creatures were the size of sheep and much faster.

I slashed at the first one's legs with my swords. The monstrous beast had a huge, bulbous body and thin, spiny legs.

Even before I caught sight of the silver and blue markings, I recalled the first nightmare Wren had described to me. I expected her to start screaming. Instead, I was rather impressed to see her launch herself at the second spider, delivering a solid kick to its head. The giant arachnid reared back as Wren landed in a crouch and proceeded to strike it with her fists in a complex flurry of blows.

Behind me, I heard Kraster yell some sort of spell. There was a flash of fire followed by a shriek of pain from an inhuman mouth.

The spider in front of me lashed out, but I managed to dodge and sink one of my blades deep into its side. The creature jerked sharply, then its legs curled inward as it crumpled to the ground.

Before I could celebrate, more spiders appeared from the back of the cave. I was too slow to get out of the way as the bulk of the first monster slammed me to the ground. Immediately, I rolled, but instead of rolling away, I rolled toward the spider. As soon as my feet were under me, I surged upward, blades first, impaling the creature from beneath. It made a terrible, gurgling sound as it died, and green ichor gushed onto my hand.

I glanced around. Wren had managed to chase off the spider she'd been fighting. Two more bodies lay at Kraster's feet. However, he was incapacitated by the web of a third spider, which was closing in on him, maw open.

I charged, but Wren got there first, attacking bare-handed with incredible agility. While she had the creature distracted, I sliced at its back legs, severing a few. It gave a screech of pain that sounded like the grating of two pieces of metal, then the spider scuttled away, half dragging itself back down the tunnel.

I freed Kraster, and we dashed out of the cave, back to where we'd left the horses.

"Am I awake? Was that real?" Wren panted.

I nodded, too winded to speak.

"It was just like my dream," she gasped. "And if those creatures are real, then it means all the others are too…"

"It's just a coincidence," Kraster protested.

Wren didn't appear convinced, and neither was I.

"I've heard of those creatures. They come from the UnderEarth," I recalled.

"Impossible," Kraster shook his head. "The UnderEarth has been sealed for hundreds of years."

"Apparently not," I muttered. "Either that or something has gone very wrong in our world."

Instead of spending the night in the cave, we got back on the horses and rode until the moon was high in the sky. We didn't stop until we'd put many miles between ourselves and the spider-infested cave.

Even though I was exhausted, and the rain had stopped, I found it hard to sleep when I finally lay down. I'd fought worse monsters than the spiders, but their very existence concerned me. Also, they'd been smaller than the ancient tales told. Had those stories been exaggerated? Or were these simply recently hatched juveniles?

Worries and concerns continued to crowd my head in the morning as we rode steadily westward. By late afternoon, Gnomania appeared so close that I felt there was a good chance we wouldn't have to spend another night in the elements. The hope of finding a tavern serving hot drinks was the only thing that kept me going.

Finally, we reached the edge of the vast city. There were no outlying towns or buildings, just the walls themselves built right up against the forest. Despite the normal scale of gnomish construction, the walls reached ridiculously high into the air. They were twice as tall as any of the nearby trees. From over the top, I could see the hint of light coming from within the city, giving proof that not everything in this world was cold and drowned by the rain.

Chapter 14

The Capital

Just before twilight, we found our way to the east gate. It was a short, narrow door, heavily watched by a score of gnomes. We dismounted as the guards surrounded us.

"You don't honestly think you're getting inside?" one of them demanded.

"We aren't admitting any of you tall folk! Not with all the happenings these days!" another shouted.

"The happenings are what have brought us here," Kraster replied coolly. "We are merchants working to keep your cities well-supplied with goods throughout these trying times."

"Merchants my big toe!" a voice squeaked. "That's a warhorse if I ever saw one!" The gnome pointed at Raspberry.

"He is," Kraster admitted. "Or, rather, was before I bought him. He was injured during training. Now he's retired from military life."

While most of the gnomes continued to eye us suspiciously, an older fellow with a captain's insignia shouldered his way to the front.

"You don't look much like merchants to me," he said after studying us for a moment. I had to stop myself from reaching up to make sure my hair was covering my ears. Wren's curly, brown locks were unruly enough that I doubted he could see through them, but my pointed ears had a bad habit of being noticed. Hopefully, in the dark, they wouldn't realize what I was.

"We just left Gnomonly the day before yesterday, and I carry a letter of commerce from one of our trade partners there." Kraster brought out the papers from Gnorman. He presented them to the captain with a flourish.

The older gnome looked the documents over with a scowl, which deepened as he continued to read.

"Everything appears to be in order," he growled. "However, I must warn you that any suspicious behavior on your part will result in immediate imprisonment, if you're lucky."

"We have no intention of disturbing the peace," my brother assured the gnome.

"See that you don't," the captain warned, moving aside.

"Of course," Kraster promised.

Provided we don't get caught, I added mentally.

As we passed through the gate, I was shocked to find that we stood on the lip of a massive crater, which encompassed the entire city. The path in front of us descended for as far as I could see, but the slanted ground hadn't stopped the gnomes from constructing houses and other structures on every square inch of space. Only two buildings stood high enough to be level with the land outside. The first was the central spire. It rose into the air even higher than the walls. The second was a huge, dark-colored building, which could be none other than the golem factory the gnome child had mentioned.

The streets were nearly as bright as though the sun were up, lit by hundreds of twinkling electric lanterns. I'd heard of the almost-magical energy before but had never witnessed the marvel for myself. Gnomania was the only place in Planosia that had it. On top of all the other oddities, it seemed that nothing in the gnome's capital city was square. Instead, the roads and buildings were constructed in a hexagonal grid.

We were unable to remount due to numerous low archways crossing over the streets. As we led our horses downward, deeper into the bustling city, hundreds of unfriendly eyes followed us.

"Maybe we should try a side street," I whispered to Kraster, who nodded.

We took the next turn, which was more of a slant, to the right. The new street had almost no lanterns, leaving this part of the city shrouded in darkness. There were fewer gnomes to see us here, but their expressions were far more hostile.

"Do we have any idea where we're going?" Wren asked softly.

"There's an inn I remember my brother-in-law talking about, The Jumbo Mushroom. It's in the northeastern quadrant," Kraster told her.

"Is that the direction we're headed?" she wondered.

Kraster nodded. He looked a bit less confident five minutes later when we found ourselves in what was definitely the slums of the city.

"I think we need to go a little more east," he said, glancing around. There weren't any intersections nearby.

A sound from behind made me turn and look back into the gloom.

"We're being followed," I breathed to the others.

"Not this again," Kraster muttered, lengthening his strides.

I wasn't in front, but could still make out a large, squarish something, which dragged itself into the middle of our path.

"Oh no!" Wren gasped.

"It's just a box," Kraster replied in confusion. "Someone must have thrown it."

"It moved itself," I warned him, knowing his eyes weren't as keen in the darkness as Wren's and mine. Kraster stopped instantly, and one of his hands filled with fire, shedding light on the cube in the street. At first, it did appear to be just a box, but then the sides parted and a large tongue came out.

Wren shrieked at the exact moment Kraster launched a fire bolt at the monstrosity. My swords were in my hands a second later. As I expected, the gnomes, who had been following us, charged. My first strike connected with one, and he went down.

Raspberry spooked and kicked another, sending it flying away. The hapless gnome struck a wall and bounced off, landing in the light of one of the few lanterns.

"They're children," I called to Wren and Kraster, who were poised to attack.

I shifted my stance so my next few strikes were made with only the flat of my blade. Wren kicked one of the gnome children in the side, knocking her over and eliciting a piteous wail.

Kraster was focused on the shifting creature that blocked our path. His first strike had left it smoking, and, after two more fiery blasts, the entire thing was engulfed in flames.

The attack ended as suddenly as it had begun. Most of the children vanished, and the monster they had been trying to drive us toward shuddered and went still, its corpse still burning brightly.

"Are you all right?" Wren asked, kneeling beside the girl she had kicked. The child staggered to her feet and rushed away, screaming for help.

"We'd better get out of here," Kraster said.

I didn't answer, because I'd caught sight of the first gnome I'd struck, a teenage boy from the look of him. He was lying in the street, not moving. I reached for him, and my hand touched something warm and sticky.

"He's bleeding," I told the other two, picking the child up and carrying him into the scant pool of light. The gnome that had landed here after Raspberry's kick had gone with the others.

The boy in my arms had a deep cut in his abdomen. I instantly applied pressure to the wound as the others gathered around.

"Is he–" Wren's question was cut off by the sounds of angry voices and many feet approaching.

"We need to go! Leave him!" Kraster ordered.

"He'll bleed out!" I argued.

"Then bring him, but we need to hurry," he urged.

I lifted the gnome child again and rushed after my brother, who was leading both of our horses. Wren brought up the rear with Valor. While moving, I continued to apply pressure to the wound, hoping it wasn't as bad as it looked. My training had kicked in when we'd been attacked, but I still felt a lump of guilt rise in my throat. After the bandits on the road, I should have known that we weren't in real danger, except maybe from the shifting monster.

"There's an inn!" Wren cried out, pointing up ahead. The building was a tiny bit taller than its neighbors and had a thatched stable and a small yard for animals. The plaque above the door declared it was called The Little Villa.

The sound of our pursuers was farther away, but we needed somewhere private to tend to the child. Kraster popped inside for the longest five minutes of my life. When the door opened again, I tucked the gnome boy out of view under my cloak.

Inside, a portly gnome lady with a mole on her chin handed Kraster a set of keys. She gave me an extra-long look as I passed but didn't say anything. For the first time in my life, I prayed my ears were sticking out.

Once we were all together in one of our rooms, I laid the boy on the floor. His skin was pale and his breath shallow.

"What do we do?" Kraster asked.

"Puvva," I breathed, turning to Wren. "Summon her."

Wren took out the teapot, and I continued to hold a bloody rag in place over the gaping wound on the boy's side. Puvva appeared a moment later, looking us over coolly with her steely gaze.

"You said you have healing abilities; so heal him," I demanded.

Puvva didn't move.

"Wren," I said desperately, "wish for her to heal him."

"I don't think it's fair–"

"Please," I begged. "Please, she can save him."

"I can't. If she doesn't want to heal him, she shouldn't have to. She's not a slave."

Fury boiled inside of me. "Wren, he's a child, and he's dying."

Wren considered for a moment. "We could–"

But I didn't hear what she said, because, under my fingers, the child's heart stopped beating. Slowly, my hands slipped from his body.

"What–" Kraster started.

"It's too late," I whispered, shooting a glare at Wren and Puvva. Wren at least seemed contrite. Puvva's face didn't reveal any emotion whatsoever.

"This is your fault," I spat at the pair. "Why wouldn't you help?"

"Puvva isn't a slave," Wren repeated. "I can't make her—"

"Yes, you could have," I cut her off. "Otherwise, you'll just accidentally use your wishes for destruction."

Wren's face went white as a sheet. I rose and staggered back away from the corpse of the child I had murdered.

Why me? Why was I always so unlucky? The cut wasn't that long or deep. I'd been just as likely to hit him in the arm or the leg, but no, I had hit him in just the right spot to have to watch him die.

"We need to get rid of the body," Kraster murmured.

"That I would be happy to help with," Puvva announced. "He can rest in the vast sea within my vessel." All three of us watched in surprise as Puvva took hold of the child and both turned to pale green mist before vanishing into the teapot.

A wave of nausea washed over me. I stumbled out the door, passing the same lady who had given us our keys.

I managed to make it outside before heaving up the contents of my stomach, which was mostly bile since I hadn't eaten much that day. After wiping my mouth, I staggered down the street, looking for a tavern.

I went inside the first one I saw. They had lots of drinks there–good, strong drinks. I tried half the menu before the gnome behind the bar told me to get lost. Kraster was in the street looking for me when I lurched out.

"Really?" he asked when he caught sight of me.

"Reelly," I slurred. "Itch been a night."

"That it has," he sighed, grabbing my shoulder and steering me back inside the inn. I fell into bed, longing for unconsciousness, but just before I dropped off for the night, there was a banging on the door. Thankfully, I was still too drunk to have a headache yet.

Wren opened the door, and several smartly dressed gnomes entered.

"I'm Constable Linkle," one of them announced. "And this is my partner, Constable Bizzet."

"How can we help you, officers?" Wren asked politely.

"There was an anonymous report of a gnome child, possibly kidnapped, being spirited into your room," Constable Bizzet replied. His voice was nasally and annoying. I wanted him to go away so I could sleep.

Through the open door, I saw the inn's owner looking at us, and knew exactly where the "anonymous report" had come from.

"There's no gnome child here, but you're welcome to see for yourselves," Wren announced, throwing the door wide open.

The constables came in and poked around for a bit, but there wasn't much to see. The Little Villa was aptly named as the rooms were tiny, even by gnome standards.

In less than five minutes, the officers had left after begging our pardon. I caught sight of them heading to Kraster's room next.

At least that stupid genie was finally good for something, I thought bitterly, pulling the covers back over my head and finally finding the blackness I craved.

I didn't feel much better in the morning but tried to be civil to Wren. While I did blame her partially for the child's death, I blamed myself more.

"What's next?" Wren asked as I picked at my breakfast. My head was pounding, proof that it had been too long since the last time I'd gotten completely sloshed. Inside, I felt all twisted up and gross. The eggs and toast on my plate were unoffending but not exactly welcome.

"I'm not sure," Kraster admitted. "I guess we need to find a way inside the golem factory."

"But how?" Wren asked.

"Rakus," I said, forcing myself to take a bite.

"What?" Kraster asked.

"We need to find Rakus," I told him.

"Who is Rakus?" Wren furrowed her brow.

"A wizard," I replied. "A wizard who might help us."

Kraster and Wren exchanged a confused look as I finished my last mouthful of breakfast, stood up, and walked out of the inn.

Chapter 15
The Wizard

Eventually, after my headache had mostly worn off, I explained to the others what Doctor Nithe had told me about her brother, Rakus. It took twice as long for me to convince them that I wasn't joking.

"A wizard," Kraster mused. "Where would we even start looking for him?"

I shrugged. "Maybe we should ask someone."

We'd left the horses at the inn. Even without them, the gnomes still stared, but it felt less ominous in the light of the sun.

"I'm not sure that's a good idea," Kraster told me.

"Who would we even ask?" Wren wondered.

I looked around. The street we were on consisted mostly of shops.

"There." I pointed to a sign painted in jewel tones. "The Wizard's Emporium," I read. "That seems like a good place to start."

Kraster opened his mouth as though to object but then seemed to change his mind. "No harm taking a look," he decided aloud.

Inside the shop were dozens of shelves filled with strange trinkets and glittering gemstones. My hope of learning anything useful about Rakus diminished as I passed a rack of "wizard staffs". I was pretty sure you couldn't just buy those, regardless of whether you were a wizard or not.

Kraster was inspecting the clothing section, which contained everything from pointy hats to "magical" robes. Again, I was certain those kinds of things couldn't be purchased, especially not on sale for just a few silvers.

The sound of Wren's voice made me turn my head. My stomach clenched when I saw her beside the "enchanted" rings, talking to Puvva.

"What is *she* doing out?" I hissed, coming over to them.

"I thought she might like to see some of this stuff," Wren replied.

I glared at the pair. There were so many things I wanted to say, but if I started speaking, I wouldn't be able to stop, and the words would not come out quietly. I knew this wasn't the place to make a scene, so I turned on my heel and stalked away.

Kraster moved to the counter and began chatting with the shopkeeper, a stumpy gnome with a black beard. Throughout the conversation, I kept seeing the gnome's shifty eyes glance toward Puvva. She and Wren were meandering closer and closer to where the shopkeeper stood with my brother.

Resting a hand on my favorite sword, I moved into earshot.

"So, he lives a few streets over?" Kraster was asking.

"Indeed," the shopkeeper replied. "Take a right at the end of the street, then another right two streets later, and you should be able to see his tower."

"His tower?" Kraster blinked.

"Well, of course," the gnome answered. "You wouldn't expect a world-renowned wizard like Rakus not to have a tower, would you?"

I refrained from pointing out that the only time we'd heard of Rakus was from a random doctor, in a backwater town, on top of a forlorn plateau. Wisely, Kraster didn't say anything of the sort.

"Thank you so much for your help," he replied instead, turning to leave.

"Don't mention it," the gnome told him. "But before you go, who is your companion?" He pointed at Puvva.

"She's–" Kraster started uncertainly. "She's hard to explain. I've never met anyone like her before and know very little of her history."

The gnome nodded, narrowing his eyes in a way that I didn't quite like.

"A genie?" he asked so softly that I almost didn't hear him.

Kraster's eyes widened. "How did you know?"

The gnome smiled with more teeth than seemed entirely friendly. "Just because most of the items in my shop are strictly novelties, I do know something of real magic, and she's dripping with it. Who is her master?"

The shopkeeper's eyes skipped me entirely, passed over Kraster, then jumped to Wren. As he watched, she lifted a silver talisman for closer inspection. The movement caused her sleeve to fall back slightly, revealing one of the bangle bracelets.

"I think it's time to go," I announced loudly. Stepping up to stand beside my brother, I effectively cut off the gnome's view of Puvva and Wren. He curled his lip at me as I turned, hoping Kraster wouldn't protest. He didn't, and Wren followed us as soon as she saw that we were heading for the door. Puvva was right on her heels.

"What was up with that guy?" I asked as soon as we reached the street.

"I don't know," Kraster shrugged, seemingly unworried. "I think it's his shtick. Act all mysterious and wise and people will be more likely to buy your magical items, or something like that."

"Sure," I nodded, unconvinced. He had easily recognized Puvva for what she was and seemed to know more about her than even Wren.

After the concerning encounter, I was a little nervous about following the shopkeeper's directions, but they turned out to be superb. Rakus's tower was where he said it would be, in a quiet part of the city, with buildings that were a little more spread out and less on top of each other.

A set of stairs led up to the tower's door, which was painted gold. The structure itself was ten stories high, making it the tallest building we'd seen, aside from the central spire and the factory. It was built from stone, completely round, and had a pointed roof. There were a handful of windows, but they seemed to be spaced randomly, with no rhyme or reason. The entire structure was slightly curved, like a relatively straight banana.

Kraster marched up the stairs and tapped with the knocker. It was brass and in the shape of two identical dragons facing each other.

After a moment, the door opened. Standing there was a gnome who I assumed was Rakus. His skin had a rich, golden brown tint like his sister's, but instead of blond curls, he had white hair and a long, white beard, as wizards often do.

The robes he wore were a deep, forest green trimmed with gold. His eyes were also gold, but a much more vibrant hue. They instantly jumped past Kraster and, for a moment, I thought they'd settled on me, but it was more likely they were looking at Puvva, who was just to my right.

"Greetings," the wizard said in a timeless voice. "I am Rakus. How may I be of service?"

Kraster licked his lips before answering. "Well, you see we– we are on a quest– of sorts– and– and were told you might be able to help us."

Rakus nodded slowly, his eyes running over all of us again. They met mine and lingered for a moment. "You're the one Phillis told me about, aren't you?"

I nodded, and the gnome beamed.

"My sister sent word that you might be stopping by." Rakus leaned forward and lowered his voice. "And that it was about dragon business."

I nodded again as Rakus took a step backward, motioning for us to come inside.

The room we entered had all the furnishings of an entry hall. There was a coat rack, which leaned forward helpfully and extended several hooks to take our cloaks. I ignored it, but Wren happily hung hers up.

Several curious-looking cabinets stood along the walls, each with dozens of drawers of different sizes in no particular order. On the floor was a round carpet that resembled a lake, complete with large, embroidered fish that actually swam in endless circles. Even more interesting to me was the lack of a staircase.

There were two other doors set equidistant from the one we'd come through and from each other. I didn't think there was anywhere for them to go but back outside. However, when Rakus opened the one on the left, I realized there was magic at work here.

We followed him into a marvelous sitting room. The couches and chairs were upholstered with gold and green fabric, and there were matching tapestries on every wall. I was beginning to sense a bit of a color scheme.

This room also had three doors, all evenly spaced from each other. There was a single window. When I glanced through it, I saw that we were high in the air and looking out over the city of Gnomania.

"Please sit." Rakus gestured to the couches. While we settled ourselves, he took a small, three-legged stool for himself. It didn't look very comfortable to me, but he perched upon the seat like it was the most natural thing in the world.

"Now," Rakus began. "Do you mind telling me which dragon you are working for and how you got involved?"

The wizard focused his attention on Kraster, but before he could answer, Wren spoke up. "The Great Shal'eth."

A shadow crossed Rakus's face, and his expression grew distant. "I haven't heard that name in a very long time," he murmured.

"He was the guardian of my town, but when we were attacked, he sent my people away and entrusted this to me." Wren held out her stone.

Rakus leapt to his feet, jaw hanging open. "Do– do you know what that is?" His eyes darted to me, then away quickly.

"It's a scrying stone," Wren replied.

"It's not *a* scrying stone," Rakus told her. "It is *The* Scrying Stone!"

Wren furrowed her brow.

134

"What did Shal'eth tell you about it?" the wizard inquired.

"Almost nothing," Wren admitted.

Rakus considered this for a moment. "You've come for Dimble's Legacy, haven't you?" he asked.

After a brief hesitation, Wren nodded.

"Can you help us get it?" Kraster blurted out eagerly.

Rakus was silent again, for much longer this time. "I suppose I must," he said at last.

Wren smiled. "That's great! I was afraid we were going to have to steal it or something."

"Oh, we are definitely going to have to steal it," Rakus assured her.

"What?" she gasped.

"The gnomes will never give it up willingly," he explained, "especially with rumors of war in the wind. They have already put Dimble's Legacy to use building hearts for their war golem army."

"But how are you going to get it, then?" Wren wondered

"I'm not," the wizard replied. "But I will help *you* get it."

"And why would you do that?" Kraster asked suspiciously.

"Two reasons," Rakus told him. "First, I knew there was a possibility this day would come, and if Shal'eth has made his move, then I must as well. Secondly," he finally looked at me again, "one of you has something I want."

"Me?" I blinked at him.

He nodded.

"What could I possibly have that would interest a wizard?" I scoffed.

"Your blood," he replied.

"Excuse me?" I spluttered, leaping to my feet and drawing my weapons.

Betrayal! Not again! I thought.

Betrayal? Again? That was a weird thing to think. Although quite a few people had tried to kill me lately, so maybe not so much.

The wizard paid no attention to my hasty actions, which was probably for the best, considering I'm sure he could have smote me dead at any moment.

"When Phillis told me to keep an eye out for you, she said that your soul is not attached properly to your body," Rakus explained.

"What?" cried Kraster.

"I'm sure it's part of my curse," I sighed.

"Curse," Rakus repeated. "Is that what you call it?"

I nodded, then raised my weapons again. "Why do you want my blood?"

"To study it, of course," he replied, still ignoring the sword blades pointed in his direction.

"How much blood would you want?" I demanded.

"Not much." Rakus snapped his fingers, and a glass beaker appeared in his hand. "I believe this should be a sufficient amount."

Kraster and Wren glanced at me uncomfortably. Slowly, I sheathed my swords and retook my seat.

"Fine," I said. "Let's talk."

Chapter 16
The Portal

An hour later, we had a tentative contract drawn up. I was going to allow Rakus to take my blood for his experiments. In return, he was going to open a portal for us directly into the factory where Dimble's Legacy was kept.

He also offered to let us spend the night with him. At first, we'd declined because our horses were stabled at The Little Villa, but then Rakus had risen and walked to one of the room's doors. When he opened it, I could smell fresh hay and see several wooden stalls.

"How is any of this possible?" Wren breathed.

"Magic," I muttered with a shake of my head.

Kraster and I left to fetch the horses, while Rakus went to see if he could procure the supplies he needed for the portal.

When my brother and I returned an hour later, we found Rakus giving Wren a lesson on how to use The Scrying Stone. She seemed equal parts nervous and eager. Puvva was still out of her teapot, playing with a bowl of water on the floor like a child.

Once the horses were stabled, Rakus took us into a room that could only be described as a laboratory. There were beakers and burners, some already lit with multi-colored flames. Against the walls were dozens of bookcases, piled high with dusty scrolls and tomes. Wren sneezed as soon as she set foot inside.

Rakus led me to a desk where our contract lay.

"Please sign," he said, handing me a quill.

I leaned forward and scrawled my full name at the bottom of the document. Rakus did the same, but while I wrote in the common tongue, he used a language I was unfamiliar with. As soon as the wizard finished, the parchment glowed with golden light and vanished in a flash.

"Wonderful," Rakus exclaimed with a clap of his hands. "Now we can get started." He gestured to the largest armchair in the room. I sat down and had to stifle a sneeze of my own as a cloud of dust escaped the ancient cushion.

"Sorry," the wizard apologized. "I've been meaning to hire a maid."

Before long, Rakus had stuck my arm with a needle attached to a tube, and I was watching curiously as my blood drained into the beaker he'd set on the floor.

"Does it hurt?" Wren asked.

"Not really," I told her. "It feels slightly strange, but of all the ways I've lost blood, this is the least painful by far."

She nodded, looking slightly nauseous.

When the beaker was full, Rakus took the needle out and gently wrapped my arm with a bandage. I didn't see what the gnome did with the blood, but a moment later he was offering me tea and biscuits.

"These should keep you from becoming faint," he promised.

I took them, but tea had never been my thing. Not wanting to be rude, I drank the bitter-tasting leaf water anyway and nibbled on the first cookie. Nibble was about all I could do because the darn thing was so hard I feared I'd break a tooth.

As evening fell, Rakus took us to his guest room. Surprisingly, the beds were large enough that even Kraster's feet didn't hang over the end.

Morning came, and, for once, we didn't have to be up at dawn. Rakus had told us that we wouldn't be entering the factory until the evening, when the workers had left for the day. I took advantage of the situation and slept in. When I did get up, I didn't feel at all worse for the wear. Perhaps the tea had been more than just tea.

Glancing around, I found I was the only one in the room. Hastily, I laced up my armor and pulled on my boots. Opening the door I'd entered through the night before, I came to a halt. Yesterday, this door had led from Rakus's study, now it opened into a different room, one with a long table where Wren and Kraster sat eating a luxurious breakfast.

"Glad to see you're finally up, sleepy head," Kraster called at me.

I scowled at him then grabbed the nearest empty plate and started filling it with food.

"I think I earned some rest after yesterday," I pointed out, loading up on a double portion of crispy bacon.

I sat down next to Wren, but before I could take a single bite, the room was rocked by a loud explosion from somewhere below.

"What was that?" Wren gasped.

"Better go and find out," I muttered, shoving two strips of bacon into my mouth and heading for the closest door. It opened a second before I touched the knob, admitting a puff of orange smoke. A frazzled-looking Rakus stumbled through a moment later.

Wren hurried over and helped the elderly gnome to a chair. "Are you hurt?" she asked.

"I'm fine," Rakus replied, speaking a little too loudly. "Never better."

The wizard turned to look at me. "Your blood is a touch flammable."

"My blood did this?" I gaped.

Rakus nodded and accepted the cup of water Wren offered him.

"How?" Kraster asked. "She's never exploded before!"

If my brother had been next to me, I would have kicked him. But when I glanced in his direction, it seemed he was serious.

"What exactly did you do to my blood?" I pressed Rakus.

"I just performed a few tests," he replied, voice at a much more normal level now. "Regrettably, I fear I have destroyed the entire sample. I don't suppose you'd be willing to give a little more?"

"I don't know," I said. "I think I'm going to need all my strength for tonight."

"I wouldn't take as much, and you'd still be in top form," Rakus promised. "Plus, if you agree, I will provide you with another service."

"What service?" Kraster wanted to know.

"Once you return from the factory, I will open a portal that will take you off the plateau."

"You can do that?" Wren whispered in admiration.

Rakus dipped his head to her. "Indeed."

"That would actually be very helpful," Kraster admitted.

"I thought so," Rakus agreed. "Especially since the city will go into lockdown once they realize Dimble's Legacy is gone."

"Why are you helping us?" I asked, narrowing my eyes. "You're a gnome. If war really is coming, surely, this isn't in your people's best interest."

Rakus hesitated. Our eyes met, and his were full of sorrow.

"I have made some poor decisions in my past, which I am very sorry for," he told me softly. "Decisions I made for *the good* of my people, which ended up being great folly. If Shal'eth has set you on this path, then I will help you as much as I can, because I truly believe there is nothing better I can do for *all* people."

I stared at him in confusion, trying to puzzle out exactly what he was saying and, more importantly, what he was not saying.

"I also choose to trust the wisdom of The Great Shal'eth," Wren added fervently.

"The ancient dragons know much," Rakus agreed. "That is why I will be sending you to see Asteropaios."

"What?" we all gasped.

"Is she still here in the city?" Wren asked.

Rakus shook his head. "No, she never remains long on the plateau, only a few days to fill our cisterns with water and charge our vaults with electricity. She's probably finishing her round of the outer villages today and will head home in the evening."

"Then how are we supposed to meet with her?" Kraster asked.

"I'm more interested in why you're sending us," I cut in.

"I will open a portal to her seat in the south," Rakus explained to Kraster, before turning to me. "You are on dragon business. Who better to help you than The Queen of the Dragons?"

"This is going to be incredible," Wren breathed.

"Until we get eaten," Kraster mumbled.

After I finally got to finish my breakfast, I again went into Rakus's laboratory so we could sign an amended contract, and he could draw more of my blood.

The room had an acrid scent. I could see scorch marks on one wall with the charred remains of a table on the floor beneath them.

This time, the vial was half the size of the one from before. Rakus stepped out while it was filling, but Wren came to keep me company, bringing Puvva with her. The sight of the genie made my stomach turn.

"Why is she here?" I asked, hoping Puvva wouldn't start breaking Rakus's instruments. That seemed to be all she was good at: destruction.

"I think she should come with us tonight," Wren replied.

"What?" I hissed. "How can you possibly believe that's a good idea?"

"She'd be a great distraction," Wren explained.

Well, I couldn't argue with that. "But if she is the distraction and then gets caught, how are we going to get her out?"

"If something happens, she can just turn to mist and put herself back into the teapot."

I gave Wren a flat stare. "And will she do that? From what I have seen, Puvva is the opposite of cooperative. She'd probably find being arrested and imprisoned amusing. Plus, you and her can't get too far apart."

I pointed to the two remaining bangle bracelets on Wren's arm. "If she gets captured, you're captured too."

"Of course, Puvva knows how important it is to escape," Wren explained.

I raised an eyebrow at her. "And if she does get captured and decides not to mist herself back into the teapot, are you willing to either wish her back or take off the bracelets and leave the teapot behind?"

Wren furrowed her brow. Before she could answer, Rakus returned, and he wasn't alone. It took me a moment to place the gnome with him as the stumpy shopkeeper from The Wizard's Emporium. Apparently, the place did sell more than novelties, since he'd come to bring Rakus the supplies for the portals.

"This is Raull Minker," Rakus introduced us. "In addition to running his shop, Raull sometimes dabbles in wizardry himself."

Wren eagerly shook hands with the dark-haired gnome. I still had a needle in my arm, so Raull skipped me and tried to shake hands with Puvva. She just stared at the outstretched appendage until he withdrew it, chuckling.

Once I'd finished filling the second vial, Rakus escorted me back to the room with the large table and insisted I have another breakfast. I wholeheartedly agreed with him and ate myself almost sick on the scrumptious feast.

When I'd taken the last bite and sat back in my chair, the table suddenly flashed with white light. The food and dirty dishes vanished, leaving a completely clear surface.

"What if I wasn't done yet?" I asked no one in particular.

In reply, the table flashed again, and the breakfast returned, every plate heaped with delicacies.

"This looks great," I told the table. "But it's almost lunch time."

The bacon, toast, and breakfast cakes vanished, replaced a moment later with sandwiches, pudding, and a creamy-looking potato dish.

"I need a table like this," I announced to the empty room.

It would have been downright rude not to eat anything after the table had performed so marvelously for me, so I took a sandwich. However, I was too full to swallow more than a few bites. Thankfully, the others came in and joined me, Rakus and Raull with them.

During the meal, I couldn't help but notice that Raull was watching Puvva like a hawk. The genie didn't eat anything but put a spoonful of pudding on her dish. She kept moving the plate, watching in fascination as the gooey substance jiggled.

I took a nap in the afternoon and woke up feeling like I'd overslept. I hadn't, but a feeling of urgency lingered, setting me on edge. After such a large second breakfast, I didn't feel hungry for dinner. Still, I forced down a few bites of chicken and warm bread.

Finally, Rakus told us it was time, and we returned to the laboratory. I quickly checked the straps on my armor, making sure all of my weapons were ready.

"Stand right here," Rakus directed the four of us, while he and Raull began marking the floor with chalk runes.

"Perfect!" the wizard announced a moment later. He dusted himself off, which only smeared the chalk on his hands all over his robes. Rakus took a large tome from one of the shelves and started reading the words in a strangely deep voice. I blinked and, for a moment, saw a flash of green and gold scales, then there was blinding light in front of me.

I squinted as the circular portal formed, opening into a dark space that appeared to be a closet.

"I will keep the portal open as long as I can," Rakus told us. "But such things consume a lot of energy. If you return to find it closed, you'll have to make your way back here on your own."

Kraster nodded and stepped through the portal. I was right behind him, Wren following me. Out of the corner of my eye, I saw Raull lunge forward.

Turning, I watched as his foot intentionally smudged one of the runes on the floor, then he seized Puvva by the wrist, pulling her away from us. The portal immediately started to collapse at an alarming rate. Wren's right arm, which held the bangle bracelets, was wrenched back into the opening, but the portal was too small for the rest of her to follow.

"Help!" she screamed, voice laced with pain.

Kraster and I had her other arm a moment later. We heaved with all our might, but it wasn't enough. The portal shrank even further, and I truly wondered what we were going to do if Wren's arm was sheared off. The fear of that happening gave me greater strength. I strained as hard as I could, my brother laboring beside me. Inch by inch, Wren's arm began to emerge, but the portal was nearly gone.

"Now!" Kraster yelled. With a sudden surge, we dragged Wren free. The portal closed completely before we'd even stopped moving.

Wren's right arm, whole and intact, dropped to her side. She was shaking and gasping for breath, face white as a sheet from the terror of what had almost happened.

Chapter 17
The Factory

Quickly, I took stock of our position. We were in a closet, but not the nice kind of closet where they kept the liquor. All I could see in the space around us were brooms, mops, and buckets.

"What happened?" Kraster panted, looking Wren over to make sure she was still in one piece.

"That Raull guy grabbed Puvva and closed the portal," I answered, since Wren was still breathing too hard to speak.

"The question is, was Rakus in on it?" I asked darkly.

"It's possible," Kraster replied. "He did agree to help us pretty easily."

"What do we do?" Wren fretted.

"We need to figure out where we are," I told her. "If he actually did send us to the factory, this may not be a total loss. How's your arm?"

"Fine," she replied, massaging it carefully. "I'm more worried about Puvva. What would they want from her?"

"A magical genie who grants wishes? Gee, I can't imagine," I said in a flat tone.

"But she's useless without the teapot," Wren pointed out. "And I've got that here with me."

"Maybe they don't know about the teapot," Kraster suggested.

"Since you two were forced apart, did she turn to mist and go back into her vessel?" I wondered.

Wren fumbled to check her pack, but shook her head as she held up the teapot. For the first time, it was completely dark without any inner light.

"What does that mean?" Kraster sounded confused.

"I'm not sure," Wren told us, glancing down at her arm.

That was when I noticed that the bangles were gone.

"I don't think it's good for her to be separated from her teapot," Wren said. "She– she might be– You don't think she could be dead?"

There was a moment of silence. Much as I didn't care for the genie, and was furious over some of her actions, I didn't want her dead.

"There's nothing we can do for her right now," I finally said, my military training kicking in. "We need to figure out where we are and if we can still complete the mission."

Kraster and Wren nodded.

I moved to the door and slowly eased it open a crack. On the other side was a dark hallway with no sign of life. I wasn't surprised. If anyone had been close by, they would have heard our struggle to free Wren from the portal, not to mention our conversation afterward, which had been anything but quiet. So either we'd gotten lucky, or the alarm was being raised. It didn't matter. There was only one way forward.

Most gnome buildings had low ceilings, but here the halls were more than twice as tall as Kraster and wide enough for a dozen horses to walk abreast.

Rakus had given us instructions on how to navigate the factory. I wasn't sure he could be trusted; however, with no other knowledge of the layout, we didn't have much of a choice.

Even still, I stopped to check around each corner and investigate every shadow, since I absolutely refused to walk into one more gnomish ambush.

Despite my fears, we saw no one until we reached an enormous room filled with war golems. Though humanoid in shape, their limbs were crafted from metal and gears. In place of a head, there was a transparent dome covering a cockpit where the pilot would sit.

There must have been nearly five hundred of the mechanical creations. Less than a quarter were finished and ready to be deployed. Some were just legs or heads. Others had gaping holes in the middle of their chests where the power unit, called the heart, would be inserted.

146

I paused in the doorway, causing Wren to trip over me. Kraster caught her arm to keep her from falling. Unfortunately, it was her right arm and must have still been sore, because she cried out in pain.

The three of us froze. For a moment, all was still, then a high-pitched voice cut through the darkness. "What was that?!"

Footsteps sounded from above us, and the glow of lantern light could be seen over our heads.

"They're on a walkway above us," I whispered, pointing up at the high ceiling.

"What do we do?" mouthed Wren.

"We need to find the place where they make the hearts," Kraster reminded us. "Rakus said the stone would be in a secret room, located in the middle of the golems."

"How is there a secret room in the middle of the golems?" Wren asked, squinting at the constructs.

The footsteps were coming closer, nearly right over our heads. We fell back and took cover in a corner filled with wooden bins.

"I know I heard something," a gnomish voice said.

I peeked out from behind the bins and saw a square section of the walkway suddenly move downward. There were two gnomes standing on it. When they reached the floor, the pair stepped off, and the piece of walkway began to rise again, pulled back into place by a pulley system.

Each of the two gnomes held a lantern.

"Sleep," I whispered urgently to Kraster. He nodded and pointed a finger at the gnomes. They dropped like sacks of potatoes a moment later. I heaved a sigh of relief and hurried to extinguish their lights.

Leaving the pair to slumber, we started searching among the cluster of golems. Even uncompleted as they were, the machines were unnerving.

"What are they for?" Wren asked quietly.

"War," replied Kraster solemnly.

"How did they know war was coming?" I mused.

Kraster shrugged. "I guess they saw the signs before we did."

"But why is the world falling apart now?" Wren murmured softly.

I didn't have an answer, because how could one have an answer to a question like that?

We reached the middle of the room, and I carefully inspected the floor for signs of a hidden door or secret staircase but without success. We spread out and made a thorough search of the area. After combing the entire field of golems without finding anything, we regrouped in the center.

"This is a problem," I muttered. Kraster nodded as we exchanged a hopeless glance. "How much longer will those two gnomes be asleep?"

"Less than fifteen minutes," he answered.

Wren was suddenly tapping my shoulder. I turned to see her eyes fixed on something above us. Looking up, I saw the walkway the gnomes had been on. It circled the perimeter of the room. Wren's hand directed me toward the center of the ceiling, where a rectangular portion was several yards lower than the rest.

"That must be the secret room," I breathed. Looking closely, I could see a hatch in the very center. It was too far away to make out much more in the dim light.

"Now, how do we get to it?" Kraster asked.

"Magic?" I wondered.

"No," Kraster shook his head. "That would require a lot of concentration, and I wouldn't be able to keep the gnomes from waking up."

"I think I can reach it," Wren offered.

We both looked at her in surprise as she hurried to the nearest golem and began scrambling up its leg. The construct stood directly under the secret room. Despite her usual clumsiness, Wren scaled the golem surprisingly well. I held my breath as she reached the top and stood on the glass dome, then she sprang acrobatically forward and caught hold of something a few feet from the hatch.

"How's she doing?" Kraster asked, squinting into the darkness.

"Pretty well," I told him. "She seems so young most of the time that I forget about her martial arts training until we're in a pinch."

Carefully, Wren began maneuvering herself closer to the hatch. I couldn't see what she was holding onto, but the fact that she appeared to be struggling to maintain her grip made me certain I would never have been able to make the climb myself.

When she finally reached the hatch, she kicked upward at it with both feet. It opened a little, and she wedged one foot inside. Hanging basically upside down, she was able to hook her legs over the edge and swing herself inside.

I heaved a sigh of relief.

Kraster glanced at me. "What–" he started, but cut off as a rope ladder dropped down from the opening above.

Kraster held the bottom for me, ready to start his ascent when I finished. I reached the top quickly and pulled myself over the lip of the opening.

I was not prepared for what I found inside the secret room. Wren had a gnome in a headlock. I quickly looked around for more assailants but didn't spot any.

"As I was saying before you so rudely stepped on my foot," Wren addressed the gnome. "I have no interest in hurting you, I just need to know where Dimble's Legacy is."

"Might want to give him a little more air if you're expecting an answer," I advised Wren. The gnome in her grip was starting to turn a little purple.

"Last time I tried that, he assaulted me," Wren grumbled, but I saw that she loosened her chokehold slightly.

Kraster joined us a moment later. "Find it yet?" he asked.

"No, but I'm sure he knows where it is." I pointed to Wren's captive.

"He's not talking, though," Wren scowled.

"I can make him talk." Kraster stepped forward, a ball of fire forming around his fist. The gnome's eyes grew wide with terror. I saw that he was very young, probably not even twenty yet.

"Easy there." I put a hand on my brother's shoulder. I was already responsible for the deaths of quite a few gnomes. They had all deserved it to some degree, but this one did not. This time, we were the thieves coming to steal something that wasn't ours.

I stepped closer to the gnome, who was now struggling wildly. "What's your name?" I asked.

"Gnomex. Graese Gnomex," the gnome whispered.

"Listen, Gnomex, I know what you're thinking. You're thinking that we've come here to take the stone to make your people vulnerable in the war, right?"

Gnomex nodded at my words.

"But that's not true," I assured him. "We're here for the opposite reason." He didn't appear to believe me. "There's something bigger going on. We don't even fully understand it, but we are trying to stop the war, and for that, we need the stone. Will you help us?"

Gnomex really seemed to consider for a moment, then doubt clouded his eyes. He shook his head. I sighed, not sure why I'd thought he would believe me.

"Wren, you keep holding him," I instructed. "Kraster and I will find the stone."

Kraster was already rooting through the drawers in the desks that lined three sides of the small room. Above the desks, the walls became transparent. From below, we hadn't been able to see into this room, but up here, I could look out in three directions. If Gnomex had been on watch, he must not have been doing a good job.

I cocked my head as I recalled how it looked from below. The room had appeared bigger, much bigger. I moved to the fourth wall, the one without windows, and felt along it until my fingers brushed an imperfection in the otherwise smooth surface. I gave it a quick push and felt a knob pop out into my hand.

"I found something," I whispered. Turning the knob, I opened a door into a second, larger room. This one had no desks, but there were several rows of mechanical devices nearly as tall as I was. From what I could tell, they were golem hearts.

"The stone has to be in here somewhere," I told Kraster, who had followed me.

We searched high and low without finding any sign of it. Still, I had a strong feeling it was close by. I walked through the rows of hearts slowly, trying to determine where the gnomes would keep Dimble's Legacy.

"Maybe we should have Wren use The Scrying Stone," Kraster suggested.

"You know why she doesn't want to do that," I reminded him.

"Because of what The Oracle said," Kraster recalled.

I nodded.

"Well, we're running out of options," he sighed impatiently.

I frowned and continued searching. Walking the length of the room again, I felt along all the surfaces in case there were more hidden doors. On the far wall, I found one. It was better concealed than the first. If I hadn't knelt to check along the floor, I would have missed the hidden trigger entirely. Just like before, a knob popped out when I pushed on the imperfection.

"Kraster!" I called in excitement, opening the door.

On the other side was a very small room, only large enough for a single gnome to work inside. A strange-looking machine stood at the far end. It was covered in turning gears and thin wires. Secured in a socket on its front was a golden stone, which pulsed faintly with warm, rich light. The rune for eternity was carved into its surface, and I knew I had found Dimble's Legacy.

The room's low roof meant I had to enter on my hands and knees. Kraster wouldn't have even fit through the doorway. The walls grew narrower farther inside, until I was forced to turn sideways. Finally, by reaching forward and straining my arm, I was close enough to touch the stone. As I popped it free of the socket, I received a slight shock. I jerked back, and the stone clattered to the floor.

"Did you just drop it?" Kraster asked from behind me.

"Sort of," I admitted.

"Sort of?" he echoed.

"I've got it." I reached out and picked up the fallen stone. It tingled slightly in my palm but didn't shock me again. I stretched back toward Kraster, thrusting it into his hand.

"Don't drop it," I warned.

He just snorted.

I shimmied backward out of the tiny room and rose to my feet. Kraster was inspecting the stone.

"Did it shock you?" I asked.

Kraster shook his head.

"Can you feel it tingling?" I persisted.

"No, what are you talking about?" Kraster looked at me like I was crazy.

"It was–" I began, reaching for the stone just as Kraster stuffed it into the pouch on his belt.

"Come on, let's get out of here. We can play with it later," Kraster told me.

The two of us rejoined Wren, who was still holding Gnomex in a headlock.

"Did you find the stone?" she asked excitedly.

"We did," I answered, noting the way Gnomex deflated in her grip.

"Please," he whimpered. "Don't take it! We need it to protect ourselves."

"I'm sorry," I said, pushing away pangs of guilt.

"It looks like there are plenty of completed golems down there to defend the plateau," Kraster pointed out.

"They won't be enough," Gnomex argued. "We need–"

"Please put him to sleep," I instructed Kraster, who nodded.

A moment later, Wren let Gnomex's snoring body drop to the floor.

"Why didn't you do that ten minutes ago, so I could help you look?" Wren demanded, crossing her arms.

"We might have needed him if we couldn't find the stone," Kraster explained.

"I don't think he would have talked," Wren pointed out. "He was pretty tight-lipped."

"There are ways to make anyone talk," Kraster said darkly, and I wondered if he was being serious or joking.

I was the first to descend the ladder back to the factory floor.

"That's not good," I whispered as my feet hit the ground.

"What's wrong?" Kraster puffed a little too loudly, trying not to fall on his face while getting off the flimsy ladder. It was a testament to gnomish engineering that the thin strands of rope could bear his weight at all.

"The guards you put to sleep are gone," I informed him.

Chapter 18
The Invasion

"At least they didn't sound the alarm," Wren pointed out, as she slid down the ladder without using the rungs. Close to the floor, she let go and landed in a crouch. I would have been impressed if she hadn't ended up with one foot on the laces of her shirt sleeve, causing her to trip when she tried to straighten.

I suppressed a laugh and turned to my brother. "The bigger problem is we have no idea how to get out of here."

"Rakus said if the portal was gone, the best way to escape would be to try and reach the ground floor and find an exit," Kraster reminded me.

Wren joined us, carefully dusting herself off. "How do we find the stairs then?" she asked.

"By looking," I replied.

We headed to a door on the opposite side of the room. I pulled it open, startling a gnome who was mopping the hallway. Instantly, I tackled him to the ground. As we landed, the gnome's head struck the floor, and he lay still. I checked for a pulse, and, for once, I was in luck, because I felt the pumping of his blood strong under my fingers.

"Come on," I whispered to the others, springing up and racing down an open hallway to the left. There were a dozen doors. We pulled each of them open in turn but didn't find a single set of stairs.

"Why are you running so fast?" Kraster panted behind me as we moved onto another hallway.

I wasn't sure myself, but I was starting to feel trapped. All I wanted was to escape. Every dead end made me a little more desperate, and I couldn't repress the feeling that something bad was about to happen.

The tramp of feet brought me sliding to a halt. I stuck my arms out to stop the others.

"They're coming this way," I mouthed, then pointed at the nearest room.

We rushed inside and closed the door behind us. Wren lay flat on her stomach to look under the door. I was standing beside her, waiting for the all clear, when I heard my brother call my name softly.

"Candra, come here." He motioned for me to join him by the opposite wall.

I scowled as I crossed the room, unsure of what could be so important at a time like this.

"Look," Kraster said. He pointed to a map of the plateau that hung on the wall. "There are tunnels."

I studied the plans for a long moment.

"What do you mean tunnels?" I asked.

"Don't tell me you don't know what a tunnel is," Kraster scoffed.

I rolled my eyes and glared at my brother as he continued talking.

"Don't you see? There are tunnels under the plateau connecting all the gnome towns and villages."

I raised an eyebrow.

"That's why we didn't see anyone while we were on the roads," he explained. "Well, at least, anyone that wasn't trying to rob us."

I nodded slowly, agreeing with his deduction.

"It looks like they have trams or something to take them between cities," Kraster went on.

For a moment, the image of bright lights and faces flashing by in an underground tunnel filled my mind, but I wasn't sure where it had come from.

"So?" I managed to ask, trying to shake the feeling of déjà vu.

"So, maybe we can use these to make it out of the city."

"No," I said quickly, the hairs standing up on the back of my neck. "I think that's a bad plan. We should try to get back to Rakus's tower. He did send us to the factory, so I think we can trust him. We would never have been able to get this far without his help."

"But what if we can't make it there?" Kraster persisted. "The gnomes don't tell outsiders about the tunnels, which means they'll never look for us there."

"I don't–" I started, but Wren interrupted.

"They're gone," she whispered to us from across the room.

Quickly, my brother pulled the map from the wall and folded it up.

We moved with more caution now as we searched the hallways. We'd given up on checking the rooms. They held only mechanical odds and ends and offered no means of escape.

Finally, after having to hide twice more, we found a hallway connected to a spiral ramp. Judging by the height of the ceiling and the gentle slope of the smooth floor, I assumed the ramp was used for moving large pieces of equipment between levels in the factory.

Almost as soon as we set foot on it, an alarm started blaring.

"This is bad," fretted Wren.

"Better now than ten minutes ago," I pointed out as I took off down the ramp. We'd completed two rotations when we encountered half a dozen gnomes heading up. I plowed straight through them, knocking a few aside. Wren and Kraster followed in my wake.

I heard Kraster mutter some sort of spell, then there was a flash of light and heat. I glanced back to see a wall of fire spring up behind us, cutting off any pursuers.

After another six times around the spiral ramp, we reached the bottom. A solid, wooden door stood directly ahead of us. I grabbed the handle and pulled, but nothing happened. I landed several kicks to where the door's weak point should have been, but the lock held firm.

"Kraster," I gasped, stepping aside. "It's your turn."

Before Kraster could raise his hands or cast a spell, another voice spoke up.

"Hello there." From the shadows stepped a gnome in a black cloak. "Please, allow me."

I drew my swords, a prickle of danger running up my spine and setting my teeth on edge.

The gnome ignored my aggressive stance. He walked to the door, produced a lock pick, and started working. The three of us stared at him dumbfounded as the door popped open a second later, revealing the darkness of the predawn hours.

He turned back to us, bowed slightly, and then gestured toward the door. "After you," he said politely.

"Who are you?" I demanded.

"More formal introductions will have to wait," the gnome replied, voice still respectful. "Rakus sent me to guide you back to his tower."

"That's excellent!" my brother exclaimed, some of the tension leaving his shoulders.

The gnome smiled at all of us warmly–a little *too* warmly. No one smiled at me like that.

While his expression was friendly, there was something about the gnome's dark eyes that I didn't quite trust. But I didn't trust anyone until I really got to know them, so that wasn't surprising. He was of average gnome height, with cropped black hair and dusky skin.

"If you will follow me," the gnome said, taking the lead.

"What's your name?" Wren asked, falling into step beside our guide. He was leading us down a nearby side street filled with shadows.

"I'm Obignobus Kelingnombie," he replied. "Most people call me either one or the other or just Gnombie since all the rest is such a mouthful." He gave her a wink, and she suppressed a smile.

I didn't think it was very funny.

A scream cut through the night to our left.

"What was that?" Wren gasped, looking at Gnombie.

"I'm not sure," the gnome replied, furrowing his brow.

The first scream was followed by another and another, until it seemed the entire city was yelling.

"What is going on?" I demanded, hands covering my ears.

Gnombie turned to me and said something, but I couldn't hear him. However, over his head, I saw for myself. An enormous spider, twice the size of a horse, was standing at the end of the street. It had a gnome woman cornered.

I didn't wait, but launched myself at the creature, blades out.

"Wait, Candra," Kraster called, but I paid him no heed. I really hated spiders.

My first blade severed one of the spider's front legs. It reared back with a terrible clicking sound. My second blade was ready for the inevitable bite I knew was coming. I thrust the weapon directly into the open maw of the monster.

My sword sank in deeper than I'd anticipated. I let go to keep from losing a hand as the tip of the metal entered the spider's brain. The creature's death throes were violent but brief.

I freed my sword and turned to see my companions hurrying up. The gnome woman was nowhere in sight. Before I'd even wiped my blades clean, I heard more cries.

"This can't be happening. It's just like my dreams," Wren breathed. Horror filled her voice.

I gave her a sharp look, but Gnombie was urgently motioning for us to follow him. As we pressed deeper into the city, I saw the signs of spiders everywhere. Huge webs had been erected, blocking certain streets. Terrified gnomes tore across our path from both right and left.

We were forced to engage a dozen more spiders. None were as large as the first I'd fought. Kraster was thrown to the ground and almost stung by one, and Wren got a nasty scrape from the hooked foot of another, but we were mostly unscathed.

At last, Rakus's tower came into sight.

My steps faltered. "Maybe we should stay and help," I suggested.

"Are you crazy?" Kraster snapped. "What are we going to do against this lot?"

"But we could save lives!" I protested.

"We're on a different mission!" Kraster argued.

A loud boom sounded from behind us. Turning, I saw a red glow on the horizon.

"The war golems have been deployed," Gnombie told us.

"Good," Kraster said. "Then we don't need to feel guilty about leaving." He gave me a pointed look.

Slowly, I nodded and followed the others, trying to convince myself that there were enough completed golems to protect the city.

When we reached the tower, Kraster wrenched open the front door. Gnombie took it from him and held it as the rest of us passed into the entry hall.

"Rakus!" Kraster bellowed.

Almost before he'd finished saying the wizard's name, one of the room's doors popped open, and Rakus hurried through it. Puvva was following after him, a blank look on her face.

"Puvva!" Wren cried, rushing forward to embrace the genie. "Thank goodness! I was so worried."

Puvva regarded Wren with a cool and distant expression.

"Who are you?" she asked. "Are you my master?"

"You don't have a master," Wren told her, still clinging to her neck.

"I most certainly do," Puvva assured her.

"I'm so sorry about what happened," Rakus addressed Wren. "I've known Raull a long time and never would have suspected him a thief."

"Is he still here?" Wren asked warily.

"No. He's been dealt with," Rakus assured her.

"Have you seen what's happening outside?" I demanded, stepping forward.

"I have." A somber expression crossed Rakus's features.

"Can't you help them?" I asked beseechingly.

"Sadly, I cannot," Rakus replied. "Despite my reputation, age has taken its toll on me. I'm afraid there is little I can do against the power of Char."

A shudder ran through me at the sound of the name. Much as I tried to fend it off, a feeling of panic started rising inside of me.

"Who is Char?" Wren asked.

I looked at Puvva. She was the only other person I'd ever heard speak that name. The genie was in the midst of transforming into green smoke as she returned to her teapot, which Wren held.

Rakus glanced my way, eyes softening as he took in my discomfort. "Char is a monster of void," the wizard told us. "She is all the more dangerous because she was originally a creature of light."

"What happened?" Wren breathed.

"Char was corrupted by darkness and imprisoned long ago," the wizard replied. "She has been struggling within her bonds for a long time. It seems she has begun breaking free. What is happening now is but a taste of the terror she will unleash upon this world."

"How do we stop her?" I choked out. My throat had gone completely dry.

Rakus's golden eyes rested on me for a long moment. "I do not know, but I believe you will find a way, which is why Shal'eth sent you to gather the stones. You found Dimble's Legacy, yes?"

We all nodded.

"Then it is even more important that I send you to see Asteropaios immediately," Rakus announced. He turned on his heel and walked back to the door he'd come through. It led us into his laboratory.

Once inside, I saw that the floor was marked now with a different set of runes, these ones hasty and not so clear as those from the first portal.

"Your horses are through there." Rakus pointed to another of the room's doors without looking back as he scrawled a few more marks on the floor.

Kraster went to retrieve the horses. Fortunately, we'd left them saddled and ready to go in case a hasty retreat was needed.

"I'm sorry, I don't have time to be more precise," Rakus apologized. "I don't know exactly where the portal will open, but it should be close to The Hall of Asteropaios."

"Aren't you coming with us, Rakus?" Wren asked.

The gnome shook his head. "I cannot. My apprentice, Axel, has been missing for nigh on three weeks. His mission wasn't supposed to be perilous, but now I feel I must go in search of him. He has much potential and might be able to help where I cannot."

"I hope you find him," Wren replied gently.

Rakus nodded his thanks and took up his tome again. I was more prepared for the flash of light this time when the portal opened, but it still left me dazed for a moment.

Kraster returned with the horses, and I grabbed Tempest's reins. Hurrying past me, my brother led Raspberry through the portal.

I was about to follow, but Rakus caught my hand as Wren and Valor went after Kraster.

"Trust Asteropaios," the gnome said to me, looking deep into my eyes. "She is wise and uncorrupted. She will help you if you are honest with her."

I nodded.

"I'm– I'm sorry." Rakus's words were so soft I almost couldn't hear them. "I'm sorry that I couldn't help you more. I wish– I wish I'd been stronger."

He turned away and spoke without looking at me. "Your journey is far from over. Do not give up, no matter how dark the path ahead. There is radiant light at the end of it."

Slightly confused, I did as he instructed and stepped through the portal.

Chapter 19
The Hall

The first thing I noticed on the other side of the portal was the bitter wind. I stumbled a step forward, feet sinking into the snow. It was just before dawn, and we appeared to be on the western side of a mountain, close to the summit.

"Where did that blasted gnome send us?" Kraster yelled above the whistling of the wind. I doubted he could see anything between the muted light and swirling snow.

"He said his calculation might not be quite correct," Wren hollered back.

"Useless wizard," Kraster snarled.

"I'm sure he did his best," Wren defended Rakus. "It's still better than where we were."

"I can't argue with that," my brother muttered.

"I think that's where we're headed," Gnombie piped up.

Kraster, Wren, and I all turned to gape at the gnome.

"How did you get here?" I asked.

"Through the portal, same as you," he replied.

"But I didn't see you with us in the tower," Wren gasped.

"I'm small and sometimes hard to notice," Gnombie said with a shrug.

Wren narrowed her eyes at the gnome. "You aren't Rakus's missing apprentice, are you?" she guessed.

"No," Gnombie shook his head. "His apprentice is named Axel. He's a human. I don't do magic, well, not much magic, at least."

We all continued to stare at him.

"Look," he started again. "It's really cold out here, and the snow may only be knee-deep to you, but it's up to my waist, so I'm going to freeze to death first if we don't make it down this mountain soon. I'm fairly certain that's The Hall of Asteropaios; can we walk and talk?"

This time, all three of us turned our heads to look in the direction the gnome indicated. Far below, but still perched high on the mountainside, was an enormous structure made from wooden beams. It had two long sections, the end of one meeting the center of the other to form the shape of a capital T. I could see a path on the far side, winding up from the valley floor far below.

"He's right," Kraster agreed. "We'd better get a move on."

My teeth had already started chattering, so I raised no objections.

Going downhill on the icy slope was treacherous. We didn't dare attempt to ride. I honestly think we would have covered twice as much ground had we been climbing the mountain instead of descending it.

My greatest fear was that one of the horses would stumble and break a leg. Tempest, who was smaller and more agile than the others, fared the best, while Valor and Raspberry were constantly slipping and sliding.

Wren suggested Kraster create a fireball to try and melt the snow.

"That's a terrible idea," he retorted. "Not only would that make the snow twice as slick, but it could cause an avalanche."

I glanced up nervously. Until he'd said the word, I hadn't even realized the potential danger we were in.

"Better keep our voices down too," I advised. "There's more than one way to start an avalanche."

Inch by inch, we worked our way down the slope as the sun began to rise on the opposite side of the mountain. When we were halfway, we took a short break to let the horses rest. Despite the cold air, the labor had kept them warm. I, on the other hand, was shivering like crazy and frozen to my very core.

During our rest, Kraster summoned fire to his hand. He held it out so all of us could share the heat.

"I think it's getting warmer," Wren said hopefully, a few minutes later.

I couldn't feel it. All I wanted was to lay down in the snow and succumb to its clutches.

"Bes' get movin' 'gain," I muttered, my voice sounding distant and slurred to my ears.

Kraster gave me a sharp look and nodded. All of us were bundled up as much as possible, but it did no good against the wind and snow.

We struck out again, working our way down the slope. It was with weary steps that I moved forward, only able to focus on putting one foot in front of the other.

When we reached the place where the snow gave way to stone, I sensed that it really was getting warmer. My nose and ears weren't stinging as badly as before. I hoped nothing was frostbitten. Soon, the sun crested the frozen peak, casting its rays on our backs. I relished the warmth it gave, even if it was only a small amount.

"Almost there," Kraster said, falling into step beside me. "You okay?" His voice was filled with concern. I'm sure his eyes were too, but I couldn't lift mine from the path ahead, or I was likely to fall headfirst down the slope. The only response I gave him was a nod. He didn't speak again but remained wordlessly by my side nonetheless.

Only once the land leveled out, several hundred feet from our destination, did I glance up to see how my companions were faring. All of them, even the gnome, seemed to have handled the cold better than me. That was embarrassing. I was half wood elf after all; wasn't I supposed to be built for the elements?

As we reached the path rising up from the land below to the main doors of the great hall, a deep voice bellowed for us to halt.

A moment later, we were surrounded by a dozen dragonborn guards. I'd always been fascinated by dragonborn. Legend had it that they were those descended from the ancient dragons and their mortal lovers. The color of a dragonborn's scales indicated what color the dragon of their ancestry had been. Supposedly, you only needed a drop of dragon blood to grow the

164

scaly skin, reptilian features, and clawed hands that distinguished the race.

"What is your business here?" demanded the largest of the dragonborn, a red male. He carried a long spear, which he pointed at Kraster.

"Please, we are here to see the magnificent Asteropaios," Wren said.

All eyes turned toward her.

"How did you get up here? We didn't see you climbing the path from the valley," the same guard challenged, then went on without waiting for an answer. "And why would Asteropaios agree to see the likes of you?" He narrowed his eyes at our tattered and rugged appearance.

"Because we've been sent to her by Rakus the wizard and The Great Shal'eth," I told him, at last feeling the fog clear from my mind.

The guard looked at me, and I could sense the ridicule in his gaze. "That does not seem likely."

"It's true!" Wren cried, drawing the attention back to herself. She pointed urgently at the trail we'd left in the snow. "Rakus sent us here from Gnomania. We had to leave quickly, due to an invasion, and the portal opened way up there. We spent all morning climbing down, which is why you didn't see us on the path below, because we came from the mountain, not the valley, and–"

The red dragonborn cut Wren off with a raised hand. "What's this about an invasion?" he asked.

"Gnomania is under attack!" Wren replied. "Rakus sent us to talk to Asteropaios because we're on a mission from The Great Shal'eth."

While her words were a little scattered, they certainly caused a stir among the dragonborn.

"Unfortunately, her highness is not here at present," the red guard told us.

Wren nodded. "We know. She left Gnomania yesterday and should be back here soon, though, right?"

The guards exchanged looks.

"That is correct," the red one admitted after a long pause.

"So can we wait for her?" Wren asked.

"Preferably inside," Kraster added.

The red dragonborn shot him a stern look but nodded to Wren and lowered his spear. "We will have your horses taken to the stable. You may proceed to the main entrance." The guard pointed over his shoulder at a pair of massive wooden doors. They were ornately carved with depictions of dragons and stars. A set of eight stairs led up to them, and on either side rose a great pillar of stone, each crafted to resemble a flowering tree. The more I observed, the more awe I felt. Every inch of The Hall of Asteropaios was carefully designed and manicured to perfection. There was nothing gaudy or out of place, just elegance and beauty.

Leaving the guards behind with our horses, we ascended the stairs. As I opened one of the doors, I could feel how heavy it was, but the way in which it was perfectly balanced on its hinges allowed it to be moved with ease.

Inside, we found a hall of marble stone. It was lined with statues, tapestries, and many other artifacts. A green dragonborn stepped forward to greet us. She wore a silver robe trimmed with blue. Although a few inches taller than me, she was short for her race.

"Greetings," the green dragonborn said, dipping her head. "My name is Everly, and I welcome you to The Hall of Asteropaios, Queen of the Dragons."

"Thank you," Kraster said, sounding slightly surprised. The dragonborn picked up on his tone.

"I apologize if your greeting by the guards was less than pleasant. There have been unsettling rumors of late, and our queen herself has warned that war is on the horizon. It has put some of our people on edge," Everly explained.

"It does seem that few places are as safe as they once were," Wren replied.

"Please do not trouble your minds with any concerns while you are here," Everly assured us. "The world would truly have to be ending before anything ill would befall the seat of Asteropaios."

We all nodded, and the dragonborn motioned us to follow her. Kraster fell into step beside Everly, while Wren and I came behind, and Gnombie brought up the rear.

"How long will you be staying with us?" Everly asked.

"We must speak with Asteropaios," I said, causing the dragonborn to glance over her shoulder. Her eyes were like two emeralds burning with inner light, but the way they looked at me was not encouraging.

"Many come seeking such an audience, but few are granted that privilege." Her words sounded rehearsed. "I'm sure you can understand," Everly went on.

Wren hastened her steps to walk beside the dragonborn. "It is very important," she told Everly. "We were sent by The Great Shal'eth. I am one of his shrine maidens, and he has entrusted me with a sacred mission."

The dragonborn's steps faltered. "If that is true, it is likely that Asteropaios will want to meet with you once she has returned."

"That would be excellent!" Kraster beamed.

When we reached the far end of the hallway, Everly rang a small bell. A door to the left opened, and a pure white dragonborn child entered.

"Alice, take these travelers to the guest quarters," Everly instructed. "They will be staying with us tonight and maybe longer."

"Of course," Alice replied, bowing from the waist. "Please come this way." We followed Alice through the door onto a spiral staircase, which led downward.

"Your chambers are this way," the child said, picking up a torch and guiding us through a network of underground hallways. As we walked, Alice pointed out the baths, the banquet hall, and the passage leading to the garden. We saw other visitors in pilgrim's garb and several more dragonborn wearing the same silver robes as Everly and Alice.

"I grew up in a place very much like this," Wren told our young dragonborn guide. "Do your parents work here too?"

"No," Alice answered shyly. "I am an orphan and was sent here by my village when I was a baby."

"Oh, I'm so sorry," Wren told her.

"It is all right," Alice replied. "It is a great honor to serve Asteropaios. She was delighted by my arrival, since white dragonborn are very rare."

"Why is that?" Kraster asked.

"Because there is only one line of white dragonborn, all descended from Asteropaios and her mate's youngest child, Anadaiza," Alice explained softly.

"So you're a direct descendant of Asteropaios herself?" Wren gasped.

If Alice had skin instead of scales, I feel certain she would have been blushing. Instead, all she did was nod.

"That's incredible," Kraster breathed.

"What is she like?" Wren asked.

"She's amazing! So kind and wise." Alice's face lit up as she spoke. "She cares about all the beings of Planosia. When she's not here sharing her wisdom with those who come to seek it, she's traveling all across the land helping whoever she can."

"Like bringing rain and electricity to the gnomes," I murmured.

Alice looked back at me and nodded. Her pale eyes were iridescent, sparkling with a dozen flecks of light. As she continued her conversation with Wren, I couldn't help but wonder what Asteropaios would think of me.

Our quarters were extremely comfortable, save for the lack of a window, but since we were underground, I supposed that was to be expected. Kraster and Gnombie had the room directly across from the one given to Wren and me.

Of course, the first thing Wren did was summon Puvva.

"Why?" I asked as green smoke filled the room.

"She was very confused back in Rakus's tower," Wren explained. "It wasn't a good time to talk, but now I need to make sure she's all right."

I sighed as Puvva's shape took form, and the genie became corporeal. "I am Puvva of the Pot," she said. "What does Master wish?"

"It's me, Wren," Wren told Puvva. The genie stared at her for a long moment.

"You were in the tower," Puvva stated. "No wish was issued, yet–" There was a pause and, for the first time, I saw uncertainty cloud Puvva's eyes. "You have only two wishes instead of three. This has not happened before and should not be."

"You've broken the genie," I couldn't help laughing.

"She's not broken," Wren snapped. "She's just confused." Turning back to Puvva, Wren continued. "Don't you remember me before Rakus's tower? We traveled a long way and–"

"Negative. Before the tower, my master was Shal'eth. I was waiting for him to designate a new master as I had just completed his final wish: to release the portion of my power keeping Char imprisoned. However, I sense those events took place over a quarter of a century ago."

I leapt from the bed where I had been reclining and gaped at the genie. "What did you say?" I breathed.

Puvva's forehead puckered. Again, she appeared uncertain.

"No, that can't be right," Wren said. "The Great Shal'eth would never wish for something like that."

Puvva blinked twice and glanced around as if unsure of where she was. "Who would never wish for what?" she asked as if she had not just spoken.

"She really is broken," I muttered, trying to push down the unsettled feeling that had arisen within me at Puvva's words.

"I am not broken," the genie stated. "But I must have been forcibly separated from my pot. It has tampered with my memories."

"Will they return?" Wren asked.

"Perhaps. With time," Puvva told her. "But I am unsure, as it has never happened before."

"Is there anything that will help?" Wren asked.

Puvva considered for a moment. "Water," was her only reply.

"There is a bathing chamber down the hall we could visit," Wren offered.

"That would be delightful," Puvva said.

"Do you want to come with us?" Wren asked me.

I shook my head.

"Why not?" Wren seemed confused.

"Water and I– we don't get along so well," I admitted.

"There's nothing to fear," Wren promised. "I'm sure it won't be deep."

"That's not really the problem," I mumbled, unsure of how to explain my aversion.

"It would certainly make you smell better," Wren grumbled under her breath.

"Excuse me?" I demanded.

"Come on, Candra. We've been on the road for weeks, so it's understandable, but you really do smell."

I glowered at her.

"I will come and sit in the steam," I told her stiffly. "But that is all, and not until after I've had a nap."

Several hours later, I found myself in the bathing chamber, which was more of a cavern. Wren and Puvva were swimming around in a pool fed by a waterfall.

"Come on in!" Wren called. "The water is wonderfully warm."

"I can see that," I muttered, watching the steam rising from the surface of the pool.

Wren swam toward where I was perched on a stone bench close to the door.

"You don't have to be scared," she chided me.

"Remember how I'm cursed?" I started.

She nodded.

"I think it's connected."

"Then this is your chance to face your fears and fight your stink!" she laughed.

I glared at Wren. Rising, I walked to the pool's edge. The stone was carved in a gentle slope. I advanced until the water was a little above my ankles but not deep enough to reach the hem of the bathing robe I'd been given.

My heart thundered in my chest. I'd almost drowned in water this deep more than once. Carefully, I leaned forward and allowed my hair to tumble into the pool until it was soaked almost to my scalp. With my face so close to the surface, I could smell the scents of rose and lavender coming from the water.

Maybe this will make her shut up, I thought. I straightened and headed back to my seat, my hair streaming water down my shoulders. Just before I reached the edge of the pool, a massive wave engulfed me from behind. I stumbled forward and managed to grab hold of the bench. I clung to it for dear life, as terror shook my body.

The water receded as suddenly as it had come.

Laughter I'd never heard before filled the room. It came from Puvva.

I spun around, sorry I'd left all my weapons with my clothes in the room where I'd changed into the bathing robe.

"I'm sorry, Candra." Despite her apology, Wren was fighting a smile. "I promise I didn't tell her to do that."

I was too upset to speak.

"It was your wish, no?" Puvva said to Wren.

"I never said to–" Wren started to protest.

"But you wished for it," Puvva interrupted. "And since I am not sure what happened to your first wish, I decided to fulfill this desire as a substitute."

Puvva lowered her voice, but I still heard what she whispered in Wren's ear. "Her stench was quite unpleasant to me as well."

I turned away and stalked out of the room, ignoring the apologies Wren called after me.

Chapter 20

The Garden

I felt much better once I was dressed and wearing my weapons again. Hurriedly, I left my room. Wren would probably turn up soon. She'd insist that my wetting wasn't her fault and that she was sorry. I'm sure both things were true, but I didn't want to deal with it. I was humiliated enough by my fear and lack of control over it.

Unfortunately, we'd arrived just a little too late for lunch, and dinner wouldn't be served for a while, so I would have to find somewhere else to hide. I turned my feet in the direction Alice had said led to the garden. With the hall built so high up on the mountain, I wasn't sure much would be growing, even in the peak of summer.

I was shocked when the tunnel-like passage brought me up into a lush paradise. This part of the building had glass walls and dozens of skylights, letting in the sunshine but not the cold. In fact, it was almost warmer here than in the bathing chamber.

The garden was set on the western side of the hall, overlooking the valley, which is why we hadn't seen it on our approach. Many of the plants were foreign to me. Somehow, they all managed to appear carefully cultivated and yet wild at the same time. Paths wound through the garden, gracefully circling flower beds and statues in no particular pattern.

To the right of the entryway was a metal staircase wrought in the form of a climbing vine. It rose high in the air and led to a free-standing platform. I would have assumed it was for viewing the garden, except it seemed to be tucked too far into the corner.

Slowly, I made my way deeper into the garden, enjoying the warmth and delicious smell of the flowers, all of which were in full bloom. More honey bees than I'd ever seen in my life buzzed through the air. They alighted on the delicate petals of the flowers to gather pollen and nectar before sailing back to their homes in the treetops.

I watched the flight of one, lifting my eyes toward the ceiling, which rose at least two hundred feet over my head. Painted there was a magnificent mural. It showed the eight great dragons intertwined together. In the center of them was a glass skylight.

Asteropaios was easy to pick out. Her blue and silver body was the largest. I recognized the twins as well. They were half the size of the others, and their green and gold bodies were pressed close together as they had been in the egg they'd shared. Morazz the Fire Drake, was next to them, his red scales tinged with brown.

Close beside Asteropaios was a long, slender dragon. Its body was white with traces of teal in the wings and claws.

"Shal'eth," I breathed as I realized the mural I was looking at was of The Constellation of the Great Dragons from the night sky. When Wren had pointed Shal'eth out to me, I had thought it was just her people's beliefs, but no. He was here, a great, just as she had said.

There was also a yellow dragon, with some of the largest wings I had ever seen, and an orange dragon, whose scales darkened to a shiny bronze along its back. At first, I couldn't recall ever having heard of them, then their names came to me. Lathaan Great Wing and Karradin the Wise. The pair had been good friends, but I wasn't sure how I knew that.

Below all of them, in the place that Kraster had called the void, was an eighth dragon. Its body was only slightly smaller than Asteropaios's, even with its exceedingly long tail. Dark scales of gray and purple coated the creature, and two cruelly hooked claws extended from the apex of each wing. Looking at her sent a chill down my spine.

"Are you well?" a husky voice asked from beside me. I snapped my head to the right and found a silver dragonborn standing there. His hands were coated in dirt. In one of them, he held a spade.

"What is that?" I asked, pointing up at the dark dragon.

The dragonborn craned his head to look upward.

173

"That is Char the Corrupter," he replied.

I nodded slowly, my throat too tight to speak.

"Do you know of her?" he inquired.

"Sort of," was all I managed to choke out.

"Would you care to learn more?" he asked. His eyes were a darker color than his body, making them hard to read.

"Are you an expert?" I hedged, trying to figure out if he was offering information or trying to get it.

"Hardly," he laughed. "I'm Rizzen, the gardener here. However, the history of the mural is well known to all who serve in The Hall of Asteropaios."

"Then tell me of Char," I said quickly.

"Of course." Rizzen dipped his head to me as he began. "To tell you the story of Char, I must tell you the story of the great dragons. Contrary to what many believe, they were not the first dragons but a dozen generations descended from them. However, those eight were chosen from among all of the others and elevated. Each was given a special gift.

"At first, Char and the others used their gifts as intended. They worked together to aid the mortals of the land and drive back the horrific creatures who threatened the lives of so many. Together, they helped to build the first kingdom of men, whose line is now lost.

"Char's gift was light, but it did not take long before she began using it to explore the dark crevices of the world. She strayed farther from the sun than she should have and remained absent for long periods of time in the UnderEarth.

"In such places, ancient monstrosities dwelt, creatures who dared not step into the light. Char was curious and diluted her gift so she could speak with them. For years, they whispered to her until her mind was full of their shadows. Soon, Char began to loathe the warm lands above and even her gift itself.

"Slowly, her light waned. She remained longer and longer in the UnderEarth, away from all that was good and wholesome, until her corruption was complete and she hated all that was not of darkness.

"Finally, the day came when Char sought out the other great dragons. She spoke of how they could rule the world on their own and make it better for the mortals. Her words were persuasive as she told them of the paradise they could create. One free of pain, sorrow, and even death.

"Only one great dragon was not invited to their meeting, for Asteropaios alone had the strength to rival Char's own abilities.

"The rest of the great dragons were enthralled by Char's honeyed words. They could not see her true plan, for the evil she intended was far beyond anything they could have imagined. All they perceived was the dragon of light, dreaming of a beautiful world that would bring nothing but happiness. So, they lent her their gifts."

"What was her true plan?" I breathed.

"Void." The single word that slipped from Rizzen's lips was no surprise to me, yet it still took my breath away.

"Not just darkness," Rizzen explained grimly. "She abhors the world so much that her only desire is for oblivion. Absolute emptiness, where nothing exists."

Despite the warm air of the garden, a feeling of cold crept over me. Even the sun, filtering down through the skylight above, did nothing to warm my skin.

"And so, Char tricked nearly all of the great dragons into treachery." Rizzen grew even more serious than before. "They betrayed the one who had bestowed their gifts upon them. I will not speak of that tragic battle, except to say that Asteropaios arrived too late."

Rizzen trailed off, and there was silence between us for a moment. I dared not break it, but, surely, this could not be the end of the story. We were still here, so, somehow, Char must have failed.

"It did not take long for the other dragons to realize Char's promises were nothing but lies. Darkness began to envelop the land with no light to push it back.

"Without their gifts, they knew they could not defeat Char. It was Shal'eth who found a way to imprison her using the four elemental spirits of the world. He and the other traitorous dragons created the elemental vessels. These they used to bind Char and reclaim their gifts."

"What if she escapes?" I couldn't help asking. Rakus had claimed the attack on Gnomania was due to Char, but that could have just been superstition.

"It would mean the end of our world," Rizzen replied gravely. "But it would take some doing for anyone to free her. The dragons took precautions to ensure that all of the vessels were well-hidden and well-guarded."

I nodded slowly. It was a good tale, but left many unanswered questions. Why was Asteropaios–and I guess sort of Shal'eth–the only great dragons left? Where had the others gone? Had Asteropaios killed them?

"Who was it that gave the dragons their gifts?" I asked, suddenly wondering what sort of being would be able to bestow power on a dragon.

Rizzen chuckled. "Look up."

I did.

The deep red sun had moved directly overhead and was shining down through the skylight in the center of the mural making it hard to look at. Still, I turned slowly in a circle, my head craned back. The opening above was sort of shaped like another dragon or a similar type of creature. The head was completely wrong, but it definitely had two wings and an odd looking tail.

It's avian in shape, I thought.

A bell rang, and I jumped.

"I must go," Rizzen told me apologetically. "Asteropaios has been sighted, and all those who serve her are summoned to make preparations for her arrival."

"Can I come with you?" I asked. "My friends and I must see her."

"I'm afraid not," Rizzen shook his head. "Your petition will be shown to her with the others, but I can make no promises."

The dragonborn hurried off before I could say more.

I didn't look at the mural again but took my time walking the paths of the garden. My imagination must have been truly taken with Rizzen's words, because the events he described kept running through my mind, almost like a memory.

Hours later, another bell rang. When I glanced around, I realized that the sun was close to setting. I headed down to the banquet hall, hoping I hadn't missed dinner. Thankfully, I had not, and I found my friends waiting.

"Where have you been all day?" Kraster asked.

"I was in the garden," I said, taking the seat across from him, next to Wren. Puvva was not with her, for which I was very grateful. Gnombie was perched beside Kraster, his feet dangling off the bench.

"They told me it was closed," Wren said.

"Really? I was there most of the afternoon," I replied.

"You must have slipped by somehow," Kraster laughed.

"It was surprisingly empty," I recalled, then changed the subject. "What have you guys been up to?"

"Gnombie's been snooping around," Kraster answered with a wink. The gnome rolled his eyes but didn't say anything.

"Kraster and I have been trying to find out how to get a message to Asteropaios," Wren said.

"And?" I prompted.

"And it's pretty impossible," Kraster announced, mouth full of pork pie. "Everyone we spoke with kept saying she would be notified of our presence in due time."

"You'd think name-dropping Shal'eth would help," I said with a glance at Wren, who scowled.

"Yes, but I don't think they've told her yet," Wren grumbled. "Asteropaios arrived a few hours ago. If she knew, I'm sure she would have sent for us by now."

"Maybe she's resting," Gnombie put in. "As soon as she landed, I believe she went directly to her cave on the northern side of the mountain."

"You saw her?" I asked eagerly.

Gnombie shook his head. "There are no public windows facing that direction, and the guards won't let you on that side of the hall from the outside either."

"It makes me question whether she's actually here," Kraster remarked. "I mean, despite all the precautions, how do you hide an entire dragon?"

"Seems like they have it down pretty well," I observed.

"But it's so important that we see her!" Wren huffed.

"We'll just have to be patient," I told her.

Wren let out a long sigh.

We didn't linger too long in the banquet hall. The food was excellent, but there was nothing to drink except water, so I didn't object when the others wanted to turn in early.

That night, I dreamed I had fiery wings and flew high above the land under the light of a golden sun. I soared among the clouds, catching at them with my claws. All was warmth and light and brilliance. Suddenly, a wall of darkness fell on me, engulfing my senses and smothering them.

Chapter 21
The Queen

I jerked awake at almost the exact same time Wren did. Our eyes met in the dark.

"Bad dream," she explained.

I nodded. "Same."

We were silent for a moment, but I got the impression that neither of us was planning to attempt sleeping again.

"Want to talk about it?" I asked.

Wren shook her head. "It wasn't that bad, just– there was a river, and I knew something horrible was hiding beneath the surface: invisible and ready to kill."

"You know how I feel about water," I told her softly. "So, that sounds pretty terrible to me."

My comment helped ease the tension, but we were both quiet at breakfast.

When the boys joined us, I discovered that Gnombie was a morning person. He was beaming brightly and talking about how amazing all the food and drink choices were.

After ten minutes, I'd had enough. I informed him that none of the choices were amazing because they didn't contain alcohol. Kraster told Gnombie to ignore me, which he did. A moment later, he was back at his happy chattering.

I tuned him out and stared at my half-eaten plate. The food had been good, I just wanted something better to wash it down with. The glimmer of white scales made me perk up. I turned and saw Alice approaching us with a letter that she handed to Wren with a slight flourish. It was written on silver paper and sealed with blue wax. Wren opened it and scanned the contents of the note quickly.

"She's going to see us!" Wren exclaimed.

"Wonderful! When?" I asked.

Wren's eyes turned back to the paper. "In less than an hour. We'd better get ready."

I had half risen from my seat when Wren's voice brought me to a halt. "It does say that we ought to limit the number of representatives from our party."

Wren glanced around.

"Well, you should definitely go, since you're Shal'eth's shrine maiden," Kraster told her.

Wren nodded, looking pleased.

"So should you," I told Kraster. "You're the best speaker."

Slowly, my brother shook his head. "I don't think that's a good plan," he said.

I gave him a questioning look.

"Right now, the human army is ravaging the land," he explained. "I heard yesterday that they've completely razed Bennton, maybe Fal Ridge too, and a couple of other villages. Everyone is terrified of where they will go next.

"If Asteropaios finds out I'm military, she won't help us and might even throw us in the dungeon."

"I don't think they have dungeons here," Wren pointed out.

"I'm sure she can make one," Kraster insisted. "Or come up with a worse punishment." Kraster snapped his teeth together suggestively.

"How would she know you're military?" I asked.

"It's pretty evident in the way he walks," Gnombie announced.

I sighed and turned to the gnome. "What about you then? Any desire to go with Wren?"

Gnombie was shaking his head before I even finished speaking. His eyes were wide in alarm at the suggestions.

"Well, I'm not going alone," Wren said, then cocked her head. "Maybe I should take Puvva."

"No!" both Kraster and I nearly screamed at the same time.

"Then you'll have to come with me," Wren announced, turning in my direction.

"Oh, I do not think that's a good idea," I protested. "You know I'm terrible with people."

"The Great Shal'eth seemed to like you," Wren argued.

"And that was my one exception for the decade," I countered. "Trust me, things will go much more smoothly if I'm not there."

"You'll be fine," Kraster told me. He continued to say it the rest of the way through breakfast and on our way back to our rooms.

"I always have to do all the hard things," I muttered, closing the door behind me.

"Hard, but amazing!" Wren's voice trembled just a little. I could tell she was equal parts excited and terrified.

As we got ready, I tied my hair back, intent on showing off my pointed ears and slanted eyes for once, instead of hiding them. Wren put on her shrine maiden uniform. I hadn't seen her wear it since the day we fled from Thea. Most of the fabric was pure white, making Wren appear younger and more vulnerable.

I didn't have anything fancy but tried to dust off my nicest set of traveling clothes. It didn't really help much.

There was a knock at our door a few minutes later. It was Alice summoning us to meet The Queen of the Dragons. With a candle in her scaly hand, she led us down the same passage I'd taken yesterday. Soon, we emerged in the garden.

The wall to the right and part of the ceiling had rolled back, exposing the plants to the elements. As a result, the temperature was much cooler than yesterday. Wren and I were guided to the base of the metal staircase.

"You may wait at the top," Alice said, gesturing to the platform.

I followed Wren up, not sure if I was going to meet my destiny or my doom.

From the top, I could see the land below stretched out in nearly every direction. The hall sat on a mountain that overlooked a vast plain which had a river running through it toward the south.

Far in the distance, across the valley, another mountain range stood almost parallel to this one.

I'd never been in this part of Planosia before. It was a long way from the human territories I was accustomed to patrolling, but I knew that once the region had belonged to the human kingdom. In fact, its capital, The Great City, had been located somewhere a little north of where we were.

However, that was long, long ago, when there was a human king on the throne, and all the cities of man were united under his banner. After the fall of King Ardit, these mountains had become home to a race of savage giants from beyond The Eastern Mountains.

In the centuries since, they had been driven out and beaten almost into extinction by the dwarves who still dwelt in the mountain range across the valley. Unlike the giants, the dwarves were natives and had dwelt in their mountains since the beginning of time.

Following the river to the north would take one into the wild country of the fae and other such nasty creatures. Out of view in the south could be found the forest of the high elves. They had settled there after breaking with their wood elf kin five millennia ago. Their domain marked the start of The Southern Forest.

I'm not sure how long I stood there, musing about the geography of Planosia. I was brought back to myself by the sound of rushing winds and concussive blasts of air as a large pair of blue and silver wings rose into view.

It is impossible to describe the feeling of standing in front of a dragon. Many people have tried, but descriptions like majestic, awe-inspiring, and terrifying do no justice to the actual experience.

The first thing that went through my head as Asteropaios landed on the ledge outside the garden and began to move toward the platform through the opening in the wall, was how easily my entire body would fit inside her mouth. From a distance, dragons are vast. Up close, they are so impossibly large that you can't take them all in at once.

Wren and I stood rooted to the spot as The Queen of the Dragons came to a halt, her head less than ten feet from the metal platform. Her deep blue eyes studied us for a long moment. I didn't know whether to curtsy, or fall to my knees, or beg for my life. Wren, who was in front, bowed deeply, hands together. I mimicked her, trusting that she was more schooled in dragon etiquette than I.

"Welcome." Asteropaios's voice was deep and ancient, touched by mystery and time. "Tell me the reason you have sought an audience with me."

"Great Queen of the Dragons," Wren began, head bent and eyes downcast. "We have come seeking aid. My companions and I have been tasked with gathering eight magical stones by The Great Shal'eth himself."

A small crackle of lightning issued from the dragon's nostrils. I tried not to cringe as I wondered if the platform was intentionally made of metal so it would be easy for Asteropaios to electrocute those who earned her ire.

Wren waited tentatively for a sign to continue, but Asteropaios spoke first. "I did receive a message from my once-mate that there was a chance a half-elf would come here seeking something dear to me."

Wren and I exchanged a confused glance, then both of us looked up quickly as Asteropaios took a step closer. She was studying Wren with an intensity that would have made me sweat, but Wren bore it well.

"Tell me, young one, do you know what you are asking for?" Asteropaios inquired.

"I– I– am asking only for your aid, such as you choose to give." Wren's reply was shaky, but diplomatic as ever.

"Such as I choose to give," Asteropaios mused, almost to herself. Her eyes clouded as she considered Wren's words.

"Yes," Wren ventured to say. "We have two of the stones, and the names of four more: Azazoth's Wand, The Gem of Aero, The Heart of Jong, and Baarthagon's Collar. The Oracle of the Three Sisters also told us of the last two, one which has passed into shadow and the other that is no more."

183

Wren sounded confused herself as she listed off what little we knew of the stones.

Asteropaios leaned forward, eyes locked on Wren. My hands instinctively went to my weapons in case she attacked. There was probably nothing I could do, but it was always best to be prepared. Plus, I'd heard dragons admire courage, although launching any kind of attack would have been more akin to stupidity.

"So, you have The Scrying Stone and Dimble's Legacy," Asteropaios concluded.

Wren nodded. I can't imagine how tight her throat was with that massive, scaly head only a few feet from her. After a long moment, Asteropaios pulled slowly back.

"And Shal'eth has sent you to me," the dragon said bitterly. "I'm sorry; I can't help you. He was wrong to ask you to retrieve the stones for him. Do you know his purpose for them?"

"I'm– I'm not sure," Wren stuttered. "I was tasked with keeping The Scrying Stone out of the hands of those who might use it for evil. We only learned of the other seven when we showed The Scrying Stone to The Oracle of The Three Sisters. She was the one who told us that the stones would be united, and whoever held them would be able to protect the world by freeing what has been bound and using a– a gift?"

Again, Wren's words were uncertain, as she related the information we had been given.

"Then we met a wizard, named Rakus," she picked up the story again quickly. "Who sent us here from Gnomania yesterday morning, because he said we should talk to you–"

"Rakus sent you from Gnomania yesterday?" Asteropaios asked sharply, interrupting the words pouring desperately out of Wren.

"Yes," Wren nodded.

"What was happening there?" Asteropaios demanded.

Wren's forehead wrinkled. "There was an attack. It started just as we were leaving. That's all I know."

"It was Char." The whisper escaped my lips before I could stop it.

Asteropaios whipped her head in my direction, and I felt her eyes on me for the first time.

"What did you say?" she demanded almost breathlessly, well, as almost breathlessly as a dragon can sound.

"Char was behind the attack," I explained. "Rakus told me as we were leaving, and then he sent us to you."

Asteropaios turned to Wren. "Is this exactly as it happened?"

Wren nodded hastily. The dragon swung back to look at me. She took another step closer, head passing Wren. I braced myself, knuckles white as I gripped the hilt of one of my swords. My nerves were screaming for me to draw it, but I remained perfectly still and let my eyes meet Asteropaios's. They were a darker blue than her body, a sapphire as deep as the ocean and the dusk.

Obviously, I wasn't meeting her gaze because I was overwhelmingly brave, but because I was frozen by the intensity of her eyes. It felt like hours before the dragon turned back to Wren, and I could breathe again.

"One of the stones you are seeking was entrusted to my possession," Asteropaios told her.

"Was?" Wren frowned.

"Yes," Asteropaios answered. "I tried to use it only for good, but a day came when I– when something terrible happened as a result of my– my despair.

"I vowed that it would never happen again, so I destroyed the stone."

Wren and I both stared at her in dismay.

"However," the dragon continued. "I have the ability to remake it."

I didn't dare breathe as she seemed to consider, gaze drifting from Wren to me, then back. Slowly, Astreropaios's eyes closed. I saw a glow coming from beneath the lids as she bowed her mighty head, tucking it almost to her chest.

"Forgive me." Asteropaios's words were so faint, I almost didn't catch them. Then, to my everlasting astonishment, two glistening tears, one from each eye, escaped the dragon's closed lids. They met and rolled down her snout before dropping onto the platform.

For some reason, the sight of the dragon's tears made me want to cry as well. I even felt my eyes brimming but blinked them dry.

There was a clunk. Instead of liquid, a glistening stone, the icy blue color of Asteropaios's scales, landed just in front of Wren. The rune for power was carved on the top.

A jolt struck me, as though the stone had held an electrical charge that passed through the metal platform.

The dragon opened her eyes, and they were filled with some strong emotion I could not identify.

"Thank you," Wren whispered. Leaning forward, she retrieved the stone.

Asteropaios dipped her head ever so slightly. When she spoke again, her voice was altered, more distant and sorrowful. "This I entrust to you, my gift, Asteropaios's Gift."

All was silent for a moment, then the dragon turned her great head toward the south and began speaking once more.

"Jong is the name of a special mechanical golem given to the dwarves many centuries ago by the gnomes to aid them in their war against the giants. The remnants of that golem still stand in the valley to the south, but be warned, he was no normal creation. There is life to be found in him still.

"You should begin your search for The Heart of Jong there. It will most likely lead you further south, into the realm of the high elves.

"Baarthagon's Collar is in the human city of Kempt, but I know not where."

I drew in a sharp breath as the dragon named the city where Kraster and I had lived until recently.

"The locations of the other stones are not known to me," Asteropaios went on. "You are probably already aware of this, but

186

one of the stones in your possession can supply you with the knowledge you seek. However, it is unwise for a mortal to attempt to wield magic meant for dragons."

Wren nodded fervently. "Thank you," she whispered.

Asteropaios gave us both one last, long look, then turned and left the way she had come.

It was several minutes before Wren and I dared to speak.

"Three down, five to go," I murmured as we headed for the stairs.

I'd been trying to lighten the mood, but Wren's forehead bore deep furrows.

"You okay?" I asked.

She nodded without saying anything.

"Let's find the boys and tell them the good news," I suggested.

Wearing a distant expression, Wren followed me out of the garden and back into the underground passages beneath The Hall of Asteropaios.

Chapter 22
The Descent

Naturally, we found Kraster and Gnombie waiting in line for lunch even though they'd each eaten an enormous breakfast. We joined them just before they passed a dragonborn collecting donations. There were too many people for us to speak freely, so I only greeted them with a nod. Once we'd contributed and loaded our plates, we made our way to a table in the back corner of the dining hall.

"She gave us another of the stones," I told them.

"What?!" Kraster gasped. "Asteropaios had one lying around and just handed it over?"

I nodded.

"Wish the last one had been that easy to get a hold of," my brother grumbled.

"Did she say anything else?" Gnombie asked eagerly.

I hesitated, trying to recall the conversation, but mostly just remembering how large and close Asteropaios's teeth had been to my person.

"She gave us a lead on the next two stones," Wren replied softly. She still seemed a bit subdued. I was the opposite. To survive a meeting with a dragon was an incredible feeling.

"Excellent! Where are we headed?" Kraster asked.

"South, first," I told him. "Probably into elven lands."

"Do either of you have any relatives there who could help us?" Gnombie wondered, glancing between Wren and me.

"The forest is inhabited by *high* elves," I responded.

"Which means?" Gnombie appeared mystified.

"Well, I'm half wood elf, so no family from me." I looked at Wren, but she shook her head.

"Even if I met my father, I wouldn't recognize him. I doubt he even knows I exist," she explained.

"So, we shouldn't be expecting any aid," Kraster noted.

"More likely the opposite," I warned. "Most races are not fond of half-breeds."

"Wait a minute." Gnombie sounded thoroughly confused now. "You mean to tell me you two aren't sisters?"

Wren and I exchanged a glance before turning to the gnome and shaking our heads.

"Cousins?" he asked. "Maybe, distant cousins?"

"We look nothing alike," I pointed out. It was true. I had the more athletic build of my wood elf kin and the height of an average human. Wren was shorter, with the slender limbs and fine features that heralded the high elves as the most beautiful creatures of Planosia.

"Sorry, but all you tall folk look alike to me," Gnombie announced, popping a sausage in his mouth.

"Then it won't surprise you at all when I tell you Kraster is my brother," I said.

Gnombie almost choked on the sausage. "What? Really? No, you're having me on," he spluttered.

I sighed and let Kraster handle the explanation. I'm not sure if Gnombie was convinced in the end.

Soon, the discussion turned to our plans. Much as we'd enjoyed the peace and safety of this place, we all felt the urgency of our quest and opted to leave as soon as possible.

In little over an hour, we found ourselves at the top of the path leading down from The Hall of Asteropaios to the valley floor. The only other pilgrims leaving the hall appeared to have set out many hours ago and were just now reaching the bottom.

The dragonborn guards were still positioned near the steps but only nodded to us as we began our descent.

"I think this is even higher than the plateau," Wren observed.

"At least we will be going down this time," I pointed out.

"Too bad they don't have a lift," Kraster said, earning him a dark look from both Wren and myself as we recalled how he'd abandoned us at the base of the plateau to walk up alone.

189

My muscles hadn't fully recovered from our last downhill trek. Thankfully, this time there was a road to follow and no snow.

"Look!" Wren exclaimed suddenly, pointing upward. "It's Asteropaios!"

All of us followed her extended hand to where the blue and silver dragon glided through the air toward the northwest. It wasn't long until she was lost from our sight by the mountain.

"Where do you think she's going?" Wren asked.

"No idea." Kraster shrugged.

"Maybe she's going to see Shal'eth," I suggested.

Wren pursed her lips. "I don't even know if Shal'eth is still alive. Those soldiers attacked and–" Wren trailed off, not looking at anyone.

"I can't imagine he could be killed so easily," I said after an uncomfortable pause. "He knew the attack was coming, and, if he was prepared enough to get his people to safety, he probably had a plan for himself as well."

Wren nodded but seemed even more perturbed than before. No one had any other words of comfort to offer her, so we continued in silence.

After the first few switchbacks, which were very steep, the road leveled somewhat, and we were able to mount. Gnombie rode double with Wren on Valor since he was the largest of the horses. The gnome seemed a little uncomfortable with the arrangement and kept fiddling with something in his right hand as though to soothe his nerves.

The ride would have been quite pleasant, except for the large clouds of dust kicked up by the horses' hooves. Despite that, we made good progress and reached the halfway point while it was still early afternoon.

Less than an hour later, there was a strange sound, like an explosion, somewhere above my head. I brought Tempest to a stop. The others, who were in front of me, halted as well. We were at the turn for one of the last three switchbacks.

"What was that?" I asked.

Almost before I finished speaking, there was another explosion.

"Landslide!" Kraster cried out.

I was off Tempest in a second, pulling him as close to the mountainside as I could. Several rocks tumbled down the path behind us, stopping mere inches away. All was quiet for a moment, then the ground beneath my feet gave way. Before I could even register what was happening, Tempest and I were sliding down into a large pit, Kraster and Raspberry beside us.

When everything stopped moving, I got to my knees and took stock of the situation. Miraculously, both Tempest and Raspberry were on their feet and didn't seem injured beyond a few scrapes.

"Kraster!" I called, spotting my brother half-buried in rock and dirt. I stumbled to his side and helped pull him free.

"What happened?" Kraster coughed. He wiped the dust from his face with the back of his hand as he staggered to his feet.

"The road collapsed," I panted.

Both of us looked up from the bottom of the twenty-foot deep pit where we stood. A moment later, Wren's head peeked over the edge of the hole.

"Are you guys all right?" she called, her voice tight with panic.

"Nothing's broken," I replied.

"Good," she said, voice wavering. "We can–"

Her words were cut off as an arrow flew over the opening and embedded itself in the earth wall beside her. Wren jerked back out of view with a yelp as another arrow struck the rock close to where her head had been a moment before.

"We're under attack!" Kraster exclaimed.

"I can see that," I replied. Hastily, I unhooked my pack and freed my bow from where they were attached to Tempest's saddle. "Any chance you've got some magic that can get us and the horses out of here?"

Kraster nodded and moved to Raspberry's side. He started to mutter something. I focused my attention on the opening above, not that there was much to see. I did hear a few cries in a strange tongue, along with some shrill snarls of pain.

The rock-shattering boom of a third explosion came from somewhere high above my head. Shouldering my pack, I moved back a few steps. Pressing myself against the side of the pit, I tried to see what was happening above, but it was to no avail.

I glanced at Kraster and was shocked to see that he had Raspberry tucked under one arm, the horse now the size of a cat.

A shadow passed over my brother. I looked up to see a harpy flying over the top of the hole, a dagger clutched in her hand. Immediately, I loosed an arrow and managed to clip one of her wings. The creature cried out in dismay as she plummeted out of sight. I heard the thud of her body striking the ground a moment later.

Quickly, I readied another arrow in case any more of the feathery monsters came into view.

"Hold on to me," Kraster ordered, wrapping his free arm around my waist. In his other hand, he still cradled poor Raspberry, who appeared rather distraught by this turn of events.

"What about Tempest?" I demanded.

"I can only reduce the size of one horse at a time," my brother explained. "They need us topside. Once we get things sorted out, I'll come back for Pest."

I nodded and held on tight as Kraster began to levitate us into the air.

It felt like an excruciatingly long time before my head was finally level with the ground. Immediately, I saw Wren and Gnombie standing back to back, facing half a dozen of the wingless, male harpies. A pair of females circled overhead, waiting for an opportunity to strike with their cruel talons. The monsters were smaller than humans and had slight builds. However, what they lacked in size and strength, they made up for in agility.

As soon as my feet were above the side of the hole, I leapt free of Kraster and charged. The harpies on the ground fell back, realizing that the odds were no longer in their favor. I ran one through with my initial charge and wounded another before he could even turn to face me.

Gnombie was stabbing here and there with his knives, which were small but deadly. I saw Wren kick a harpy in the head so hard he staggered away and right off the edge of the path, shrieking in terror as he fell.

One of the female harpies landed in front of me. Her pointed face was twisted in rage. She held a spear equal in length to my sword. Unfortunately for her, I had two swords.

The harpy caught my first attack with the end of her spear, but I easily twisted my blade free and used my second one to sever the shaft of the weapon. The harpy shrieked in dismay and tried to leap away. My next blow sent her stumbling back into range of Wren's fists.

Just as it looked like the fight might almost be over, the second female threw a small pouch at me. Quickly, I ducked, and it sailed over my head. I didn't see where the pouch landed, but when it did, there was another explosion. This time, the blast was so close it almost knocked me off my feet.

I turned in panic, ears ringing, and saw a billowing cloud of dust rising from the pit Kraster and I had just escaped. Hardly able to stand, I staggered to the top and looked down. The bottom of the pit had vanished completely, leaving only a gaping hole.

There was no sign of Tempest.

More harpies were clambering over the rocks toward us as half a dozen explosions sounded from somewhere higher up the cliff face. Rocks and clods of earth came raining down. The trail above was mostly destroyed.

Fury rose in me. I raced back into the melee, landing blow after blow on the creatures until those still standing retreated. Animal-like, they scrambled up the stone wall, using the talons on both their hands and feet.

My companions and I were left panting on the path, then a great rumble shook the mountain beneath our feet.

"I think we should run!" called Gnombie.

Kraster hurried back toward the pit, but I put a hand on his shoulder to stop him.

"Tempest is gone," I murmured.

"Are you sure?" Wren gasped in horror, her eyes huge with shock.

I nodded, not trusting my voice.

The ground started shaking harder, sending down a hail of debris from above.

"We need to get off this mountain!" Kraster yelled.

Leading the way, my brother hurriedly pulled Raspberry into a trot. The horse was full-size again and looked ready to bolt at any moment.

The rest of us followed, occasionally having to duck out of the way as a large stone or small rockslide threatened to crush us. I continued to look upward, trying to determine what was happening above. However, the path was tucked too closely against the cliff to allow me to see anything. Only when we reached the next turn was I able to get a good view of the rest of the mountain.

There were hundreds of winged harpies in the skies and, most likely, many more on the ground. The great hall wasn't visible from our angle, but from the clouds of black smoke choking the air, I feared that it had been set alight.

"Asteropaios's people are under attack!" I gasped.

"We have to help them!" Wren looked at my brother desperately. "Can't you do something?" she pleaded.

"We'd never make it in time, even if they hadn't destroyed the road," he told her solemnly.

"This is just like the plateau! Innocent people being attacked for no reason. Why is this happening?" Wren cried despairingly.

"The stones, probably," Kraster murmured.

"If they are that powerful, why are we the ones collecting them?" Wren demanded.

"Maybe Shal'eth thought we'd go unnoticed," Kraster suggested.

"Or because we happened to be in the right place at the right time," I said. "Except for you, Wren. I think Shal'eth chose you for this mission long ago."

"But why me?" she asked.

I had no answer for her.

Half an hour later, we reached the bottom of the slope and headed out into the plain beyond. I couldn't keep myself from looking back, trying to see what was happening on top of the mountain. Dark smoke was still rising from the summit, concealing nearly everything, but there appeared to be fewer harpies in the sky.

I wasn't sure if that was a good or a bad sign.

We reached the river as the sky was starting to darken. A glow came from where The Hall of Asteropaios had been located, but from such a distance, it was impossible to see if any part of it was still standing.

"It's like they knew she'd left," Wren whispered almost to herself. She too was gazing back at the mountain.

"What?" Kraster asked.

"The attack didn't start until just after Asteropaios left," Wren recalled. "It was like they were waiting for her to go and knew as soon as she was too far away to help."

"Well, I don't think they would have gotten very far if they'd attacked while she was there," I pointed out.

The others nodded.

"They must have a spy," Wren persisted.

"Because it's so hard to see when an enormous dragon flies away from its mountain," Kraster scoffed.

Wren shot him an angry glare.

"I don't know they're reason for the attack or how they figured out that Asteropaios was gone," I broke in. "But we should just be glad we got away with the stone before they did. Otherwise, she might never have re-created it, and our quest, or mission, or whatever you want to call it, would have failed."

Wren appeared pensive for a moment, then asked, "Why do you think Asteropaios gave us her stone? At first, she said no, then changed her mind."

I shrugged. "When I understand how dragons think, I'll rule the world."

Kraster let out a chuckle. "That'll be the day."

"Speaking of day," I said. "We are out of it. Might be time to stop for the night."

The other two nodded, and Kraster started to unsaddle Raspberry.

"What about moving a little closer to the water?" Wren pointed to the river, several dozen feet away.

I took one look at the dark water and shook my head. "Here's good."

"You've probably noticed, she's a little scared of water," Kraster told Wren.

"I did notice that," Wren replied softly.

"You'd be scared too if you could drown in water half the depth of a gnome," I muttered.

Then all three of us looked at each other because there were only three of us, and we had no idea where our gnome companion had gone.

Chapter 23
The Grove

"The teapot!" Wren cried.

"Check the stones!" I ordered.

A moment later, Wren had confirmed that the teapot was still in her bag, along with The Scrying Stone and Asteropaios's Gift.

"Nothing else seemed to be missing," my brother reported, holding up Dimble's Legacy.

"You don't think he got lost, do you?" Wren fretted.

"I have a feeling not," I told her.

"He may have decided to scout ahead," Kraster suggested.

"Without telling us?" I asked.

"Maybe," Kraster answered. "It's hard to say. We haven't known him very long."

"I don't think I trust him," Wren admitted.

"Even though Rakus sent him to help us?" Kraster asked.

"I trust Rakus," Wren replied. "But not Gnombie. It sounds harsh, but I can't shake the feeling that he's keeping secrets from us."

"I think a lot of people are doing that," I pointed out. "I'm pretty sure Shal'eth, The Oracle, Rakus, and Asteropaios all have a pretty good idea of what's going on but are leaving us in the dark on purpose."

"That can't be true," Wren protested. "The Great Shal'eth has never been anything but open and honest with my people."

Kraster and I exchanged a look. I knew he was thinking the same thing I was: Wren sounded woefully naive.

We decided not to light a fire, as we didn't want to attract the attention of any stray harpies. I took the second watch and sat looking back the way we had come. It might have been my imagination, but there still seemed to be a dim glow on the mountain top. From time to time, I thought I heard the echo of more explosions too.

After several hours had passed, I realized that the sound of running water was louder than it had been half an hour ago.

There was no moon and only a little starlight, but I rose and walked slightly closer to the river, trying to determine what had caused the change.

I'd taken about a dozen steps when icy water engulfed one of my feet. I leapt away with a yelp. Ending up on my butt, I scooted backward toward our camp.

"Kraster!" I scream, real terror in my voice. There was water here. Cold water. Water I couldn't see that was coming for me. I would be snuffed out.

"Kraster, there's a flood! We need to get to high ground!" I shouted.

"Candra? What–" I heard his groggy response.

I scrambled to my feet and back to where he and Wren were sleeping, then started gathering our supplies.

"The river," I explained. "It's risen, and it's still coming. We need to find high ground!"

"How?" wondered Wren.

"No time to ask stupid questions," I snapped, stuffing my bedroll into my pack.

Carrying as much as I could, I started moving away from the river. Only when I felt the earth under my feet begin to slant upward did I relax. A little further on, there was a flat section where I dropped everything I was holding before hurrying back for another load.

The others helped me move the camp, grumbling as they did so. Finally, all of our stuff and the two horses had been relocated to the high ground.

I sat down for the rest of my watch, twice as attentive as before. When it was over, I didn't bother waking Kraster, who was supposed to watch next. I knew I wouldn't be able to sleep after my scare.

The light of dawn revealed a vastly swollen river bearing loads of debris among its waves. I stared in shock as part of what looked like a wall rushed past in the strong current.

When the others woke, Wren was quick to point out that the water hadn't reached our first campsite. Somehow, the fact that it was mere feet away from where we had been sleeping didn't seem to bother her. My brother remained silent but was in a good mood, since he'd gotten to sleep through his watch.

Kraster risked a fire to cook breakfast while Wren and I prepared the horses. It took all my inner strength to keep the tears from my eyes as I saddled Raspberry. Even the stallion seemed to be looking around, searching for his lost companion.

"Oh no," Wren gasped.

I turned to see her standing beside Valor, staring out at the flooded river. There were bodies in the water now. Mostly harpies, but I did see the occasional flash of a dragonborn's scales.

"What happened?" she breathed.

"I think– I think they brought down part of the mountain," I realized out loud. "All those explosions must have freed the springs feeding the bath chambers, which weakened the structure until it fell."

"That place was beautiful and peaceful, like my village. Now both have been destroyed. But why? What was the point?" I glanced at Wren to see her wiping tears from her face as she spoke.

I just shook my head and started to turn away when I noticed something white in the water. My heart seemed to stop as I realized it was the body of a white dragonborn child.

"Alice," I whispered, and that was all, because there was nothing more to say.

Breakfast was a somber affair, as was our day's journey. The plain continued on for mile after mile of grassland. Down a horse, we opted to walk, which meant we didn't cover many miles. As afternoon slipped into evening, the river calmed, until it was almost within its banks again.

The campsite we picked that night was tucked up on a small hill. I took the first watch because, with my lack of sleep from the night before, I was sure waking up after only a few hours of rest would be a struggle. The night was quiet, but rather cold, especially considering it was the middle of summer and we were far in the south. I stayed wrapped in my cloak to keep from shivering.

Once my watch was over, I snuggled down into my bedroll and fell asleep quickly.

The sound of hoofbeats woke me in the morning before Wren could. I sat up and saw, to my astonishment, that Tempest was racing toward our camp with Gnombie on his back. As the pair grew closer, I squinted, certain I was dreaming.

Something wasn't quite the same about my horse. His coat, which had always been a glossy black, was now so dark no light seemed to touch it. The eye sockets were filled only with shadow, and the beast seemed to run without actually touching the earth despite the sound of its footfalls.

Gnombie brought the animal to a halt right in front of where I stood, flanked by Wren and Kraster.

"Hello!" he greeted us warmly. "I found a friend of yours."

"That's– that's not my horse," I told him.

"Sure it is," he insisted. "He may not be quite the same as he was before, but it's him all right."

Gnombie held out one of the reins, which I accepted hesitantly. Tempest, if it was indeed him, stood unnaturally still, not so much as flicking his tail.

"How did you accomplish this?" Kraster gasped.

I was glad he asked. My throat felt too dry to speak.

"You don't spend half your life around a powerful wizard and not pick up a few tricks," Gnombie told my brother with a wink.

Slowly, I put out a hand and touched Tempest's neck. The horse didn't react. His fur felt soft but cold.

"Thank you," I said uncertainly to Gnombie, wondering what was actually standing before me.

"You are most welcome! I am pleased to be of service," Gnombie replied with a little bow, before hurrying off to help Wren finish cooking breakfast.

I noticed that, though she asked several times about where he'd been and what he'd seen, the gnome dodged all of the questions thrown his way.

After eating, it was decided that Gnombie would ride double with me. He insisted that Tempest would never notice the extra weight. I could see Wren's relief that the gnome wouldn't be sharing her horse this time.

I went to Tempest and squinted. The beast wore the same saddle and bridle as before. Those appeared completely normal, but as I looked closely at the horse in the full light of morning, I realized I could see through him.

I stroked the horse's neck again, assuring myself that he was corporeal and not some kind of wraith. I mean, maybe he was a wraith, but he was definitely the touchable kind.

"Is something wrong?" Gnombie asked, sidling up beside me.

"I'm not sure," I admitted, eyeing both the gnome and the horse warily.

"Everything is going to be better now," Gnombie assured me. "You'll see."

I considered for a moment, but decided that we weren't going to get very far by walking, so I carefully swung into Tempest's saddle and reached down to pull Gnombie up behind me.

The shadowy steed obeyed me just as he had before, heeding my every signal and command as we fell into line behind Wren on Valor.

The river was much quieter today, gurgling along peacefully to our right. All morning, we continued traveling through the same grasslands as the day before. However, around noon, there started to be some small scrub and even a few trees.

In the afternoon, we stopped to water the horses. Well, all the horses except Tempest, who apparently didn't need that kind of thing anymore. Instead, I waited among the trees of a small grove, far back from the river's edge.

I caught sight of something golden on one of the branches. Pushing the leaves aside, I discovered a ripe apricot. I picked the fruit and took a bite. It was one of the best things I'd ever eaten. From the sweetness of the juice to the firmness of the skin, it was utter heaven. After I tossed the pit away, I carefully licked the juice from my fingers, then went in search of more.

When the others returned, I'd already tucked half a dozen into my pack.

"Those look so good!" Wren exclaimed when I showed her.

"These trees must be why it was said that The Great City was set in The Land of Golden Fruit," Kraster announced, picking several apricots off a nearby tree.

"The Great City was here?" Wren asked.

"Farther to the north, on the other side of the river somewhere," Kraster told her. "But I don't think we're too far from it. Or, at least, what remains of it."

"Apricots," I mused. "Who would have thunk it?"

"They are really good apricots," Wren observed. "I would definitely name a kingdom after them."

"Of course you would," I chuckled. "I'd name it after something much better."

"Beer or wine?" Kraster teased me.

I threw one of the apricots at him, striking my brother squarely in the shoulder.

"Mead," I announced. "It would be The Land of Golden Mead."

Kraster bellowed with laughter. Gnombie cracked a smile too, but not Wren. Ever since our meeting with Asteropaios, she'd been wound tight as a clock.

We picked fruit until our bags were full, then carried on, going slightly slower since the horses' loads were heavier now. Several times, I caught Wren glancing at me like there was something on her mind, but she remained silent.

Only once we'd stopped for the night, and Kraster and Gnombie were working to build the fire, did Wren come to my side.

"Do you think the legends are true?" she whispered.

"What legends?" I asked, matching her soft tone.

"That one day the line of the king will return, and The Great City will be rebuilt, and all the people of the land will unite, and there will be peace." Her words came in a great rush as though she had been holding them in for hours, which I had a feeling was exactly the case.

"Sure," I said. "Anything is possible."

Wren nodded slowly, forehead furrowed.

"Why are you asking?" I inquired.

"Because– because–" She had to lick her lips before she could go on. "Because I think the lion of Lion's Hill has awoken or will soon. Isn't that only supposed to happen when the heir of the old king appears?"

"This is because of your dream about the flying lion," I realized.

"There is a prophecy that someone will light the oil lamp beside the statue just by touching it," I told her. "Then the lion is supposed to come to life, but I don't know about an heir…" I trailed off to consider. A moment later, the exact words of the prophecy came back to me, and I quoted:

"The flame shall be lit
The lion shall waken
The lost returned
The crown retaken

A brilliant dawn
A triumph roared
A golden king
A line restored"

Wren looked at me with wide eyes. "It's all true," she breathed.

"What do you mean?" I wondered.

Wren dropped her gaze. "I dreamed it," she whispered.

"Yes, you told me about that," I reminded her.

"No. I mean, yes. I mean, I did, but I dreamed again. I dreamed of *him*. A young man with golden hair who picked up the lamp, then both it and the lion erupted in flames. I've never witnessed anything more incredible!"

"It was just a dream," I told her. "Nothing more."

"But lately, my dreams have been coming true," she pointed out.

"Well…" I hesitated before continuing. "Your dreams have been kind of generic: monsters lurking in the shadows, random attacks, a hidden terror… All of it could easily have been prompted by our daily activities. Anything more than that is just coincidence.

"It's not that I think you're lying, but I think that things have been happening, and then you believe you've dreamed them."

"No," Wren shook her head slowly. "I haven't told you all of my dreams. Some of them have definitely been coming true.

"At first, I thought along the same lines as you," Wren explained. "But it's happened too many times to be a coincidence. Now I'm afraid The Scrying Stone is affecting me.

"I haven't been using it. At least, I haven't been doing it on purpose, but what other explanation is there?"

"What– what are you saying?" I spluttered. "That your dreams are actually visions of the future?"

"Yes," she replied. "I think so."

"But none of the other stones are doing anything," I pointed out.

"Not yet," Wren countered. "We haven't had them very long, and we don't know what to look for. Plus, my mother used The Scrying Stone. Maybe it thinks I'm her."

"It's a stone," I reminded Wren. "I don't think it thinks at all."

"We don't know that," Wren insisted. "When Mother Imin gave me the stone, she said not everyone could use it, but I would be able to because of my mother's blood. That means I must be connected to it somehow."

"Fine," I conceded. "You're using the stone to see the future. Maybe we should use that to our advantage and try to find the other st–"

"No!" Wren cut me off. "I'm not supposed to be using it at all! Both The Oracle and Asteropaios warned me not to."

"That isn't exactly what I remember. They just said it might be a little risky," I recalled.

Wren hesitated before speaking again. "Rakus gave me some instruction, but I'm afraid." Her voice was so soft I had to strain to catch it. She paused, and I waited patiently for her to continue. "Sometimes, when I dream of the future, I get the feeling that *something* is watching me."

Wren licked her lips. "I can't really explain it, but I know that whatever it is, it's evil, and cold, and dark."

There were strands of panic laced in my friend's words.

"What do you think you should do, Wren?" I asked her.

"That's the problem," she sighed. " I don't know. I don't dare keep The Scrying Stone anywhere but on my person for fear of it being stolen."

Wren glanced toward Gnombie for a moment.

"I could–" I started, but Wren interrupted me.

"It's not fair of me to pass this burden onto anyone else. I was chosen for this task, and I must see it through."

I could tell from the set of her jaw that I wouldn't be able to convince her otherwise.

"How can I help you?" I asked.

"I don't know that either," Wren admitted. "I just wanted to tell someone and hoped that you would believe me." She gave me a sad smile.

Personally, I wasn't sure what I believed. All this about magical stones and seeing the future was fine for someone like Wren, raised at a shrine and trained in meditation and mental control, but I'd grown up in the woods and served in the military. I believed in what I could touch, feel, and, like as not, start a fight with.

"You should share more of your dreams with me," I decided. "They might help us avoid disaster in the future."

Wren nodded. "I don't want to tell the others," she admitted. "I'm afraid they'll think I'm crazy."

"Okay, we'll keep it between us for now," I agreed.

Wren beamed. It was the first time I'd seen her smile in days. Even though our conversation had made her feel better, it left me with a pit of worry in my stomach, because I knew that most of the dreams she'd had on this trip so far had been nightmares.

Chapter 24
The Golem

Several days later, we were traveling through a small forest of mostly oaks and beeches, with the occasional cluster of apricot trees. Over their leafy branches, we got our first sight of Jong. The golem was enormous, at least ten times as large as the ones we'd seen in Gnomania.

At first, all we could make out over the treetops was the curve of the head, which we might have mistaken for a mountain if not for the glint of metal. Slowly, as the day wore on, the shoulders came into view, but we were still far away when we stopped for the night.

Even though I had been riding Tempest for the past few days, I wasn't entirely comfortable with the creature. He didn't react to being scratched in his favorite spot and wasn't interested at all when I offered him a sugar cube from the sack I carried. Indeed, I hadn't seen the horse eat a single thing since Gnombie brought him back to me. The longer I observed the animal, the more I was certain that this wasn't Tempest but something wearing his body. However, I decided to wait and see what happened, since it would be a great inconvenience to be without a horse at the moment.

I was also keeping a closer eye on Gnombie. It made me nervous that he was included in the watches. One night, I pretended to be asleep during his shift to see if he would do anything, but the gnome just sat there, poking at the fire with a stick. Eventually, I dozed off, but woke a little later, thinking I'd heard voices. I sat up quickly to catch him in the act. Gnombie was completely alone, still in the same spot as when I'd fallen asleep, so maybe it was a dream.

The next evening, I watched as he and Kraster went to the river together to see if they could fish up anything for us to eat. The pair were chatting and laughing together jovially.

"Is something wrong?" Wren asked, and I realized I'd been scowling at them.

"No, everything's fine," I told her, smoothing out my features.

"Are you sure?" Wren persisted. "You aren't–"

"I know what you're thinking," I interrupted. "And I am not jealous that my brother seems to enjoy being with our new companion. He knows I'd never get close to the river unless absolutely necessary. Otherwise, I'm sure he would have asked me to fish with him instead."

"That's not what I was going to say," Wren replied quietly.

She glanced to the right, where the horses were tethered. Raspberry and Valor were contentedly cropping grass. Several feet from them, Tempest stood facing us. He seemed to be watching over the campsite with his empty eye sockets. It made me shiver, knowing that somehow the creature could see without eyes.

"Like I said a few days ago, I'm a little uncertain of Gnombie," Wren continued. "Something seems off about him. He turned up in the middle of an attack and– well, he was pretty calm about the whole thing."

"I don't know," I shrugged. "Rakus sent him to us, so–"

"But did he?" Wren asked.

"He didn't say a thing about Gnombie, not even once. And I don't remember seeing Gnombie in the tower with us before we stepped through the portal."

I considered that for a moment.

"I didn't see him either, but he must have been there," I protested.

"I'm not saying he wasn't," Wren explained. "Just that I didn't see him, neither did you, and I don't think Rakus did either." She gave me an expectant look, but I remained silent.

"Why was he trying so hard to stay out of sight?" Wren went on. "If he really was friends with Rakus, you'd think he would have at least said goodbye, but he didn't. He just slipped through the portal behind us without a word."

I blinked at her.

"You think I'm being paranoid," she guessed. The tone in her voice told me that she was asking herself the same question.

"I'm not sure," I admitted. "This whole journey feels shrouded in shadow."

"Yes," she agreed. "How can we know who is really on our side?"

"We can't," I answered. "We just need to keep doing the same thing we have been doing. If Gnombie is here to help us, he'll prove himself. If not, at least we'll know which way to expect the knife to come from."

Wren sighed but nodded.

We didn't speak much more after that. Kraster and Gnombie had been successful and were heading back toward us with several fresh fish. Despite both of our misgivings, we passed another peaceful night.

The next day, we emerged from the forest in the late morning to find Jong standing before us. He was taller than any structure or building I'd ever seen and was dwarfed only by the mountains on either side of us. The sun was shining, with just a few wisps of cloud in the sky. The dark silhouette of the golem stood out in sharp contrast to the brightness of the day.

Even though we had a clear sight of Jong, it took us several more hours to reach his feet. They were half buried in the dirt, where he stood about fifty yards from the river. A good deal of the golem was covered by metal plates fitted together in the shape of a giant. However, there were several parts, including one of the arms, where only the metal skeleton beneath remained. The entire thing was eaten away by rust, with little of the original color visible.

The golem had both arms raised slightly. There was nothing in them now, but a gigantic battleaxe, broken into several pieces, lay on the ground close to the metal feet.

Jong's head was horrifying. The left side had been carefully sculpted with noble features. The eyelid was closed, making that half of his face appear asleep. The other side was much the opposite. Most of the metal plates had fallen away to reveal the mechanical workings underneath, including the teeth, which were longer than my arm. The metal eye was completely exposed as well, and it stared down at us with a terrible intensity.

In the center of the torso, there was what appeared to be a small panel. It was slightly open, hanging by one hinge, or I might not have noticed it.

"That's probably where the heart was," I surmised, pointing it out to the others.

"Was?" Kraster asked.

"Asteropaios implied that the stone wasn't here anymore," Wren explained. "But she did say this is where we should start looking for it."

Kraster glanced up at the towering golem. "And how do we do that?" he asked.

"I can climb up there," Gnombie volunteered. "I'm quite agile."

He wants the stone, I thought, and gave Wren a desperate look.

She understood and spoke up at once. "Maybe it would be better if I did it."

Gnombie seemed about to protest, but Wren didn't give him the chance. Instead, she slipped out of her pack and began scaling the nearest leg. The sections without plating were easy for her to climb, as there were plenty of handholds. She hesitated when she reached the torso, which appeared mostly smooth. Somehow, she managed to get a grip on the flat metal and slowly pull herself up to the golem's chest, right below the open panel.

Carefully, she reached up and swung back the door. I took a step forward, ready to catch the stone if it happened to fall out.

"Anything?" Kraster called.

"No," Wren replied. "It's empty, but there is a place where a stone would fit perfectly."

I let out a huff of disappointment, wishing we had been lucky enough to secure another stone so easily.

"Should I check the head while I'm up here, just in case?" Wren asked.

"Might as well," Kraster told her.

"It's kind of high," I muttered to him.

"She'll be fine," he insisted.

Wren moved even more carefully as she slowly searched for handholds on the broad chest of the golem. My tension eased once she reached the shoulder and was able to perch upon it. Her chest rose and fell as she waited there, catching her breath.

"I'm going to try and get inside," she called down to us a moment later. I had to strain to see her as she began to start climbing again. I braced my hand against the golem's leg and leaned back, trying to keep her in view.

Just as Wren put a hand on the enormous nose, Jong's left eye blinked. Wren let out a squeak of alarm as she fell. I shouted in dismay and leapt backward. Kraster pointed a finger, but before he could mutter any kind of spell, Jong's arms moved, and the golem caught Wren in one of his large hands.

There was a creak as the elbow bent, bringing Wren up to the golem's face.

"Who are you?" Jong's voice rang out loud and clear. Wren instantly covered her ears.

"I'm Wren," she answered. I was barely able to catch her words.

"What was that?" bellowed the golem. I winced, imagining how much louder his voice must be to Wren, who was so terrifyingly close to his mouth.

"Wren," she cried out, voice shrill. "I'm Wren!"

"Wren," Jong repeated her name. "Never heard of you." There was a whirring of gears as his eyes moved up and down in their sockets. Carefully, he inspected Wren.

"Not a giant," he mumbled. "But not a dwarf either."

"If you please," Wren called. "I'm sorry I was climbing on you, but I didn't realize you were alive. If that's not rude to say," she added quickly.

"Alive? Of course, I'm alive," Jong announced.

When he spoke again, his voice was softer and more distant. "I've been alive a very long time. Never won't be alive.

I've just been sleeping. Sleeping for ever so long, and you woke me up."

Jong raised Wren even closer to his face, staring at her with his mechanical eyes.

"We have to help her!" I hissed to Kraster.

"What are we supposed to do against that?" he countered. "If we launch any kind of attack, that thing could crush Wren like a grape."

I glanced up and bit my lip. My brother was right; there was nothing to do but hope Wren could talk her way out of this one.

"I did not mean to disturb you," Wren promised. "My friends and I were seeking your heart. It is a great source of power and something that we thought could help save our people."

"My heart," Jong mused, then looked down. "Your friends? Oh yes, I see them." Jong waved at us with his free hand. "Hello, Wren's friends," he called.

I waved back politely, wishing Wren hadn't pointed us out to the golem. It would only require one of his massive feet to flatten the three of us and our horses as well.

"My heart was taken long ago," Jong said sadly.

"Really?" Wren asked. "Do you know who took it?"

"It happened while I slumbered," Jong replied somberly. "You see, during the final battle between the dwarves and the giants, I made my stand here, on this riverbank. Dozens of foes came against me, but I slew them all with blow after blow of my axe."

Jong glanced down to where his weapon lay in several pieces.

"I see quite a lot of time has passed since I last held Skullspliter," he observed. "She will need to be mended if I am to again make such a stand as I did that day. There was no giant that could defeat me, not even their king, The Iron Juggernaut, Demir Tetsu, fourth of his name.

"I was weary by the time he reached me, but it is not in my nature to back down from a challenge. Our weapons met many

212

times. Finally, I struck him through, and he staggered. But, alas, I looked down to find his blade in me as well and my legs unable to move.

"Though my foe was impaled by my axe, it was not a death blow. Before the king of the giants could escape, I pulled his blade from my body and threw it, severing his head from his shoulders.

"The dwarves triumphed that day, and the giants were driven from the hills around us." The golem looked at the mountains on either side of the valley.

"After the celebration, the dwarves attempted to fix the damage caused by King Demir's sword, but failed. They promised to send to the gnomes for one of their engineers to come and repair me. Until such time, they shut down my power levels, allowing me to hibernate.

"However, they must have forgotten about me. I woke a few times from my slumber, usually due to a landslide or passing caravan. Oh, did I ever give them a fright," Jong chuckled, then his face grew serious.

"I slumbered for a long time then, with few wakings, as the trees grew into a forest, and the river carved itself a deep channel. All the while, my body was rusting away."

The golem's head tilted forward slightly as he surveyed himself. Slowly, his eyes came back to rest on Wren. "I am not what I once was and expect that I shall soon slumber forever."

"Who took your heart?" Wren asked. Her voice was filled with pity.

"The last time I woke," Jong started, "I saw an elf standing on the ground before me. She had very cold eyes, but there were tears on her cheeks.

"As I watched, she rose into the air, flying to the compartment that held my heart." The golem tapped his chest with a finger.

"I began to speak to her, but she commanded me to be still, and I found I could not move. A moment later, she drew forth my heart, yanking it free of its physical and magical tethers.

"Never before had I felt pain, so I cannot judge, but it seemed excruciating to me. Still, I could neither move nor speak. The last thing I knew was darkness closing in and being wrapped in pain. I thought death had finally found me, but then I woke to your touch, and the pain was gone."

Jong smiled at Wren, not a pleasant sight considering the number of exposed teeth in his mouth.

"I'm very sorry to hear that you went through all of that," Wren said. "But can you tell me anything else about the elf?

"Of course," Jong replied. "I can still picture her as if she were here just yesterday. She had dark hair and blue eyes. She wore a deep crimson cloak, and there was a green rune inscribed on her brow."

"A rune?" Wren asked.

"Yes, the ancient rune for life. The same rune that is carved into the cavity in my chest where my heart was placed long ago," Jong explained. He carefully lowered Wren so she could see for herself.

"That can't be a coincidence," I muttered to Kraster, who nodded.

"Thank you for answering our questions," said Wren gratefully. "I'm sorry, but there doesn't appear to be anything my friends and I can do for you."

"Tis all right, small one," Jong told her. "I believe I was granted life once more because I was meant to tell you these things. I was created to help win a war that has long since ended. I will rest now. Forever."

The voice of the golem grew faint, and the lid slid down over his left eye. The other remained open, but the stare was sightless once again.

Carefully, Wren freed herself and climbed to the ground. Her face was grave when she reached us. I also felt moved by the tale of Jong, the only golem ever given true life, who was abandoned when he was no longer needed.

Chapter 25
The Forest

Despite Asteropaios all but telling me it would be necessary, I dreaded the thought of going into the forest lands of the high elves. There was only one elf, wood or high, who had ever treated me with any kind of decency. We'd met in Thea, just before this crazy quest had begun. I'd been a little drunk at the time, and all I really remembered was that her name was Lucille, and she had orange eyes.

I was certain the treatment I could expect from her people in the south would be far from pleasant. If they were anything like the wood elves that had lived in Owen's Falls, they would consider me pond scum on a good day and even worse on a bad one.

Wren didn't seem nearly as worried as I was about our reception. I chalked that up to her sheltered life. At the moment, she had enough on her mind, so I didn't burden her with my concerns.

After leaving Jong behind, we continued south, following the Konno River. Kraster kept reminding us that we would need to cross it at some point. According to the map, he was correct, but I insisted that we hold off. I felt certain that if we traveled far enough, we were sure to come to a bridge or a ford where the crossing would be less lethal to those of us rivers wanted to drown.

Finally, late in the afternoon of the fourth day, we did find a bridge. The oldest, weakest-looking bridge I'd ever laid eyes on.

"Absolutely not," I said as soon as Kraster glanced my way.

"We have to get across, Candra," my brother insisted.

"On that?" I asked. "No, thanks."

"Look," Kraster started, taking a superior tone. "It's not ideal and probably won't hold the horses, but it might hold you, and the rest of us can swim."

"So, I get to walk the treacherous path of death alone?" I snarled.

"Basically," he replied.

I rolled my eyes.

"We have to get across," he repeated. "This may be the only bridge, since the elves aren't reported to have built anything on this side of the river."

I hesitated, hoping some other solution would pop into my head, but it didn't.

"Fine," I snapped, dismounting from my horse.

I approached the bridge like it might attack at any moment. The water flowing beneath it was calm, but that didn't fool me. I knew what kind of currents could be hidden under a serene surface.

Placing one foot on the first of the wooden steps, I carefully tested the strength of the planks. They squeaked and bowed, but held. I glanced back at the others, who were readying the horses for their swim.

Steeling myself, I stepped up onto the bridge. As soon as I did, it seemed that the river began flowing faster. I slowly moved forward, checking each piece of wood before trusting my weight to it. Once, a plank snapped, giving me a harrowing view of the churning waters below. Foam crested the waves now. I didn't remember seeing that before I'd started crossing.

I didn't dare look back to where the others were. If the river had dragged them under, I would be no help at all. I did wish I'd insisted they cross first because, as I neared the middle, the river turned into a rapid. I steadied my breath and skipped the next beam, which was clearly rotten.

As I neared the two-thirds mark, the railings on both sides of the bridge ceased entirely. Holding my breath, I tiptoed down the very middle, knowing that the central support beam was just below me. As long as it wasn't broken or damaged, it would be the most structurally sound part of what remained of the bridge.

The wood groaned and creaked but held as I made it forward several more feet. Then there was a snap and the terrible sensation of something cracking. Without waiting to find out what it was, I raced forward, hoping to reach the other end of the bridge before the entire thing gave way. Only once did my foot break through a plank. I scratched my leg on the jagged edges of wood as I wrenched it free and threw myself forward, off the bridge, and onto the bank in front of me.

My trembling knees gave way, and I ended up on the ground, gasping for air. Sweat ran down my temples. I felt as weary as if I had just fought a battle.

After I'd remained like that for several minutes, I dared to look over my shoulder. The river seemed calm again, and I could make out the three horses swimming strongly toward me. The bridge was now missing most of its middle section. The sight made my heart plunge into the pit of my stomach, and I fought for control of my terror.

It's fine, I told myself. *You don't have to go back across. You never have to cross again.*

By the time my brother and the others reached me, I had myself more in hand. Kraster untied Tempest from the leadline he'd attached to Raspberry and returned him to me. To my surprise, the horse was completely dry. If we had to cross any more rivers, maybe I would chance the crossing on Tempest's back and see if whatever magic had protected him from getting wet would protect me too.

I helped the others wring the water from our supplies. After a brief discussion, we decided to make camp for the night so the sun could dry our belongings. Even though we had nearly two hours of daylight left, most of the bedding, clothing, and blankets were still damp as the light began to leave the sky.

"Too bad the sun's not warmer," Wren lamented.

"It's much nicer here than it ever is on the plateau," Gnombie pointed out.

I nodded, remembering that pretty much the only time I'd actually felt warm there was when I'd been fighting for my life.

"We should reach the outskirts of the elves' territory in the next few days," Kraster stated, looking at the map. It was thin enough that the parchment had dried all the way through.

217

"Although," he continued, "this map is old, and elves rarely share their actual borders willingly with humans."

"So we could be in their land now?" Wren asked.

Kraster nodded. "It's possible."

"I doubt it," Gnombie said.

We all looked at him.

"The high elves have a penchant for beautiful things. They use magic to make all the land they inhabit reflect that," the gnome explained. "You'll see when we get closer."

Wren slept fitfully that night. She began crying out during my watch, which was the last one. I gently shook her awake. Her eyes flew open, wide and shimmering faintly teal in the darkness. The glow faded almost immediately, and I wondered if I hadn't imagined it.

"What did you see?" I whispered.

"A city," she replied. "Everything was blue and white. It was full of tall spires–"

"The Coral City," I breathed.

Wren nodded. "Yes, I think that is what it was called. It– it was besieged and– and burning. There was fire everywhere, and the spires– they were falling, one after another."

"Was it because of Greyward?" I asked, already knowing the answer.

"I believe so," she replied. "I think I saw him, but he was different. His eyes– they were soulless and full of–" she paused, searching for the right word. "Full of emptiness."

I was very glad Kraster was asleep and didn't have to hear the future of his old mentor. I'd always respected Greyward, despite his dislike of me, but Kraster had all but worshiped him.

"This vision could come true any moment," Wren worried. "Where will Greyward go next? How much of the world must he burn before he is content?"

"I don't know," I replied somberly. "If he is seeking the stones like we are, then he must believe one of them is in The Coral City. Once he has obtained it, I'm sure he'll move on to try and find more."

"But that will lead him to us eventually," Wren gasped.

"It might, but we will be much harder to find than a city," I assured her. "He doesn't have The Scrying Stone, so our movements are invisible to him."

Wren nodded and looked to the east, where the crimson light of dawn was beginning to spread.

"If he has some of the stones, we will have to face him, though, won't we?" she asked softly.

I didn't reply because she was right. Our quest would likely lead us back to Greyward, and I had no idea how the four of us could stand against his army. Wren and I sat in silence until it was time to start making breakfast.

Later that day, we began seeing signs that we were nearing the high elves' domain. The vegetation grew even more lush and green. The horses feasted on it the next few nights. Well, Raspberry and Valor did. The long, soft grass was comfortable to sleep on and wonderfully fragrant, allowing us several luxurious nights camped under the stars.

It was odd to look up at The Constellation of the Great Dragons and think of the mural I'd seen in the garden. The past was painted there just as it was written in the sky above.

Several days later, we entered a wood of towering trees unlike any of the other forests we had passed through. The trees had slender, nearly branchless trunks that rose high into the sky. Their bark was so smooth and silver, they seemed to reflect light. Above, the tops of the trees spread wide to form a perfect canopy of glowing green kissed by the sun. While the leaves did tint the light, they didn't stop it completely, making the forest well lit instead of gloomy.

We found a path of dark brown soil. It was free of weeds and lined with white stones.

"So pretty," Wren breathed, her eyes taking in the realm of her father's people.

I had to agree with her; although my wood elf blood clamored for the wildness of nature and not the order that it had been sculpted into here. Still, it was a vast improvement over the

219

cities and towns of humans, where nature wasn't even an afterthought.

The path split only once, and we randomly picked the right-hand trail as it seemed the larger of the two. When evening fell, we stopped for the night.

With the darkness came a great wonder, for the forest began to fill with fireflies. It was the most breathtaking sight I'd ever seen as hundreds of the winged insects danced on the breeze, glowing with amber light.

All of us sat up late, spellbound by their beauty. The gentle background hum of crickets, cicadas, and katydids only added to the magic. Despite all of that, I did not sleep well and woke with the anxious feeling of being an intruder in a sacred place.

Around noon, we reached a village. Unlike wood elves, high elves didn't live in the trees, but in elegant, stone houses on the ground. There was no clearing where they were built. Instead, they were scattered throughout the forest. The trees in that area were more sparse and boasted larger limbs to maintain the canopy coverage.

The road branched to each building and circled around a well in the center. Here, the path was lined with flowers of all colors, carefully worked into gardens that filled much of the space between the structures. Elegant banners of cloth hung from each dwelling, displaying a precisely embroidered family crest.

At our approach, five elven figures turned. Almost as one, they moved in our direction, coming to stand on the road between us and the town. Each was garbed in a flowing robe bearing designs of trees and flowers.

The one in front raked her gaze across our party. Her deep-set eyes were the only sign of her great age. I'd intentionally ridden in the rear all day, but I doubted her keen sight missed anything.

"Hello," Kraster greeted her and the others, another female and three males.

The elf in front didn't respond, so Kraster continued. "We have come in search of one of your number. An elf with the magical powers of a mage, who–"

"Why would we give up one of our own to you?" the elf asked.

"We wish her no harm," Kraster vowed. "We simply want to inquire–"

"Outsiders are not welcome here," the female elf interrupted again.

"We apologize for the intrusion," Kraster cut in smoothly. "If we could simply explain, I think you would come to understand that we are on a mission of great importance."

The elf crossed her arms. She performed even that surly gesture with such grace that I felt a twinge of awe.

"We have been sent by Asteropaios herself," Kraster hurried on before he could be stopped again.

A laugh, like the ringing of a perfectly tuned bell, broke through the clearing. It was from the second female elf. The others began laughing as well, all except the speaker, whose eyes once again ran over us.

"Leave," she commanded. "Take your lies and go. We don't want any of your kind here."

"We can't do that," Kraster replied, his voice less friendly than before.

The elf's eyes hardened. "You have no right to trespass here."

Kraster was silent for a moment, then Valor took a step forward.

"But I do," Wren announced. The eyes of all the elves fell on her. Several more had appeared, seemingly attracted by the laughter.

The female elf's deep-set eyes studied Wren for a long moment. I held my breath, hoping her lineage would be enough to secure our passage.

"If you want a place here, you'll have to speak to the council," the female elf spat.

"We would like that very much," Wren said mildly. "Can you tell us the way?"

The elf curled her lip in distaste. Even so, her features and beauty were unmarred.

"If that is your wish, then it is your right," she all but snarled. "However, I do not think it will have the outcome you desire."

The other elves had grown quiet. The speaker turned, and her companions parted instantly, their movements like a dance. She led us across the village to a path on the other side.

"Follow this road to The Tree of Karradin," she instructed. "That is where you will find the council."

"How will we know which tree it is?" Wren asked.

"Trust me, you will know," the elf told her scornfully, before turning and walking back the way she'd come.

"Thank you for your help!" Kraster called over his shoulder. The elf gave no sign that she'd heard him.

We continued all afternoon, encountering neither turnoffs nor other travelers. We camped in a patch of ferns that evening and watched the fireflies come out as they had the night before. Tonight, the song of the bugs was a little louder and less welcoming, making my anxious feeling from the morning return.

Even still, I doubted we would be attacked. It wasn't the high elves' way. They had other schemes for getting rid of those they deemed unworthy.

Over the next few days, the woods all started to blend together, as we rode on for hour after hour. Idly, I wondered if we'd entered an endless loop, designed to entrap unwanted guests.

Just when I'd concluded that we'd be lost forever, a bird's song broke from the trees ahead. The sound of it was a melody the likes of which I'd never imagined existed. A moment later, a second bird joined the first. Then another and another could be heard, until the woods reverberated with the song, a thousand voices strong. I strained my eyes, trying to see the creatures producing the music. For a while, they eluded me, but then I caught sight of bright plumage and darting, feathery shapes.

The trail turned sharply to the right, bringing us to the top of a rise where we could see above the canopy. Far in the distance, stood a vast tree, twice as large as Jong himself. Its enormous branches stretched over the other trees gathered around it. Instead of silver, its trunk was a warm, inviting, coppery gold, and the leaves a rich orange.

"That must be The Tree of Karradin," Wren breathed in wonder.

We all agreed with her, as nearly every other tree in this forest was indistinguishable from the rest. However, that did seem like just the kind of thing the high elves would pull: declare one tree as special, even though it was really the same as the others, then try to have strangers figure out which one it was as some kind of test.

The path took us down a slope into the cover of the canopy once more. It seemed to be leading us directly toward the enormous tree, further proof that Wren had been correct.

The trees in this second part of the forest were shorter and sprouted branches at regular intervals. These didn't produce more than a handful of leaves. As soon as we reached the bottom of the slope, the birds we'd been hearing became fully visible to us, perched among the boughs. They were all the colors of the rainbow, and no two appeared to be the same in shade or form, though their voices blended flawlessly.

We spent two more nights in the woods, steadily moving forward along the path, which was now straight as an arrow's flight. On the evening of the second day, we started seeing signs that we were nearing another elven village. We voted to make camp and not approach until morning, so no one could accuse us of sneaking up on the inhabitants.

Also, it would keep the high elves from having to offer us shelter for the night, a courtesy I was sure they would only extend grudgingly. As we'd already witnessed, hospitality was not something they enjoyed practicing.

Morning dawned, and I felt practically ill with worry. I, once again, remained in the rear as we approached the village. Gnombie was riding with me, which had become our norm.

Before long, we were under the enormous branches of the copper colored tree. Each of its limbs was larger than the trunk of a hundred-year-old oak.

A stone archway marked the entrance to the village. Two sentries were stationed there. They were armed with spears and shields that looked delicate yet deadly.

"Halt!" called the one on the left. His voice echoed like a gong.

We pulled our horses to a stop as the elves gracefully crossed their spears over the path. In unison, they advanced toward us.

"What business do you have here?" demanded the second sentry. His long, honey-colored hair was pulled back with a bronze pin.

"We wish to speak to the council," Wren told them.

"We do not permit outsiders such privileges," sneered the first sentry. His hair was also blond, but a lighter, wheat color.

"I'm not an outsider," Wren replied. "Because I'm half high elf, I have the right to speak with the council, do I not?"

The two sentries exchanged a quick glance. "What's your family name?" the sneering one with the pale hair asked.

"I have taken my mother's title instead of my father's name." I sensed Wren was attempting to project confidence and make them believe that she belonged here.

She didn't understand these people. Whatever homecoming she was expecting, I doubted she'd get it. They were more likely to denounce her than to accept her.

"I am Wren, Shrine Maiden of The Great Shal'eth, and I am here about his business," Wren went on. Her voice grew steadier when she invoked Shal'eth's name.

"And the others?" the second sentry inquired. He lowered his spear, seeming more interested now that she'd brought a dragon into the conversation.

"My faithful guardians," Wren answered.

The sentries looked at each other again, and I sensed their uncertainty. Maybe Wren would be able to convince the high elves to help us by using her patron's name.

The first sentry nodded over his shoulder, and the second hurried off with graceful strides in the direction of the village.

"We will see if the council deems you worthy of being allowed an audience," the remaining sentry told us. He didn't appear happy about it. Silently, I wished he'd been the one to leave.

We waited a long time, maybe a whole hour, before the sentry with honey-colored hair returned. His pace was unhurried, and he wore a slight scowl.

"They are to be admitted," he said to his companion in elvish, which I was fairly certain none of my friends spoke.

The other sentry's eyes widened. "Really?" he gasped.

The second elf nodded. "Please come this way," he said in the common tongue, motioning us forward.

We dismounted and followed him through the archway. I caught my breath at what I saw beyond. This was more of a city than a village.

The trail we were on met up with another, which appeared to circle the base of the huge tree. A dozen yards to the left of the path, the ground sloped up, forming a vast hill from which the trunk grew. White buildings were on the level ground around us. They'd also been constructed on the slope of the mound, all the way up to the base of The Tree of Karradin.

Carefully cultivated patches of flowers grew between the structures. There were more of the colorful birds along with other woodland animals, such as deer, rabbits, and squirrels, happily foraging in the long grasses.

"You may leave your animals here," the guard told us when we reached the entrance to a long building. Inside, I caught sight of several other horses, all of them willowy in build with champagne coats.

A pair of young high elves, a boy and a girl, came out of the stable. They could have been twins, having nearly identical coloring and features. The male took hold of Valor and Raspberry. The female approached me, then balked as she drew near Tempest.

"What is that thing?" she asked in elvish.

"He's– special," I answered in the same language. "He won't be a problem."

Despite my assurance, the elf child backed away, shaking her head. I turned to look at Tempest, unsure of what to do with the creature. Suddenly, it did the strangest, most terrifying thing I'd ever seen. The beast leapt toward me, literally jumping into my shadow and vanishing from sight. All three elves cried out, as did Wren and even Kraster.

"What's happening?" I demanded, turning on Gnombie.

"Sorry, forgot to mention that ability," he said.

"Ability?" I gasped. There was a strange pressure at the base of my skull. I could feel Tempest there, as if a thin strand of thought tethered the creature to me.

"Yeah," Gnombie went on. "Nifty, right?"

"How do I get him out?" I demanded.

"Just how you put him in, by desiring it," he explained.

Everyone was staring at us, so I swallowed my discomfort.

"You are going to tell me exactly what this creature is when we get done here," I growled at the gnome.

"Sure, sure," he agreed.

I turned to face the others. "Let's go see the council," I announced.

Chapter 26
The Council

The sentry with the honey-gold hair led us up the slope until we'd nearly reached the base of The Tree of Karradin. There, we came to an entrance way in a stone wall. Several turrets stood on either side, but they were obviously decorative instead of functional.

The double doors were opened for us by two more sentries. We entered to find a long foyer leading to a flight of marble stairs. The floor was carpeted by orange leaves, as was the circular, open-air platform we stepped out onto at the top of the steps.

It was built directly under the vast tree, so that the branches above gave the illusion of a vaulted ceiling. The platform was ringed by ornately carved chairs. In these sat those who I assumed to be the council members. All of them had deep-set eyes that spoke of great age and wisdom. Each wore a long robe. I quickly checked to see if any of them had the life rune on their forehead as Jong had described. While a few did have runes emblazoned on their skin in shimmering paint, none were the one I was looking for.

Curiously, sitting between two chairs was a black wolf, the likes of which I had never seen before. It watched me with intelligent eyes of brilliant green.

Wren, who had worked so hard to appear bold earlier, took a few shy steps forward. Kraster followed her as did Gnombie. Even though there was nothing I wanted more than to run, I went to stand with them.

"Greetings," Wren began, voice a little uncertain. "I–"

A male elf, who wore a circular pendant with the image of the coppery gold tree painted on it, rose and interrupted Wren. "You stand before The Grand Council of the High Elves of

Karradin's Vale, and you deign to speak without first having been asked a question?"

"I'm sorry," Wren replied. Confusion laced her words. "Is that not what we were brought here to do?"

"The insolence," muttered a female elf to my left. She also wore a pendant, on hers was painted a yellow rose.

"We will ask the questions," the first elf spoke again, words dripping with condescension. "My name is Elhanan, leader of The Grand Council. And you," his lip curled with distaste, "come to us using Shal'eth's name and expect us to believe that he would ever choose a half-breed to further his will?"

Wren let out a little gasp. I didn't react because, honestly, it wasn't a very good insult. Out of all those I'd received throughout my life, it was a two, maybe a three, if I added bonus points for the scornful delivery.

"Yes," Wren managed to say, voice quavering. "And not only The Great Shal'eth, but Asteropaios, as well."

A murmur sounded from the elves of the council.

"I cannot tell you why I was chosen," she continued. "It was not something I sought or ever imagined would happen to me, but it did. So, here I am, coming to you, my kin, for your help."

"Kin?" asked the elf to the right of Elhanan. "I don't think anyone here has claimed you. Therefore, you are no kin of mine."

"But– But I'm half high elf," Wren said quietly. "That makes us kin."

"Let us find out if that is the case," Elhanan addressed the other council members before turning to Wren. "If you please, provide the name of your closest relative living among us? If they claim you, then so shall we all."

I knew where this was going and that it would end with Wren's humiliation.

"I– I do not know the name of my father and doubt that he has any knowledge of me. My mother was a shrine maiden and acolyte of The Great Shal'eth. Thus, she never took a true partner."

Laughter resounded from all directions. Wren hung her head, looking at the ground.

I started laughing too. I laughed long and hard. Until all the others had finished, and I was still going. Until every eye was on me, including those of my companions.

"It's funny, right?" I said, stepping forward to replace Wren in the front of our group, as I stalked toward Elhanan. They hadn't taken our weapons, and I had a lot of them displayed on my belt. There were probably mages among the council members who could have downed me with a single word, but at least Elhanan was getting an eyeful of my sheathed blades.

"Just hilarious," I went on. "The world is burning, and you sit here, quibbling about breeding lines. Fantastically funny, that."

Elhanan and I were eye to eye. Thankfully, he was short for a high elf, or I would have come off as rather ridiculous.

"You don't even know what we have come all this way to ask. To ask in the name of two of the great dragons. To ask for the good of all races, even yours." I looked Elhanan up and down. There was fury building in his eyes, but that didn't stop me.

I turned my back on him and addressed the other council members. "Are you ignorant of what is happening in lands other than your own? The gnomes have been attacked. The Coral City is under siege. The Hall of Asteropaios has been razed."

I paused to let my words sink in.

"We are aware, actually," the female elf with the rose pendant replied haughtily. "Their concerns are not ours."

"Maybe you're next," I told her.

"We are in no danger here," Elhanan chortled behind me.

"Are you certain?" I asked.

"Quite," he answered smugly.

That was when I did something insanely stupid. In one motion, which I had performed a hundred times, I turned and threw a dagger. It sailed past the place where Elhanan stood and struck the chair behind him, embedding itself in the exact spot his head would have occupied if he'd been sitting.

There was a flash from my left. I threw myself flat, rolling to the right. A wave of hot air whiffed above me at the same time a handful of ice shards struck the ground by my side.

Scrambling to my feet, I saw that there were two casters, both readying themselves to strike again.

"Get out of here!" I bellowed to my companions, unsure of whether or not they would be spared. I dove forward, partly to draw the fire of the magic users and partly to make myself harder to hit. The council members in front of me scrambled out of the way, except for Elhanan, who raised his hand and pointed a finger at me, the words of a spell beginning to form on his lips. Quickly, I swiped his legs from under him. He dropped like a sack of potatoes, a very graceful and beautiful sack, albeit.

This is easier than I expected, I mused to myself. *I guess practicing in serene glades didn't prepare them for an actual battle.*

As soon as the thought crossed my mind, I felt a shooting pain in my leg. Looking down, I saw a shard of ice sticking out of my left calf.

One of the two mages was grinning at me with wicked satisfaction. She took a step forward, raising her arm to make another attack, this one aimed at my heart.

However, I had one trick left to play. I closed my eyes and summoned Tempest just as Gnombie had instructed.

A wave of darkness rippled out from me. Those still on the platform reeled back in horror as the shadow transformed itself into the shape of a horse. I grabbed two handfuls of mane and heaved myself up. Without any direction from me, Tempest bolted for the stairs.

I saw Kraster standing there. His arms were raised as he worked his own magic, which probably explained why I had only been hit once. We locked eyes, then I grabbed his wrist and he leapt. This was something we'd practiced many times. A moment later, Kraster was behind me on Tempest. The beast didn't seem to notice his extra weight.

"The others?" I asked.

"They ran when you said to," he replied grimly.

We caught up with them a moment later, still running. They were nearly at the stable. I dropped Kraster beside Wren and took

Gnombie up behind me, since he was the slowest. We rode ahead to prepare the horses. I silently prayed that Valor and Raspberry would still be saddled.

They weren't.

I sprang from Tempest and darted into the stable, my leg screaming in pain. The two young elves emerged as I seized the nearest saddle.

"Is something wrong?" asked the boy.

"We need to leave quickly," I told him, trying to sound cheerful, but I felt certain it came out as manic.

The pair leapt into action, and the horses were ready to go by the time Wren and Kraster arrived. I'd just finished tying a piece of cloth around the puncture wound in my leg when they burst in.

"Thank you so much!" I called over my shoulder as I hobbled back to where Gnombie and Tempest stood waiting. Wren and Kraster followed me out with Valor and Raspberry.

"What do we do?" Wren asked fretfully.

"We'll figure that out later," Kraster answered, giving me a stern look. "Right now, we need to be anywhere but here."

She nodded, and we all mounted. Kraster took the lead, spurring Raspberry back the way we had come. The sentry we'd left behind at the archway stepped forward with a curious expression. A moment later, he had to throw himself out of the way to avoid being trampled.

We galloped for half an hour before Kraster finally pulled up. Raspberry was blowing hard, as was Valor. Turning to the right, we entered the forest, letting the horses walk for another fifteen minutes before we finally alighted.

"What was that?" Kraster snarled, coming to face me.

"I wanted to show them that they were wrong," I told him. "I felt I made it pretty clear that I wasn't actually trying to hurt anyone."

"You threw a knife at their leader!" he bellowed.

"I did not!" I shouted back. "If I'd thrown it at him, I would have hit him."

Kraster ground his teeth in frustration and glared at me. I prepared myself to start dodging fireballs.

"I think it was their pride that you injured," Gnombie spoke up in the sudden silence.

"I don't think they were going to help us anyway," Wren added glumly. "They didn't even let me explain what I wanted."

"Well, at least they probably weren't planning to kill us," Kraster spat, but I could see his fury dissipating. I'd never known my brother to be angry at anyone for long, least of all me.

"So do we flee or continue our search?" Gnombie asked no one in particular.

"We have to stay," I told him. "Maybe try to find another of the smaller villages or—"

I stopped speaking when I caught movement out of the corner of my eye. Turning, I saw the black wolf, who had been with the council members, standing a few yards away. Its green eyes were fastened on me. Behind the creature stood a high elf male. I recalled that he had been seated beside the wolf. His wooden pendant was painted with an image of the full moon. He had straight, black hair with a glossy sheen and dark eyes.

I drew my swords and prepared for an attack.

"Peace," the elf said, raising one hand in greeting. His voice was soft yet commanding, and I felt myself not wanting to fight.

"Who are you?" I growled, resisting the urge to lower my weapons.

"I am Aki," he replied. His eyes wandered to the others and settled on Wren. Slowly, Aki took several steps forward. I braced myself as he passed, then glanced back to keep an eye on the wolf. The creature had gone. I didn't feel that it had simply concealed itself in the woods nearby but that its role was finished, and it had departed.

"You have the look of my son," Aki spoke very quietly, gaze locked on Wren.

"Really?" she breathed. "Is he here?" Her brown eyes grew larger, and she stumbled forward until the two were less than a foot apart.

"He died," Aki told her sadly. "It happened seven years ago, but, in the decades before, he traveled often." The high elf hesitated for a moment then continued. "You truly know nothing of your father?"

Wren shook her head. "I'm sorry, I don't. My mother spoke of him very little before she passed away."

Aki's eyes softened, and there was a moment of silence. I attempted to quietly resheath my blades but didn't succeed.

Aki glanced at me, then addressed all of us. "I have come to see if I may be of service to you. My people are wrong to think they will escape destruction if the rest of the world falls."

"We are looking for a special stone," Wren explained eagerly to Aki. "It's called The Heart of Jong. He told us himself that a high elf took it, and that she bore the rune for eternal life on her forehead."

Aki's eyes widened. "I have heard of whom you speak and know where she resides, but you must not go there."

"Why not?" Kraster asked.

"Morana was a mighty sorcerer, one of our finest for nearly two hundred years. That was before my time, but it is said that her heart was her downfall, for she fell in love with a human man named Abigor. He was a mighty warrior, extremely skilled with the longsword. Many spurned her for her choice, but she was happy enough until her son was born.

"He was a beautiful child with golden locks and a musical laugh. However, from the moment of his birth, dread crept into the heart of his mother.

"'K'halid' she called him. Everlasting. Though she knew it would not be so on account of his human blood."

Aki glanced at Wren and then at me.

"There is nothing harder for a parent than experiencing the death of their child." His voice was choked. "Morana knew it would be her fate to watch her son grow old and pass away in less than a century, all the while hardly aging herself.

"As the bitterness of reality ate away at her, she began to lose her reason and descended into madness. She studied every tome and all of our most ancient scrolls, trying to discover a way to preserve the life of her son.

"When she could find no answer, Morana demanded the council aid her in learning soul magic, a taboo form of the cursed dark arts that can lead only to tragedy.

"The council refused, telling her that what she wanted was against nature. She vanished for a time, and they never learned where she'd gone or what she'd done. When she returned, she was jubilant and seemed in her right mind again.

"Morana announced that she had found a way to allow her son to live until the end of the world. Not only that, but she told all the others of mixed descent that she could help them as well."

Aki paused and took a long breath. "The council should have intervened and stopped her," he went on quietly. "But they did nothing when Morana took her husband and child, along with those of mixed blood who desired to join them, and headed west. Several of her followers returned over the next decade, bearing tales of terror and nightmare.

"The council chose to ignore their words and turn a blind eye to all her doings. Now, none who venture too close to her territory ever return," Aki warned. "I am sure the years have done nothing to cure Morana's insanity. She was dangerous when she left, and her powers can only have grown in the time since."

"She resides in the west?" I murmured. "Then that is where we must go."

"I beg of you not to." Aki looked at each of us in turn, eyes coming to rest on Wren last.

"We must," she told him softly. "We have been sent by dragons."

Aki's eyes hardened slightly. "Dragons are not always the glorious heroes we want them to be."

Wren gave Aki a sad smile. "It doesn't matter. The world needs us; we cannot falter now."

Slowly, Aki nodded. "I understand." He reached out both of his hands and placed them on Wren's shoulders, then leaned forward and rested his forehead against hers. Both of them remained still for a moment, their eyes closed.

I turned away from the intimate scene.

Had my mother felt the same as Morana? Did that explain her behavior? I kind of doubted it.

"Thank you for helping us," Wren said.

"Promise me you'll be careful," Aki replied.

"We will," vowed Wren.

"I will set a few wards around this clearing so that no one will find you tonight," Aki told us.

"I set a few of those myself as we fled," Kraster admitted sheepishly.

"They were well done," Aki assured him. "Had I not had an excellent guide, I might not have found you. However, I am more familiar with the magic of this place and will be able to assure you a night of rest."

Chapter 27
The Puppets

Aki had spoken the truth. We passed the night in perfect peace; even Wren did not have a single dream.

"How shall we prepare for today?" Kraster asked while we saddled the horses.

"I'm not sure we can," I admitted to my brother. "We know so little about what's going to happen when we find the elf who took the stone."

"Aki said her name was Morana," Wren recalled. "She must like half-breeds if she took them all with her. Maybe she'll help us."

"From what we've heard, I don't think talking to her is a good idea," Gnombie pointed out.

"I agree," Kraster said. "I vote we try to take the stone without being noticed, if possible."

"I hate the idea of stealing again," Wren fretted.

"We aren't stealing," Kraster countered. "The stone isn't hers. If anything, she's the one who stole it."

"But–" Wren started to protest.

"I don't think there's any point even trying to make a plan one way or the other until we assess the situation," I told them, cutting Wren off before an argument could break out.

"If she's not used to anyone coming into her territory, hopefully, we can take her by surprise," my brother went on as though I hadn't spoken.

"There's no way it will be that simple," I scoffed. "But you keep on living in your dream world."

He shot me a scowl, but I knew he didn't mean it.

Ten minutes later, we were riding west, cutting through the forest instead of following any set path.

"We should have asked Aki for a map," Wren sighed.

"I think he would have given us one if he thought we'd need it," I replied.

"Candra's right," Kraster put in. "I have a feeling that we'll know the place when we find it."

Despite my brother's assurance, we rode the entire day and saw very little change in the forest. It was all the same silver trees as before, with the beautiful birds frolicking overhead. Toward evening, the land started slanting upward, but it never grew rocky or hard to traverse.

We found a level place to camp for the night. Everything was peaceful until Wren woke up screaming. I was on watch and hastily covered her mouth. The others stirred but went back to sleep a moment later.

"What was it?" I whispered.

"I– I dreamed," Wren replied. She was trembling and appeared more shaken by this nightmare than most of her others.

"What did you see?" I demanded.

"There was a river with a fortress on the far bank," Wren started. "I've dreamed of it before. More than once, actually."

I nodded, listening intently.

"I saw a boat crossing the river, but– but there was something in the water," her words came out hoarse with terror. "It followed the boat."

"What was in the water?" I pressed. It horrified me to think about what might be concealed under the surface, but I had to know.

Wren looked at me, eyes full of terror. "I don't know," she breathed. "I saw it, and it was horrible, but now I don't remember. It– it dragged the boat down. The passengers tried to escape, but one by one, they vanished, screaming as they were pulled down."

I pushed away the dread filling my body. Wren's words were too close to some of my own nightmares; dark dreams of drowning somewhere without light.

Even though I was on completely dry land, I felt the air in my lungs constrict.

"Well, we aren't anywhere close to a river right now," I reminded both Wren and myself. She nodded, finally calming down and dozing off again a short time later.

In the morning, Wren seemed to hardly remember her terror. She was all smiles as she prepared breakfast with Kraster.

Traveling was much the same as the day before, but I did notice that there were fewer and fewer birds.

Slightly after midday, I caught sight of something bright green through the silver trunks ahead. A moment later, we came to a place where the trees of the high elves' forest stopped abruptly, and a very different kind of vegetation began.

The new flora was wild. Its leaves, branches, and stems were a hundred different shades of green and yellow, with plenty of browns and some dark reds thrown in. There were tall trees, short trees, bushes, brambles, flowers, moss, and grass, all growing together in a twisted mass of life.

"I've never seen anything like this," Wren breathed.

"I think I have," Kraster said. "I saw some of these in a book about plants that went extinct a long time ago."

"Then it seems we have reached our destination," Gnombie observed.

I nodded my agreement, nudging Tempest forward. As we crossed the line into the strange forest, the temperature grew warmer. In the wood of the high elves, the air had been pristine and earthy. Here, I smelled flowers, nectar, and even the tang of wild honey. The sounds of insects and birds were everywhere. However, these were definitely not the same birds as before. Some of their calls were the melodies of songbirds, others were the sharp cackles of crows.

The undergrowth proved quite a challenge to the horses, but after a dozen yards or so, we found a trail. It was made of cobblestones, many of which were broken. Others were missing altogether. Despite its state of disrepair, the plants didn't encroach on the path. The air, which at first I had enjoyed for its warmth, began to feel heavy and stagnant, without even a hint of wind.

I stopped Tempest when I saw an opening through the trees ahead. Kraster, next to me on Raspberry, did the same.

"I think we should leave the horses here," he whispered.

I nodded and dismounted before helping Gnombie down as well. While my brother and Wren tethered Raspberry and Valor in a patch of tall bushes, I put Tempest back into my shadow. A slight shiver ran through me as the horse merged with my being.

Instead of approaching by the road, we moved into the forest about a stone's throw away. The going was slow since the undergrowth was extremely thick. We tried to move quietly, but Gnombie was the only one who really succeeded. His small, nimble body glided silently forward with practiced ease. The rest of us did our best with only a few stumbles here and there.

After fifteen minutes, we were close enough to see into the clearing. I peeked out from behind the trunk of an ancient oak and saw numerous buildings made of stone. Most appeared to be small cottages, or, at least, they had been once. The roofs were no longer fully intact. Large holes showed where the thatch had rotted away.

The cottages stood along the same path we had been following. It continued on, winding through the scattering of dwellings before leading out of sight behind a larger building. This one was also made of stone. It was almost perfectly square and had no windows. The roof was in one piece, even though the wooden shingles were warped and weathered with age. At the far end, a single turret rose from one corner.

I was about to step into the clearing when Kraster caught my wrist. He nodded at a pair of half-elves who stood at attention close to the place where the road left the forest. Their clothes were worn to the point of being rags. The two were perfectly still. I couldn't even tell if they were breathing. Finally, I saw one blink, but that was the only sign of life either gave.

"Something is very wrong here," I breathed to Kraster.

"Oh, you think?" he whispered back.

"What do we do?" I asked.

Kraster moved his hand through the air, and a deer stepped out of the forest close to the road. I knew it was one of my brother's illusions, but the creature looked completely life-like. Slowly, it began approaching the two half-elves. One of them followed it with his eyes for a moment, then his attention snapped forward again.

The deer paused.

Kraster moved his hand slightly, and the deer continued walking. It headed directly for the half-elves. Neither moved a muscle as the animal traversed the five yards between them and the edge of the trees. When it reached the closer of the two, the deer stretched out its nose and lightly nuzzled his arm. The contact seemed to go unnoticed.

Kraster scowled and curled his hand into a fist. The deer crossed the path to stand in front of the second half-elf. The beast lowered its head, pointing its antlers at the half-elf's chest.

There was no reaction.

Kraster tightened his fist, and the deer bumped the second half-elf. Nothing. The deer bumped him again, harder this time. The half-elf swayed ever so slightly, then went completely still. He didn't so much as look at the animal.

With a sigh, Kraster snapped his fingers, and the deer vanished. The half-elves didn't flinch.

"What now?" I whispered.

Kraster shook his head.

"Right," I muttered. "Cover me."

Without giving him a chance to react, I stepped out of the woods. I could practically hear Kraster grinding his teeth in frustration at my rash behavior, but I was not planning to spend the entire afternoon sitting in the bushes while nothing happened.

"Hello," I called, raising a hand to the two half-elves. One of them looked at me without turning his head at all.

As I grew closer, I could see that the clothes they wore were once guard uniforms. I also noted that their skin was a grayish, unhealthy hue.

"Lovely weather," I tried again, only a few feet from them. That was when the smell hit me. The odor spoke of unwashed bodies, rotting meat, stagnant water, and generally every other unpleasant thing you can imagine.

"Either of you gentlemen from around here?" I asked, trying not to gag as I stepped onto the path.

As soon as my foot touched the stones of the road, both of their heads snapped toward me. My mind started to summon Tempest, in case I needed a quick getaway.

"Welcome to town," one of the two said in a flat, emotionless voice.

"We hope you enjoy your stay," the other added.

"Thank you," I replied uncertainly. "Is there anyone else here?"

"Of course," the first half-elf said. "There's an innkeeper in the inn, a blacksmith at the forge, a baker at the bakery, a farmer in the fields, a—"

"Where's the inn?" I cut him off.

"Down the road a ways." It was the second guard who answered, and this time, he looked directly into my eyes. His were silver in color and tortured in expression. They bore into me with a desperate intensity that made me want to run.

"Thank you," I said again with a small nod. I moved between the pair to see if they would let me pass. They did.

"One more thing, miss," the silver-eyed half-elf said. I paused and looked at him. He didn't turn to me, so all I saw was his profile. "Best get indoors before nightfall." The words seemed to have been choked out of him, and a shudder passed through his body, then he went rigid again.

"Thank you," I repeated with greater sincerity. He seemed to have just offered me a warning at great personal cost.

I continued down the road and caught sight of a few more half-elves who had been concealed from sight by the buildings. There was a female with long, brown hair hanging up a tattered shirt on a laundry line. A moment later, she took it down, only to put it back up again. The process was repeated over and over, her movements exactly the same each time she completed the cycle.

A little further on, I was able to spot the forge and the bakery. At one, a lanky half-elf male raised his hammer and struck the horseshoe lying on the anvil over and over again, creating a dull thud in a perfect rhythm.

In the other was a slight female who looked like she was three-quarters-elf. Her presence shocked me, as she was the first quarter-breed I'd ever seen. Half-breeds usually couldn't produce children, even if they could find a mate. Her very existence was something truly rare.

The quarter-breed paid no heed to my stares. She was busily kneading a piece of dried-out dough that looked more akin to a rock. Beside her stood a male using a wooden paddle to put trays into an unlit oven, only to take them out a moment later, before putting them right back in again.

Never in my life had anything truly creeped me out, but this was on another level. I turned around to find Kraster, Wren, and Gnombie walking toward me.

"What is this place?" Wren asked softly.

"I don't want to know," I told her. "Let's go find the inn."

I figured it was worth a look, even though I doubted it would be any different from the rest of the town. The silver-eyed half-elf had implied that nights were dangerous here, so finding shelter was high on my list of priorities. We had several hours of daylight left, but I preferred to know my options in advance.

We passed a few more cottages, then came to what could only be the inn. It was a squat building with large windows whose shutters were in the process of falling to the ground.

The door was slightly ajar. I slipped inside without touching it, followed by the others.

A half-elf innkeeper stood at the counter, polishing a metal tankard with a dirty rag. That tankard was spotless and shiny, but the two dozen others on the counter beside him were covered in a grimy layer of dust.

The smell here was even worse than it had been outside.

"Welcome," the innkeeper greeted us. "Can I get you a drink?" he asked.

"Ale, please," Kraster said.

The half-elf didn't move; he just kept polishing. He looked back up at us a moment later. "Welcome. Can I get you a drink?"

Kraster glanced at the rest of us. "What is happening here?" he murmured.

"I think they're all stuck," Wren whispered.

I nodded. She definitely wasn't wrong.

"How do we get them unstuck?" Gnombie asked.

"I assume this all has something to do with The Heart of Jong," I said.

Kraster nodded. "I believe there's more to it than that. Aki said Morana was a strong mage. She's probably built some kind of enthrallment spell with the stone as her power source."

"That makes a lot of sense," Gnombie remarked. "We know the stones are quite powerful."

"So when we find the stone, we can help them?" Wren asked.

"Maybe," Kraster answered.

"That might have to wait," I told them. "We aren't supposed to be out after dark."

"Why?" Kraster narrowed his eyes.

"One of the two at the front said it. I mean, he *really* said it, and I believed him," I explained.

"We need to go back for the horses!" Wren gasped on the verge of panic.

"Calm down; the sun isn't setting just yet," I soothed her.

"But where are we going to put them? Or us, for that matter? This place is hardly defensible," Kraster pointed out.

"There was one building we passed earlier that might work," Gnombie said.

I nodded, recalling the solid stone structure with the turret.

"Let's go check it out," Kraster suggested, and we all headed for the door.

I hardly noticed the smell as we headed back the way we had come. All of the townspeople were still doing the same things they had before. Their rhythm and motion never altered in the slightest, although several of them turned their eyes toward us for a brief instant.

There was no indication of what the windowless building might be. We circled it and found only a single door made of iron and bolted fast.

Gnombie tried to pick the lock with his tools, but it was too old and rusty.

"How are we going to get in?" Wren asked.

"From the top," Gnombie suggested, putting his lockpick away. "There's sure to be a trap door up there.

Wren glanced at the lone turret.

"I'm not sure I can make that climb," she admitted.

"I think I can do it," Gnombie said, dropping his pack and moving into position to start scaling the curved wall of the turret.

"Be careful!" Wren called after him a little too loudly for my taste.

It didn't take Gnombie long to reach the parapet and vanish from sight. A few minutes later, we heard the iron door rattle, then it swung inward, revealing an armory.

"Looks like a great place to spend the night," Gnombie observed, as we crowded inside.

"You're sure it's empty?" Wren asked.

"Seems to be," Gnombie answered.

We checked the whole place just to be safe. The walls were lined with weapon racks and hung with shields. Several suits of armor lay in piles on the floor, every piece eaten with rust. The center of the room was clearly a training space. There were faded lines on the floor marking off a sparring circle.

The only light came from the door, which we'd propped open, and the archway leading to the stairs for the turret. Several iron chandeliers hung from the room's ceiling, and there were dozens of sconces containing the remnants of burnt-out torches along the walls.

"We still need to get the horses," Wren reminded us.

"Are you sure we shouldn't check out the rest of the town first?" Kraster asked. "We might not even need to stay overnight."

Wren glanced outside. "I'm going to get Valor," she said in a tone that left no room for argument.

Kraster hurried after her retreating figure. They returned shortly with Valor and Raspberry. The room didn't feel quite as large with the two stocky animals inside.

I took a torch from my pack and lit it before setting it in a sconce. The light coming from the archway had faded to almost nothing. Outside, long shadows were spreading across the clearing.

"I think it's time to close up shop," I announced, unpropping the door and letting it swing shut. Gnombie came over and helped me fasten the bolts.

"Is there a way to lock the trapdoor in the turret?" I asked, heading for the hallway next.

Gnombie nodded. "It has a sliding bar, and there's a door just before the stairs. I had to pick the lock to get it open."

"Good," I replied.

Once both doors were locked and the bedrolls were laid out, there was nothing to do but wait. I found myself straining to hear anything from outside, but all was silent. Far too silent. There was no wind. No sound of the village inhabitants or the singing of birds, nothing but an eerie calm. I wondered if the half-elves were still performing the same, repetitive actions and if they would continue to do so throughout the night.

"What do you think is going to happen?" Wren asked as we sat around eating dinner.

I was so tense, waiting for any sound from beyond the armory walls, that I hadn't tasted a single bite.

"If it's anything like what we saw out there today, something unnatural," Kraster told her.

Wren looked down at her plate. There didn't seem to be much more to say.

A heartbeat later, the shrieking started.

Chapter 28
The Child

I slammed my hands over my ears as the cries grew louder and louder. The horror I felt was mirrored in the eyes of my companions, each of whom held their own ears in turn. After a moment, the sound died down to a low moaning. Cautiously, I lowered my hands.

Without warning, the screaming started again. At the same time, there was a thud against the door as though a fist had struck it. The first thud was followed by more until it seemed that dozens of creatures were beating on the outside of the door.

My eyes met my brother's. "Should we-" he started.

"Most definitely," I replied, springing up.

Together, we dragged the closest of the weapon racks in front of the door before moving on to the next. Once the barricade was complete, we took positions across from it. Me, with swords drawn, and him, with hands raised, as we prepared to engage anything that managed to break through.

Thankfully, the door held. It felt like hours that we stood there, waiting for our defenses to be breached. Slowly, the pounding grew less and less until it stopped completely.

Kraster and I hadn't moved in a long time. When I looked at Wren, she was wide-eyed and horrified. Gnombie was sitting beside her, a dagger clutched in each hand.

"Some of us should try and get a little rest," I suggested in a strained whisper. "Gnombie and I will watch first."

The others agreed. Kraster and Wren lay down, while I started to pace. The torch burned low, and I lit another. The sounds from outside went from screams to wails. At one point, I thought I heard weeping, but I quickly realized it was coming from within the room.

I turned sharply to see Wren curled on her side. Gently, I placed a hand on her trembling shoulder.

"You all right?" I asked.

"I dreamed of *them*," she whispered.

"Them?" I wondered.

She nodded. "It's the townspeople. They are in terrible agony. They want– they want– but they already are, and it's not enough."

Wren was gasping for breath now, weeping openly. Even Kraster was awake and staring.

"I think it was just a bad dream," he tried to soothe her.

Wren shook her head and buried her face in her hands. "We must free them!" she cried. "They need our help!"

It took the rest of the night to calm Wren. I didn't get more than an hour's worth of sleep and felt groggy when Kraster's pocket watch told us that morning had come.

"We cannot spend another night here," I murmured to my brother as we moved the weapon racks away from the door.

"I agree," he replied. "We need to get what we came for and go."

I held my weapons at the ready while my brother cracked the door open. The sunlight nearly blinded me as it streamed through the narrow gap. Outside, all was as it had been the day before.

We left the horses in the armory and headed toward the silver-eyed half-elf. He was standing in the same position as yesterday.

The others hung back, allowing me to approach him alone.

"Thank you for the warning," I said. He didn't acknowledge me.

"I hate to trouble you," I went on. "But can you tell me where we will find the person responsible for this town?"

"The lord rests, the lady sleeps, and the child plays," he answered. The words were a little strained.

"Can you tell me where?" I pressed, hoping I wasn't causing him any pain.

"The estate," he answered. "There's a statue and a well. You'll find–" the half-elf cut off sharply. His eyes closed for a moment, then they opened again with a vacant stare.

"Thank you," I said, turning away.

I repeated his words to the others, and we set off along the path, heading deeper into the sprawling town. It was larger than I'd first thought. There were many cottages and shops, most manned by at least one half-elf, all of them caught in some pattern of motion or standing rigidly at attention. We passed a cobbler who had driven a nail so far into a piece of leather that the head wasn't even visible. Yet, he continued to strike it with his hammer. A willowy female stood in her garden, which was wild with weeds, and poured nothing out of an empty watering can on a patch of particularly thorny briars. There was a farmer who had created an enormous trench by hoeing the same row in his field over and over again. We also saw more guards in uniforms like the first two, but these paid us no mind.

Finally, the road led us up a small rise. When we reached the top, I could see that the path going down on the other side came to an end as it circled a small patch of ground containing a statue, a well, and a couple of benches.

The only building nearby was a small manor house. It wasn't very large compared to those found in human towns, but it was certainly a step up from the cottages in the rest of the village.

I headed confidently for the front door of the manor, the others close behind me.

"Don't go in there. Mommy is sleeping," a high-pitched voice said. I whipped around to find a half-elf child of maybe seven or eight standing beside the well.

Wren covered her mouth when she saw him, for, while his face was very beautiful, and he had lovely blond curls, his eyes were pure black. Not just the irises, but all of them. On his forehead was emblazoned the rune for life, which glowed with a green light. Unlike the other inhabitants of the town, his skin had a healthy tone. The clothes he wore were old and a bit ragged, but they were finely made and included a doublet and short cape.

248

"When will your Mommy wake up?" Wren asked nervously.

"I don't know." The boy shrugged and took a few steps forward. "She's been asleep a long time. A really long time."

"Are you K'halid?" I asked, recalling the name Aki had given us.

"I am," the child beamed. "How did you know?"

"We've heard about you and your parents," I replied. "Is your father here too?"

"No, he died," the child answered. "Mommy was very upset. She said it wasn't supposed to happen, but it did because he was human and the magic didn't work on him like it was meant to."

"The magic?" I asked, hoping the boy would tell us more.

K'halid nodded. "Mommy brought Daddy and me here a long time ago. A bunch of others came with us. They weren't much fun because Mommy set them to work. They had to make us things, grow our food, and build our home." The child pointed to the manor house.

"She said they should be happy to serve us because she was going to let them live forever. A few ran away, so she tightened up the rules and forced them to work harder. Daddy wasn't happy about that, and they quarreled, but she told him that I was all that mattered, not the others.

"For a while, everything was nice. We spent all our time together exploring and playing games. Then Daddy died, and Mommy got really sad. She buried him in the crypt under the house and had a monument built for him."

The child gestured to the statue beside the well. "She said we must never forget him, but I wish she had, because she cried so much and was no fun. I tried to play with some of the others, but they were too busy since Mommy made them work so much. She only let them rest when the sun went down."

"How did she do that?" I wondered. "Do the guards watch them?"

K'halid shook his head. "She used her magic and a stone."

"A stone? What stone?" Kraster asked eagerly.

"A green stone," the child replied. "She always had it with her and wore it around her neck. But one day, when she was sleeping, I went into her room and took it without waking her. She's been asleep ever since.

"Things were different after that," K'halid scowled. "The others don't bring us food or clothes or toys anymore."

"Then what do you eat?" Wren gasped.

"I don't," K'halid told her.

"How long ago did you take the stone?" I asked.

"I'm not sure, but it was a really long time," he answered.

"Maybe a few days?" Kraster suggested.

The child shook his head once more. "No, way longer than that."

"A hundred days?" I pressed.

"Longer," K'halid said. "Much, much longer. Years and years, I think."

I swallowed the bile that rose in my throat. "And the others have been doing the same thing over and over again ever since?" I asked quietly.

"That's right," he replied. "It's awfully boring, but now that you're here, you can play with me!"

"I don't think we can do that," I told him.

"We need you to give us the stone," Kraster added.

"No!" K'halid shouted, a flash of anger crossing his young face. "You can't have it!"

"K'halid," I started, using a soothing tone. "I think you know that things here have gone very wrong, and you can't fix them. Maybe we can help you."

"No!" he screamed again.

"What if we help you wake up your Mommy?" Wren suggested. I cringed slightly. If K'halid's mother, Morana, had created all of this just so she could live forever with her child, I doubted she'd hand the stone over without a fight.

K'halid considered for a moment, then his face twisted with rage. "You're lying!" he shrieked.

With the speed and strength of someone five times his size, the child ripped a rock from the path that bordered the statue and hurled it at Wren. It struck her in the head and knocked her to the ground.

I drew my blades as Kraster hurried to Wren's side.

"I don't want to fight you," I called. "But I will if you make me."

I hated the idea of attacking a child, but when I looked at K'halid, I didn't see a child. I saw an innocent life twisted and ruined. He'd lived hundreds of years under the influence of corrupted magics. That would curdle anyone's brain.

If nature had taken its course, this child would have died centuries ago. In order to preserve him, his mother had turned him into an abomination.

"I'll kill you all!" shrieked K'halid. He grabbed another rock. An arrow from Gnombie caught the child in the chest before he could throw it.

Instead of stopping the boy, the arrow only seemed to give him more strength, and he hurled the rock. Gnombie had to leap out of the way to avoid being crushed.

Without hesitation, I charged. K'halid turned to face me as I swung low, trying to take him out at the knees. One of my swords embedded itself in his leg, the other he caught in one of his hands. No blood came from the places where the metal bit into his skin. Instead, his wounds began to leak green light similar to what was coming from the rune on his forehead.

K'halid's hand held the blade of my sword tightly. He struggled to pull it from my grasp, but I managed to hang on. As I'd observed earlier, he was incredibly strong despite his small size. I wrenched my second blade from the child's leg, watching the wound heal almost instantly. Quickly, I swung for K'halid's back. It was a clumsy blow, due to the angle, but I managed to clip his shoulder and shear away his cloak.

A moment later, I was tossed aside as the sword was wrenched from my hand. Just as I hit the ground, a ball of fire struck K'halid in the face, eliciting a howl of fury from the child. I scrambled to my feet and charged again with only one sword this time.

A second arrow flew by my head and struck K'halid in the side. Still, he remained on his feet, appearing more angered than injured by our attacks.

It seemed impossible to wound or incapacitate the child, so I went for a death blow. Rushing in, I struck at his head. K'halid ducked my thrust and grabbed my second sword from the ground where he'd dropped it after Kraster's attack.

Before K'halid could come at me, another firebolt hit him. The boy whipped around to face my brother. When he turned, I saw something green glowing through the hole I'd torn in the back of his shirt.

Kraster cried out suddenly as my sword left K'halid's hand and impaled my brother in the leg. Quickly, I darted forward and took hold of the back of the child's shirt. Before I could do anything else, he twisted, fist raised, and punched me hard in the gut. I staggered backward, the shirt ripping away in my grasp. K'halid raised his hand for a second blow, but Gnombie saved me with another arrow.

As the child stumbled from the impact of the shaft, I got a clear view of K'halid's back. Embedded at the base of his neck was a shimmering green stone. Instinctively, I reached up and seized it. A tingle that was almost painful ran through my body.

K'halid screamed and began to struggle wildly, but I held on tight. I was jerked to and fro as he fought to free himself. Taking a deep breath, I pulled as hard as I could. The stone came loose, and the child dropped to the ground.

"No! No! No!" he sobbed. Slowly, the color of his skin started to change until it matched that of the others in the town. I thought he would die, but he only lay on the ground, rocking and whimpering.

I turned to my companions. Wren was unconscious, a trickle of blood escaping from the cut on her temple. Beside her, Kraster was sitting on the ground while Gnombie carefully pulled my sword out of my brother's leg.

252

I stumbled over to them, winded from the battle. Gnombie dropped the weapon and started tying a tourniquet just below the knee. Kraster's wound wasn't bleeding too badly, so I moved on to Wren. She moaned and rolled over when I touched her shoulder. Her eyes opened, and she lay there, blinking up at me.

"You okay?" I asked.

"My head hurts," she wheezed.

"I'm not surprised," I told her. "Can you move?"

Without waiting for her response, I gently pulled her into a sitting position. She moaned again, then leaned over and threw up into the grass beside us.

I didn't let go of her until she was able to stand on her own.

"I need some of my herbs," she said. "They'll help."

Quickly, I retrieved her bag. Wren took out a handful of leaves, which she started chewing. I left her and went back to Kraster.

"How bad is it?" I asked.

"I've had worse," he replied.

"Thanks for holding on to this for me," I said, retrieving my blade and cleaning his blood from it.

"I hate you," Kraster muttered, fighting a smile. "That was the stone you took from him, right?"

I opened my left hand to show him where it rested on my palm, still glowing with green light. The rune for life was carved on its surface.

"But the curse of this place isn't broken yet," Wren pointed out, staggering to her feet.

I glanced at K'halid, still miserably huddled on the ground. Looking back the way we'd come, I could also see the last pair of stationary guards we'd passed. They remained as rigid as before.

"That's because the spell hasn't ended yet," I said.

"What more is there to do?" Gnombie asked, perplexed.

"I'm not sure, but we probably need to find Morana for that. Which means it's time to go inside." I glanced over my shoulder at the manor, dreading what we would find within.

Chapter 29
The Remnants

The hinges creaked terribly as I shoved the doors of the manor house open. Inside was a large room that seemed to have served many purposes for Morana and her family. There were over a dozen windows letting in an abundance of sunlight. I could also make out a wooden table where a few dishes were laid.

There were several overstuffed chairs set between a fireplace and a bookshelf, along with a collection of marvelous wooden toys scattered across the floor. Everything about the place was warm and inviting, or it would have been if age and time hadn't done their work so well. The table had a thick coating of dust on its surface, the chairs were full of holes where the stuffing leaked out, and the books were yellowed and moth-eaten. There were also scuff marks on the grimy floor where someone had recently played with the wooden toys.

Kraster went rigid as soon as he stepped across the threshold.

"What's wrong?" I asked.

"There's a vast amount of power tied to this place," my brother replied with a slight wince.

"I wouldn't have guessed," I scoffed.

"It's not normal magic," he clarified, speaking quietly as if something might be listening. "It's stagnant and twisted and sad– and angry."

His serious tone in the face of my mockery warned me that the danger was far from over.

We began carefully searching the manor, finding all the things you might expect in the country house of a noble. When we moved up the winding staircase to the third floor, Kraster's head snapped to the right.

"In there." He pointed at a pair of beautifully carved doors.

I pushed on one, and it slowly swung inward, protesting loudly on rusty hinges. I shuddered at the sound. When I stepped into the room, I instantly covered my nose and mouth with my hand. The smell was horrible, just as bad as in the town and tavern, giving me a clue as to what I would find. However, I was still not prepared for the sight that greeted me.

On a large, canopied bed lay a sleeping high elf woman who could only be Morana. Her skin was pale and papery, nearly as white as her long hair, which spread over her and the bed by the yard. It was easy to see that she was very old, even for an elf, who could live for centuries.

Most shocking of all was that there was a hollow in her chest similar to the one on her son's back. Morana's was empty, the skin around it dark and necrotic.

"I guess we found the mother," Wren said sadly. "Is she dead?"

"No," Kraster shook his head. "If she were, all of this would be over. She's the last piece. Her death will end the enchantment on the others."

"But what will happen to them?" Wren worried. Her brown eyes darted to me, full of entreaty.

"Wren," I said softly. "It's too late to help them. All that's left is to end their suffering."

My friend's eyes widened. "But–" she started.

"They're already dead." Despite the fact that Kraster interrupted Wren, his words were gentle. "That's the problem with soul magic. It is a curse, hollowing out those touched by it. All of the villagers died a long time ago, but their souls are still bound to their corpses. There's nothing we can do now except free them, so they can finally be at peace."

Moisture filled Wren's eyes, but she didn't argue anymore.

"So we just– kill the elf?" Gnombie asked.

"I think that's for the best," I answered. "Her body doesn't have many more years, and it would be cruel to try and wake her. Even if she never cared about the pain of the half-elves, she'd be devastated to realize she slept her life away and to learn of the fate of her beloved son."

The others nodded their agreement.

I drew a long knife from my belt and approached the bed. I hesitated when I saw Morana's eyelids flutter, but the eyes never opened. I ended it for her quickly, conflicting emotions filling my mind.

This elf had been careless and selfish. She had enslaved dozens of others for her own convenience. However, she had been driven by a mother's love for her child. All she'd done was to protect him no matter the cost. It was tragic that all her plans had ended in devastation.

The moment Morana no longer breathed, Kraster heaved a sigh of relief. I also sensed the magic lift from the room. Until I felt the pressure of it vanish, I hadn't even realized it was there.

The peace lasted less than a heartbeat, then a shriek echoed through the manor. It sounded far away, but not nearly far enough.

"It's like last night," Wren whimpered, hands slamming over her ears.

"I thought you said this would fix things?" I demanded of my brother.

"I thought it would," he replied. "Most of the magic is gone."

"What's left?" Gnombie asked.

"The angry part," Kraster warned.

"Lovely," I muttered, cleaning my knife on the bed sheet before putting it back in its sheath and taking out my swords.

"Lead the way," I ordered Kraster.

The rest of us followed him to the ground floor. There, he stopped and looked around.

"Are we close?" I asked.

"It's– below us." He sounded confused

"But we can't go any farther down," Wren pointed out.

"At least not inside the manor," I observed. "What about the well?" The others looked at me in horror.

We left the building and headed for the patch of lawn where the well, the statue, and the benches stood. K'halid was where we'd left him. His body was still, and his lifeless eyes were blue instead of black.

I peered down the well but couldn't make out much. The rope from the bucket had rotted away long ago. I was just taking my own rope from my pack, when Gnombie spoke up.

"I think I found something," he called to us.

We turned to see him standing by the base of the statue. The pedestal alone was several feet above his head. The gnome had managed to pop one side open, revealing a narrow staircase.

"That's super creepy," Wren announced.

"But way more convenient than climbing down the well," I said.

Kraster lit a torch, and the four of us crept down the stairs. I didn't hear a sound as we reached the bottom and emerged in a long, narrow hallway. There wasn't anywhere to go but forward, so we went forward. After fifty yards, the hall ended in a small alcove where a massive stone coffin rested.

"Whatever it is, it's inside," Kraster whispered. Though his voice was soft, the hallway echoed terribly, and another cry came from within the coffin. It was impossibly loud considering the thickness of the stone it had to penetrate.

Wren pressed back against the wall while Gnombie notched an arrow.

"We have to do this," I said aloud, more to convince myself than the others.

"Any idea what's in there?" Gnombie asked Kraster.

"None," he replied.

"There's something written on the top," Wren observed.

I stepped forward and looked at the polished stone of the coffin.

"It says, 'Here lies Abigor, Master of the Longsword, beloved husband and father, may he forgive me.'" Bile rose in the back of my throat.

"It's Morana's husband?" Wren gasped.

"But he was human," Gnombie said. "How is he the only one still alive?"

"K'halid did say Morana's spell didn't work quite right on him because he wasn't part elf," Wren recalled.

"So, he's not quite like the others, but he's some sort of undead?" Gnombie asked.

"Yes," I muttered darkly. "And she didn't have the strength to put him to rest herself, so she buried him here for eternity."

My sympathy for Morana was fading quickly. Maybe we had let her off too easily and should have woken her to face the consequences of her actions.

"Well, let's get this over with," Kraster muttered. "Everyone ready?"

I nodded, eyes fixed on the coffin.

Kraster took a deep breath and lifted his hands. As he did, the stone lid began to rise into the air inch by inch. With another motion, it moved to the left and lowered itself to lean against the coffin's side.

Everything was still except the heart inside my chest, which was racing like a warhorse in the midst of a cavalry charge. Slowly, I stepped forward, preparing to look into the coffin.

When I was still a few inches away, the thing inside sat bolt upright. What had once been human flesh was now rotten and decayed. I gagged but still managed to take a swing at the undead creature. I overshot, missing my target and stumbling forward slightly. The abomination glared at me with furious eyes. The lids were gone, giving the face a ghastly and horrible appearance.

"You!" he rasped through ragged lips. "You murdered her! You murdered my love!"

The stagnant air inside his lungs, mixed with the dust of the tomb, hit me directly in the face, flooding my senses with the horror of the situation and maybe something more.

Instantly, terror seized me. It was unlike anything I had ever felt before, except the few times in my youth when I had been pulled underwater and thought I would never see the sky again.

All of my military training and years of experience vanished as I turned and fled down the hall. I only dared glance over my shoulder once and saw the thing that had been Abigor chasing me, a great longsword in his hands. Fresh panic filled my mind. I dropped my weapons as I put on an extra burst of speed, desperate to escape.

Behind me, I heard Kraster calling out, but I didn't stop. I couldn't stop. All I could do was run.

Halfway to the stairs, I heard the twang of a bow and a grunt from my pursuer. The sound of his footfalls faltered for only a moment. I didn't slacken my pace either. Maybe once I reached the sunlight, I would feel braver and turn to face the foe behind me.

A burst of light and heat at my back told me that my brother was wielding fire. Fervently, I hoped the monster had been reduced to ash, but, even without looking, my brain screamed that he hadn't.

I reached the stairs and surged up them three at a time, stumbling only once or twice. One of my knees was bloodied when I scraped it against the wall, and I twisted an ankle as I attempted to climb even faster, but no pain could stop me. I had to get away. Had to escape and reach the surface.

At last, I emerged into the afternoon light, breathing hard and trembling. I staggered forward and tried to find the courage to draw a dagger since my swords were gone.

"I will avenge my beloved!" the horror bellowed, sounding close to the top of the staircase.

Again, fear shot through me. I was about to start running when I remembered Tempest. I summoned the horse from my shadow. Taking hold as the creature sprang forth, I pulled myself onto his back and put heels to his side, urging him away. I didn't care which direction we went as long as it was far from that place.

Tempest sprang into a gallop, bearing me back into the town. I didn't notice anything as we raced along, leaving the underground passage far behind. The horse moved with greater speed than usual, seeming to sense my terror and desire for haste.

As suddenly as the fear had come upon me, it ended.

I pulled Tempest to a halt. We'd passed through the entire town and now stood on the very path that had brought us here the day before. Slowly, I turned my horse around.

The two guards were still on either side of the road, only now they lay on the ground. I slid from Tempest's back and approached the half-elf who had warned us of our peril.

His silver eyes were sightless, the pain and anguish gone forever. Gently, I reached out and closed them.

After a quick survey of the rest of the village, I found that all the others were in the same state. I left them, heading back to where I'd abandoned my friends.

"There you are," Kraster called with obvious relief when he spotted me coming down the slope to the estate.

He, Wren, and Gnombie were standing beside a fire. In the flames, I could make out the bodies of Abigor, K'halid, and Morana.

"What happened to you?" Wren asked, studying me carefully.

"I'm not sure," I replied. "It was very strange."

"You can say that again," Kraster put in. "I have never, not once in my life, known you to run from a fight and leave me to finish off the enemy.

"I took care of him for you, by the way, so you're welcome."

I grimaced at his words.

Kraster laughed slightly. "I was so surprised, I almost forgot how to cast."

I rolled my eyes at him. "I have no idea what happened," I admitted.

"I did sense a flare of magic when that thing started speaking," Kraster told me. "So, I don't think you are entirely to blame for your retreat."

"What about now? Are you sensing any more magic?" I wondered tentatively.

"Nope," he replied.

"The air smells different, too," Wren added.

I took a deep breath and realized she was right. The air was clear and cool, with a faint breeze.

"Then I guess it's time we take our leave," I said.

"Yes, please!" Gnombie agreed eagerly.

"But where to next?" Wren asked.

"To Kempt," I told her, and, at the same moment, Kraster said, "Home."

Chapter 30
The Nightmare

That night, we camped in the forest, not the strange forest where we had found the trapped village of half-elves, but many miles away from it, among the high elves' silver trees.

We traveled long into the evening, until all of us were about to drop from weariness. I felt certain the screams from the night before would never again be heard, but there was no point in taking any chances. Just because we believed all had been laid to rest in the accursed town didn't mean there weren't other ghosts waiting to emerge.

During breakfast the next morning, my brother brought out the map.

"The fastest way to Kempt is due north," Kraster said. "I won't know exactly where we are until we reach the Tarllen River."

"We'll want to cross that as soon as possible," I put in.

"Why?" asked Gnombie.

"Because the Tarllen River flows out of Hawnkenquack Lake," I replied.

A moment later, both Gnombie and Wren were laughing. Kraster and I exchanged a glance.

"What lake?" Wren giggled.

I scowled at her.

"It's not actually named Hawnkenquack Lake," Kraster explained. "But those who live in the city have called it that for centuries, ever since the monstrosity appeared."

"What monstrosity?" Gnombie asked. Wren was still trying to get her face under control, but Gnombie had grown serious when he realized I wasn't joking.

"The Hawnkenquack is a giant goose that claimed the lake southeast of Kempt several centuries ago," Kraster told them. "It's horribly bad tempered and has driven away everyone who lived nearby. Only the very foolish venture to the lake in search of discarded feathers."

"You're telling me there's a giant goose that has terrorized the countryside of Kempt for hundreds of years, and I'm only just now hearing about it?" Wren demanded.

"It's no secret," Kraster explained. "I'm surprised no one ever mentioned it to you. Plenty of people from Kempt visited Thea."

"What is it really though?" Gnombie pressed. "It can't actually be a goose, or it would have died long ago."

"Who knows," I shrugged. "Some say it's an ancient king cursed by a dark spirit. Others, that it is a goose who ate magic dust from a wizard's table. Still more that it's a creature not of this world who fell from the sky."

"I want to see it!" Wren piped up.

"Absolutely not," I told her. "The one thing that all the stories agree on is that the Hawnkenquack is extremely dangerous and highly territorial. We will not be going anywhere near its lake."

"Fine. I'll go see it by myself when all of this is over," Wren pouted.

I let out a sigh but didn't bother trying to talk her out of the crazy notion.

"Anyway, we are headed north," Kraster said, turning the conversation back to where it had started. "That should keep us well away from the high elves and any patrols they might have sent after us."

Everyone nodded.

Before long, breakfast was finished, our bags were packed, and we were headed north. No one spoke much, with the horror of the last few days weighing heavily on our minds. All in all, it was the most uneventful day yet.

We were still in the forest when evening fell. I assumed it would take at least a couple more days to reach the plains beyond.

Around the third watch of the night, Kraster woke me for my shift.

"She's been awake for hours," he said, pointing at Wren.

"Another dream?" I whispered.

He nodded. "She won't talk about it. At least, not with me." Kraster shrugged and headed for his bedroll.

I rose and stretched, feeling my back pop in a few places. Slowly, I made my way over to Wren. She was huddled on her side, facing away from the fire.

"I dreamed of it again," she whispered.

"The souls from the town?" I asked worriedly. I'd hoped that our actions had freed them. They deserved to be at peace after so many years of torment.

"Not the town," Wren whispered. "It was the river. This time, I saw the monster."

A lump swelled in my throat as foreboding filled my heart.

"Monster?" I choked.

"It looked like a dragon," she replied. "But it had more than one head."

My eyes widened. "What?" I gasped.

"I saw three of them," she whimpered. "But there might have been more. The necks were slender and snake-like, and the mouths were full of fangs. The thing turned and looked at me, and– and I think it saw me."

"You were dreaming," I tried to assure her, and myself. "Maybe it wasn't real. Even if some of your dreams are visions of the future, it doesn't mean all of them are."

Wren hesitated. "Maybe," she replied.

I gave her a questioning look.

"It's hard to explain. I still have regular dreams sometimes, but the others– they are vivid and feel like memories. Lately, I think they've been getting more powerful. That's why I can't shake the horror of the monster. I sense it every time I close my eyes."

"And you're sure it's because of The Scrying Stone?" I wondered gently.

She nodded. "I have no other explanation. After what happened to Morana and her son, I don't think I'll ever be brave enough to use the stone intentionally, but I can't seem to stop these visions. What if I become like them?"

With that, Wren dissolved into tears.

I leaned forward and awkwardly patted her on the shoulder.

"Where are you carrying the stone?" I asked.

In answer, she reached into the small pouch at her belt and pulled out the teal stone.

"Maybe don't keep it so close to you at night," I suggested.

"But Asteropaios's stone is in there too, and it's never bothered me," protested Wren.

"We don't know that," I countered. "You didn't realize The Scrying Stone was affecting you at first."

"That's true," Wren admitted.

"We should all be more careful moving forward," I said. "Kraster has Dimble's Legacy, and now that I've got The Heart of Jong, it's possible we might all start experiencing strange phenomena."

"Like what?" Wren asked.

"I have no idea," I told her. "But I would imagine these stones are more powerful than we even understand."

Wren nodded seriously.

"I still think you should put the stone in your pack so it's not so close to you at night," I advised her.

"But what about Gnombie?" she whispered.

I pursed my lips. The gnome had still given no hint of his true allegiance. On the surface, he appeared to be our willing and helpful companion, but underneath, something else was lurking, making it hard to even fathom a guess at his true intentions.

"The Great Shal'eth entrusted this stone to me, and I must endure the dreams if that's what it takes to keep the stones safe," Wren declared.

I nodded slowly. "Just be careful," I told her. "You were specially chosen for this mission, and we need you."

Wren gave me a small smile. Soon, she went back to sleep while I finished my watch.

As the sky lightened, I couldn't shake the feeling that something was different about this morning. Only once Kraster sat up and yawned loudly did I realize that it was too quiet in the woods.

At some point during the night, the sound of crickets had died away, and when morning came, not a single bird could be heard heralding the sunrise. I mentioned it to the others, but they had no answers.

Even more than the lack of bird song, the woods felt different as we traveled through them. My companions and I remained mostly silent. Our horses' steps seemed overly loud to my ears as they echoed strangely among the trees.

Just before noon, I saw the body of an elf lying on the ground. Dismounting, I went to his side. I touched his neck, but his skin was cold.

"He's dead," I told the others over my shoulder.

They weren't looking at me. Instead, their horror-filled eyes were staring at something over my head.

Slowly, I straightened and turned, then the breath left my body. In the glade just beyond lay hundreds of bodies littering the forest floor like leaves.

Runes

Future

Eternity

Power

Life

About the author and the party

Danielle N. McDonough is an author who loves all things to do with imagination, fantasy, and storytelling, so it is no surprise that she enjoys playing Dungeons and Dragons. In fact, it was one of her party's adventures that inspired the story for The Cursed Half Moon.

Although Danielle (Candra) has been friends with the members of the party for many years, D&D has brought her closer to each of them in a special way. Anna was the one who first invited Danielle to try D&D in 2017, where she instantly fell in love with the game. This is also when she met Charles (The Dungeon Master). The two have been in an active D&D group together ever since.

In turn, Danielle introduced Makenna (Wren) to D&D when she put together a small game for her birthday party. Afterward, Danielle got Collin (Kraster), an experienced player, invited to the D&D group Makenna was joining, as she knew Collin had a crush on Makenna. With a little coaxing, the two started dating, fell in love, and got married.

When everyone came together for the adventure that inspired this book series, The Teapot McGuffin, as it was originally called, Joe (Gnombie), Danielle's brother-in-law, was invited to join. This was Joe's first D&D campaign, but not his last. All of them look forward to playing together many times in the future!

www.daniellenmcdonough.com

www.ingramcontent.com/pod-product-compliance
Lightning Source LLC
Chambersburg PA
CBHW072347020726
47506CB00004B/1045